LICENCE TO HOWL

BOOK 2 OF THE WOLFBRAND SERIES

HELEN HARPER

CHAPTER ONE

'Do I get a sporty car with an ejector seat?'

'No.'

'How about a watch that shoots poison darts? Do I get one of those?'

'No.'

'A pen with a hidden microphone?'

'No.'

'A gun?'

Sarah Greensmith stared hard at him. 'Mr Webb,' she said heavily, 'this is not a film and you are not James Bond. I am not M. There is no Q. And you are not a sex symbol.'

'That remains to be seen.' Devereau linked his hands behind his head and offered her an easy grin. 'Martini,' he said, 'shaken, not stirred.'

Greensmith rolled her eyes and muttered something uncomplimentary under her breath while a pair of Lycra clad joggers bounced past them. Her eyes tracked them until they disappeared out of view. Devereau paid them little attention. He wasn't stupid; he knew they met in places like this rather than any official MI5 buildings because nobody wanted to acknowledge that he was now working for the British government. He was a werewolf, and an ex-criminal. He wasn't the type of recruit that tended to do much for PR.

'What about training?' he inquired.

'You don't get any training either.'

He raised an eyebrow, surprised for the first time. 'Seriously?'

'We need you to be you. It's why we have recruited you in the first place. Any training we provide will take the sheen off Devereau Webb, career criminal and lonely supe. It would make you look like a stooge. The less training you have, the more genuine you appear. We can't allow anyone to gain even the faintest inkling that you are not anything other than what you present yourself to be.'

'A drop dead gorgeous crime lord with a fondness for the full moon?'

She gritted her teeth. 'Don't make me regret hiring you.'

Devereau had the distinct impression that she was already regretting it. 'What happens if I'm captured by an evil mastermind and tortured to force me to reveal everything I know?'

Greensmith held up two fingers. 'First of all,' she told him, 'you won't know anything. Second, in that scenario it wouldn't matter how much training we gave you. Everybody talks under torture. That's why it's so effective.'

He watched her delve into the bag which sat beside her on the park bench. She started rummaging through it. 'Suddenly,' he said, 'I'm no longer so sure that I want to be part of MI5.'

'Too late. You've already signed on the dotted line.' Her expression cleared as she found what she was looking for. 'Here it is.' She slid over a large brown envelope. 'This is for you.'

'What is it?'

For the first time, Sarah Greensmith smiled. 'Your first assignment.' She pointed at the envelope. 'Information has reached us that a certain Member of Parliament has been compromised as a result of an evening he recently spent with a sex worker.'

Devereau shrugged. 'So? I imagine that sort of thing happens all the time.'

'This particular MP has considerable dealings with the Ministry of Defence and he's party to a great deal of sensitive data. Our tip off tells us that he's being blackmailed by a gang out of South East London as a result of his dalliance. Your job is to either confirm or deny the allegations.'

'And put a stop to the blackmail?'

'No. All you have to do is find out whether it's true or not. We will take care of the rest.'

Devereau opened the envelope flap and took out the papers within. 'Alexander Carruthers,' he read aloud. The enclosed photograph was of a pompous looking man in his fifties. He had ruddy cheeks and appeared to be wearing a cravat. He looked like the very definition of an Eton educated British politician.

'That's the MP,' Greensmith said.

'Anything on the sex worker?'

'She's not important. We're confident that she's not part of the blackmail and is unaware that it's taking place.'

Devereau hesitated. Then he glanced through the rest of the papers. 'The Wasps?' he asked.

'That's what the gang calls themselves.'

'They sound like an amateur football team.' His lip curled in disdain.

'Well, if you manage to infiltrate them and discern the truth of the matter, then you can tell them that for yourself.' She sniffed. 'This is an important matter. There is the potential that the safety of our country is being compromised by this gang. They present a very real threat and we are counting on you to help us out.' She fixed him with a steely-eyed stare. '*Can* we count on you?'

'In spades.' He winked at her. 'You have nothing to worry about.'

'I certainly hope not.' She stood up and prepared to leave. 'That will be all for now, Mr Webb.'

He doffed an imaginary cap at her. 'Cheers, Moneypenny.'

* * *

THREE HOURS later Devereau Webb swaggered into the grimy pub on the corner of Bell Street and took up position at the bar. Initially, the bartender, a short brown haired man with a wiry build and corded muscles visible on his sleeveless arms, barely glanced at him. Never one to be described as a shrinking violet, Devereau cleared his throat. 'Pint of beer, mate.'

'Not your mate,' the bartender replied. Then he glanced up and took a proper look at his latest customer. It took less than a second for the man to pale dramatically. 'You're Devereau Webb.'

Devereau didn't smile and didn't offer an autograph. 'Get me what I asked for.' He leaned slightly over the counter and permitted the faintest shadow of lupine whiskers to emerge around his jaw.

The bartender swallowed and grabbed an empty glass. Devereau grunted in satisfaction as he filled it with amber liquid. In truth, he would never normally be so rude. In his experience, you caught far more flies with honey than vinegar. However, he'd spent the last hour or so reading what Greensmith had given him and then scoping out the pub from a safe distance. It didn't take a genius to work out that this less than salubrious establishment wasn't the sort of place where punters were expected to mind their Ps and Qs. If he was going to get anywhere fast with his first mission, he had to fit in. Play-acting as a grizzled werewolf with a nasty temper wouldn't be hard, especially not with the full moon barely two days away. He'd only been a werewolf for four months but that had been plenty of time to discover how the lunar changes affected his mood, especially when he was working on an empty stomach.

He took off his coat, draping it on a nearby bar stool. Devereau grabbed the sticky, faux leather bound menu sitting on the bar top next to him and scanned its contents. It was highly doubtful that the kitchen here had passed any food hygiene requirements. It was more likely, in fact, that any inspectors had been intimidated into giving the pub a pass. However, beggars couldn't be choosers and Devereau had a façade to maintain. He shrugged to himself and barked again at the bartender as soon as the pint was presented to him.

'Five of those burgers,' he ordered. 'No salad. No sauce. No buns.' He paused. He liked all those extra components but he was trying to make an impression. In fact, he might as well go all out. 'No cooking either,' he added. 'Just give me the patties on a plate.'

'Raw?'

Devereau tilted his head. 'Did I,' he inquired silkily, 'or did I not say no cooking?'

The barman took a step back, colliding with several stacked glasses as he did so. 'Five raw burgers,' he muttered. 'Coming right up.'

Devereau reached for his wallet but the man shook his head. 'On the house.'

'Are you trying to suggest that I don't have the means to pay for my own food and drinks?' Devereau asked.

The bartender's eyes widened. 'N – n – no. I meant no offence. I'm sorry. I - '

'Relax.' He smirked. 'I'm only playing with you.'

The bartender stared at him mutely. Satisfied that he'd done enough for now and rather impressed with himself so far, Devereau lifted his glass and turned round to survey the rest of the pub while he took several long gulps of the beer. There weren't many customers. He glanced at the two middle aged geezers in the corner who were pretending not to look at him.

Both wore high vis jackets and stained clothes that spoke of hard labour, probably somewhere on a nearby building site. To their right, there was a spotty kid playing the bandit machine with intent concentration and jangling a collection of coins in his right hand. And finally there was a white haired elderly lady in the corner with a gin and tonic on the table in front of her. She was watching him with narrowed eyes.

'Fancy a little of what you see, darling?' Devereau called, splaying his arms out for her supposed delectation.

She bared her teeth at him. He bared his own teeth back – and his were considerably sharper.

'You threatening me mum?'

Devereau glanced towards the source of the strongly accented voice. It was a man in perhaps his forties, wearing a flat cap and a shabby tweed suit, and looking for all the world like he'd just stepped off the stage as an extra in *Oliver*. Devereau knew a thing or two about carefully cultivated images. He also knew from Sarah Greensmith's information that this was Ronnie Hitchens, the owner of this grubby establishment and de-facto leader of the Wasps. Well, he pondered, that had been even faster than he'd thought.

He masked his thoughts and snorted. 'I think she's the one threatening me.'

Hitchens looked over. Then, surprisingly, he grinned. 'Yeah,' he said. 'That's probably right.' He raised his voice. 'Ma! Stop staring at the supe! You're freaking him out!'

The old woman glared. 'You let all sorts of riff-raff in here, Ronnie.' She pursed her lips in disgust and turned away.

Devereau took an overly casual sip of his beer. 'You run this place?' he asked.

'Yeah.' Hitchens looked him up and down. 'Whatchoo doing here? We don't usually get the likes of you walking through those doors.'

'I was in the area and I fancied a pint,' Devereau told him.

Then, with a hint of a challenge in his voice, he added, 'Is that a problem?'

Ronnie Hitchens held his hands up. 'No problem at all. I don't care what you or who you are. Your money's as good as the next man's.'

The old woman coughed.

'Or woman's,' Hitchens said quickly.

'Here's your food,' the bartender said, sliding a plate across the bar top towards Devereau before stepping hastily away.

Devereau nodded in brief acknowledgment and, using his fingers, picked up the nearest beef patty and took a large bite.

If Hitchens was disturbed by his choice of meal, he didn't show it. 'Tell me something,' he said, 'man to man. Why'd you do it?'

Devereau swallowed his mouthful. 'Do what?'

'You were the Shepherd. You had a good thing going. Why'd you ruin it by becoming a supe?'

'You know who I am?'

Hitchens met his eyes. 'Everyone knows who you are.'

Devereau reached for a second burger. 'Maybe,' he said, 'I felt like a new challenge.'

'Uh huh.'

'Or maybe,' Devereau continued, 'I wanted to feel what it was like to have some real power.'

Hitchens' eyes gleamed. 'You've got power?'

'Hardly any. Not yet anyway.' Devereau smiled. 'Lots.'

Hitchins wasn't giving up yet. 'I heard your old lot chucked you out. That the Flock don't want a Shepherd who's also a wolf.'

'Some people don't know what's good for them.'

Hitchins chuckled. 'Ain't that the truth.' He shook his head in amusement. 'Ain't that the truth indeed.' And then, with a right hook so swift that Devereau didn't see it coming, he punched him in the side of the face. Almost simultaneously, something hard and heavy hit the back of Devereau's head. The half eaten patty slid from his hand and landed on the dirty floor. A moment later he joined it, his knees buckling. He groaned from the bursts of pain on both sides of his skull while Ronnie Hitchens bent down, his face looming over him. 'You ain't got that much power at all,' he commented. 'And you definitely don't know what's good for you either.'

Devereau blinked. His vision was blurring. He stared at the feet of the two labourers who were directly in front of him and tried to focus, in a vain bid to hold onto the last slip of consciousness left to him. All he needed to do was call on his wolf and then Ronnie fucking Hitchens would see what he was really about. He reached for the animal inside him, attempting to stir it into action yet again. But as the two pairs of feet became indistinct and he tasted the unpleasant metallic edge on his tongue, he knew he was already out of time.

* * *

THE WATER which splashed in his face was icy cold. Devereau choked and spluttered, gasping for air. He jerked his arms, in an unconscious bid to wipe the water from his face. Unfortunately, however, his hands appeared to be bound fast behind him. He shifted his body. There was rope round his waist and chest, tying him to the very chair he was sat upon. At least his legs and feet appeared to be free.

'Wakey wakey! Rise and shine!'

Devereau shook his head to rid himself of the dribbling water, sending a shower of droplets into the face of Ronnie Hitchens, who was smiling unpleasantly towards him. Hitchens took out a spotted handkerchief from his pocket and dabbed at his skin with it.

'Attacking a werewolf is not only dangerous,' Devereau hissed, realising from the smell that he'd been shoved into a small back room of the same pub, 'but downright foolish. You're going to regret this.'

'We shall see about that,' Hitchens replied calmly. 'It's not as if you have a clan at your back who will spring into action on your behalf. You're a lone wolf. You don't have a pack of your own. Even the humans who once followed you have fallen by the wayside.' Hitchens dropped the handkerchief unceremoniously on the floor. 'So unless you're planning to break free and rip my throat out, I reckon I'll be fine and dandy.'

Right now that was exactly what Devereau was planning. When he reached for his wolf again, however, nothing happened. And he could still taste something unpleasant on his tongue. This was not supposed to happen.

As if he knew what he was trying – and failing – to do, Ronnie Hitchens smirked. Then he grabbed a nearby chair and swung it round, perching himself on it back to front with his legs straddling the seat and his arms draped casually over the chair's back. 'So now that you know you're not going anywhere, why don't you answer a few of my questions?'

'You've not asked any yet,' Devereau growled.

Hitchins fixed him with a cold eyed stare. 'Why'd you come into my pub?'

'I wanted a drink.'

He lifted one arm and smacked Devereau around the face. It wasn't a particularly hard knock but it was unpleasant all the same. 'Try again.'

'The warm inviting exterior drew me in.'

Hitchins hit him again, this time with slightly more force. Devereau felt his teeth rattle. He spat out a glob of blood onto the floor. Ick.

'You might think you're being clever but it won't help your cause,' Hitchens murmured. 'For one final time, why did you come here?'

Devereau exhaled. 'You are under the delusion that I'm

friend-less and there's no-one at my back but I can assure you that's not actually the case. Clan or no clan, there are plenty of supes who owe me favours. Not just wolves either. There are several vampires who will do just about anything for me.'

Hitchens sighed. 'I didn't ask for idle threats. I asked for an explanation as to why you're here.'

'And,' Devereau retorted, 'I'm giving you one. You're not patient enough to listen to all of it. A few days ago, one of the vampires who's in my debt came to me with a proposition. She had come into some information regarding your little operation here. She knew that I was looking for a new group to work with and she suggested that the Wasps here might be a good bet. I'm no longer so sure about that.'

Ronnie Hitchens' eyes narrowed at his mention of his gang's name. 'No blood fucker would ever know about us.'

Devereau snorted mildly. 'Of course they know about you. They know a lot more about what goes on in this city than anyone else does. Anyone who underestimates the bloodsuckers,' he continued, 'is an idiot. The things that Lord Horvath knows would make your toes curl up. He's got eyes and ears everywhere.'

A muscle ticked in Hitchins' cheek. 'So, if we say for argument's sake that you're telling the truth, why would you want to work with us?'

'Because,' Devereau said, 'my own Flock left me, as you already know. The vamps and wolves I know are fine. They're good people. But they're under the government's thumb. They can't take a shit without the police landing on top of them.' He met Hitchens' gaze. 'And I miss fucking with the police. Being a werewolf is fun but my soul is crying out for some real action.' He managed a facsimile of a shrug. 'Don't worry though, I've got several other possibilities. I'm not throwing all my eggs into one basket. You're not the only little gang on my list.'

'Oh yeah? Who else are you looking at then?'

'Smack me around all you want,' Devereau told him, 'but I'm not going to tell you who they are. Not if I want to end up working with any of them. And I wouldn't tell any of them about you. There's a code.'

'Yeah,' Hitchens said quietly. 'There's a code.' He paused for a moment as if thinking. 'What makes you think *we*'d want to work with *you*?'

Devereau's eyes gleamed. He was finally getting somewhere. It was the first time he'd been interviewed for a job while tied up. Hell, it was the first time he'd been interviewed for a job *at all*. 'You need some muscle in your team.'

'Muscle?' Hitchens scoffed. 'We took you down easily enough.'

Devereau grinned. 'Did you?'

A tiny frown began to crease Hitchens' forehead. Then Devereau sprang up and, still tied to the chair, kicked Hitchens in the chest with one foot. Hitchens toppled backwards, landing clumsily on the floor with his own chair on top of him. Devereau laughed coldly and tensed his muscles, yanking hard against the rope holding his arms in place. It wouldn't take much to break free. A few attempts and he'd manage it. He kicked the fallen Hitchens in the ribs and strained against the rope again. Hmm. Then he ran backwards at the nearby wall, angling his collision so that the wooden chair at his back took the worst of the impact. It splintered into several pieces – and seconds later, Devereau was free of his bindings.

Still on the floor, Hitchins groaned. Devereau walked over and smiled down at him. 'I won't hold any of this against you,' he said. 'And I won't hurt you any more. To be honest, I'm pleased that you were smart enough to knock me out to begin with. It proves that you're able to think on your feet and adapt. That's the sort of thing I'm looking for in my new gang.' He circled round Hitchens. 'It's not your fault that you don't know how strong I really am. I could teach you a thing or two about more effective restraints. I have a lot to offer you. But,' he sucked in air through his teeth, 'I'm not sure on reflection that you've got a lot to offer me.' He bent down and slid Hitchens' wallet out from his back pocket. There was no cash inside it. There was, however, a single piece of folded up paper. 'What's this?' He smoothed it out and scanned the scrawled words. 'A.C.' He glanced down at Hitchins' face. 'What does that mean? And is this a phone number here?'

Hitchins groaned again. 'No.'

Devereau's smile grew. 'Yes.' He reached into Hitchins' other pocket. Then he whistled. 'Nice phone. It's one of those ones with facial recognition, right?' He grinned and held it up to Hitchins' face. Almost instantaneously the phone unlocked. Devereau wasted no time in tapping in the phone number.

It was answered within three rings. 'This is Alex Carruthers. I don't know why you're calling me again. I've already given you twenty grand. If you want more –'

Devereau hung up. 'Who's Alex Carruthers? And where's the twenty grand he gave you?'

Hitchens didn't immediately answer. Devereau grabbed him by the throat and hauled him up to his feet. 'I don't like repeating myself.'

'He's just some MP! We got some dirty pictures of him with a blonde woman who he paid for sex. That's all.'

'Blackmail?' Devereau sighed. 'That's unimaginative.' He shook Hitchens. 'Where's the cash you squeezed out of him?'

'In a safe under the bar.'

'What's the combination?' He tightened his grip on Hitchens' throat.

'Three five oh two four.'

Devereau tutted loudly. 'You gave that up far too quickly. My instincts were right.' He sighed as if deeply disappointed. 'The Wasps are not the gang for me.' He released Hitchins, who collapsed back down onto the floor again. 'Never mind.' He shrugged to himself and headed for the door.

* * *

NOBODY STOPPED him as he left the pub. The builders watched him warily and Hitchens' old mum, if that's who she really was, scowled in his direction. There was no sign of the teenager who'd no doubt done the smart thing by disappearing out of the front door, but the bartender remained in place, watching him with a white face as he grabbed his coat from where it still lay hooked on the bar stool. Devereau smiled pleasantly before ambling outside. Then he delved into his pocket and pulled out his own phone, calling Sarah Greensmith.

'It's me,' he said into the phone. 'The Wasps have definitely been blackmailing Carruthers. They've already tapped him for twenty thousand. It's in a safe behind the bar.' He told her the combination. 'I suggest you get someone to their pub tout suite to scoop them up.'

Sarah Greensmith didn't immediately say anything.

'Are you there?' Devereau inquired.

'Yes. Yes, I'm here. I'm merely surprised, that's all. That was fast work, Mr Webb.'

'I aim to please. Next time,' he murmured, 'try and give me something more challenging.'

'I wouldn't worry about that. Your next assignment will be longer and will involve overseas travel.'

Devereau felt a frisson of excitement. Excellent.

'I'll be in touch after the full moon,' she told him.

'I'll pack my suitcase and look forward to hearing from you.' He smiled to himself and ended the call before glancing up at the sky. It was just as well he'd finished up his work for the day. Rain was on the way and he still had a few errands to run.

He supposed that the sensible thing to do would be to wait here until Greensmith sent someone to mop up the mess he'd left behind him. He wasn't going to waste his time, however. The entire operation had been a set-up from the beginning. The two builders nursing their pints might have had appropriately stained clothes but both their shoes had been brand spanking new and were entirely unsuitable for hard labour. The bartender, who'd done a reasonable job of acting scared, hadn't been worried in the slightest. Devereau was a werewolf; he could literally smell fear – and there had been nothing on the barman to smell beyond traces of aftershave and stale beer. Part of his lack of fear had probably been because Devereau's drink, or perhaps the raw burgers, had been laced with some sort of chemical poison that had prevented him from turning into a wolf. No way a small time London gang could get hold of something like that. Not at short notice. MI5 could though. They'd probably fucking developed it in their own secret laboratory. It was hardly surprising that they'd worked out a way to tame werewolves, even if only temporarily. It was an unpleasant discovery but one which Devereau was glad he'd learned about.

The final nail in the coffin – and the one which had damned the whole thing – was Alexander Carruthers. MI5 hadn't done quite as much research on Devereau as they'd thought they had. He had pursued some dealings with Carruthers several years ago. He'd broken into the MP's second home near Westminster and divested him of several rather ugly but lucrative pieces of artwork. He knew from the photographs he'd seen in Carruthers' house that the MP was completely, one hundred percent, unstiltingly gay. Alexander Carruthers wouldn't pay for a blonde female sex worker's services any more than Sarah Greensmith herself would. Whoever had been on the other end of that phone, it certainly hadn't been the Member of Parliament. Greensmith – and by extension MI5 – had been testing him. Could he withstand pressure? Could he lie convincingly when he needed to? Would he steal money if he was given the chance? Was he a loose cannon? He'd been very tempted to throw it all back in Greensmith's face and tell her that he wasn't as stupid as she thought he was. And that she wasn't as clever. However, it served his purposes to know more about MI5 than they knew about him. It was only to his advantage if they under-estimated him. Devereau Webb had agreed to work for the secret services and serve his country as required. But he would never ever trust them.

CHAPTER TWO

'Can I come with you?' Alice asked.

'Nope.' Devereau gave his niece a flat look. 'You know you can't. Stop asking.'

'Martina gets to go.'

From the corner chair, where she sat with her legs tucked underneath her, Martina grinned.

'Martina is a werewolf.'

'You could make me a wolf like her. Then I could come.'

'If I did that,' Devereau grunted, 'your mum would kill me.' Literally.

Dr Yara appeared in the doorway. 'They are here,' she announced.

Devereau nodded and got to his feet. 'Natasha will be here to pick Alice up shortly.'

Yara smiled. 'Is no problem. I wait.'

'Thank you.' He glanced at Martina. 'Have you called your dad?'

The young girl waved her phone at him. 'I texted him. He texted back and told me not to eat anyone.'

Devereau kept his expression schooled into a blank mask.

Martina's father was an idiot. She needed support and love, not pointless warnings or admonishments even if they were wrapped up with misplaced humour. It wasn't the time to comment, however, and it wouldn't do Martina any favours. She only stayed with him for the three days over every full moon and her blood ties, especially given her history, were not his to break. It had been a few days since Greensmith's daft test and Devereau had a free pass until the moon completed its cycle so he had been able to give Martina the attention she deserved. However, with only one night left before she returned to her dad, he was keen not to rock the boat. None of them could afford to allow Martina's riotous teenage hormones to get the better of her composure. Like him, she was a werewolf who wasn't supposed to exist. Unlike him, she had to struggle with puberty and adolescence as well as her lupine form. They weren't states of existence which tended to blend well and at this time of the month it paid to tread on eggshells around any werewolf, let alone one barely into her teenage years.

'Come on then,' he said. 'Let's make a move.'

Martina bounced up and stretched. Her eyes were already glowing yellow in anticipation. Devereau nodded at her and the pair of them turned to join the small motley group of waiting werewolves outside his door.

They fell in together, forming a small band as they walked with purpose towards Regent's Park, where they could allow the lure of the moon to inhabit them completely without fear of injuring any innocent humans who happened by. From her window his pixie neighbour, Millicent, waved at them. They all waved back. Devereau insisted upon it.

Morty sidled up towards him. Once upon a time, he'd tried to kill Martina. When he'd failed, his old employer had forcibly turned him into a wolf. Fortunately, since then, Morty had learned the error of his ways and had a new job working as a personal trainer. He'd garnered himself some well-heeled human clients and was establishing a decent reputation for himself. Morty knew as well as Devereau did that his status as a werewolf meant he'd never be fully trusted by humans, however. Such was the nature of the beast.

He cleared his throat nervously. 'Uh…'

'Spit it out.'

Morty scratched the side of his neck. It was growing visibly furry and Devereau knew without looking that his fingernails had already become misshapen claws. Dusk was too close and it was all any of them could do to maintain even a vaguely human body at this point.

'I've been approached by Lord McGuigan. He's offered me a spot in his clan as a ranked wolf.'

It had only been a matter of time. In fact, Devereau fully expected that it wouldn't be long before all the ragtag wolves who'd been part of the slave ring that he'd busted a few months ago would be picked up the four werewolf clans. He took it as a success rather than a failure. He'd turned a group of near feral supes into functioning members of society. He also knew that McGuigan's approach meant the clan lords and ladies were as keen as ever to ensure that Devereau had no followers of his own and no power to speak of. They still saw him as a threat. They were right to think of him that way.

'Are you going to take him up on it?' he asked.

Morty swallowed. 'That depends on you.'

'There are four clans,' Devereau told him. 'Not five. Clan Webb does not exist. You'll do well with a real werewolf clan behind you.'

'You're not angry?'

He half smiled. 'No. Although,' he paused briefly, considering that it was worthwhile saying aloud, 'regardless of which clan you choose to end up with, I hope you'll remember me and the times we've had together.' Translation: don't forget what I did for you and don't ever fuck with me.

'I will always be in your debt, boss,' Morty said.

Good. Devereau nodded. 'Then I wish you well in your endeavours.' He pointed to the leafy trees on the fringes of Regent's Park just up ahead. 'Of course, it does mean that you won't be able to come here anymore.' Only Devereau had the rights to the use of this particular park over the full moon. The clans had to make do with the far smaller St James's Park. Devereau didn't feel the slightest flicker of guilt about the situation. He flashed the other man a grin. 'You'd better make the most of it while you can.' He broke into a run. Almost immediately Morty and the others followed him, with Martina all but nipping at his heels.

They sped past the small cluster of police officers, who were there ostensibly to keep the werewolves inside the confines of the park but whose actual jobs were to keep curious humans out. Devereau bit back the temptation to burst out of his clothes. After all, he'd need them later if he didn't want to be strolling back home stark bollock naked. It wasn't that he was modest or shy. It was simply that it was bloody freezing at this time of year. He pulled off his shirt, kicked off his shoes and divested himself off his trousers and underwear. The others did the same. Barely had his clothes landed on the ground when he allowed his wolf to take over. The surge of power and adrenaline as the change happened was incomparable.

His bones snapped and altered shape. His muscles bulged. His blood fizzed and, from head to toe, his smooth skin yielded to thick gold tipped fur. Devereau paused for a beat, on four paws now rather than two feet, and inhaled the twilight air. The power of the full moon resounded towards him. It was like nothing else in the world. He enjoyed the single solitary moment. Then he became aware of the others, watching and waiting for his cue. In belated acknowledgment, he tipped his head back and opened up his lungs, howling into the darkening sky. He wanted to sing to the moon like she sang to him. A heartbeat later, his small group of wolves, from Martina to Morty and beyond, joined in.

THEY TORE THROUGH THE PARK. Martina caught the scent of a squirrel and darted off in one direction. Two of the younger male werewolves who had been supe slaves like Morty began to snarl at each other, a missed step by one causing a minor collision that was developing into a full blown fight. Devereau could step in and prevent any bloodshed but it would be better for them all if he allowed the spat to continue. They all had to blow off steam and if it resulted in a few minor bites and some blood loss along the way then so be it. They all had to learn. This was the way of the wolf.

He turned to his right, opening up his stride and bounding along the grass with the cool dew seeping into his paws. There was a bite to the air that pleased him. Devereau bounded ahead, expending as much lupine energy as he possibly could. I am wolf, he thought. Watch me *soar*.

The mingled scents from the animals in the zoo behind him drifted over. The wolves were not permitted anywhere near that area but even from this distance he could smell their unease. They knew what was happening. Even the largest of the beasts contained within those pathetic, miserable cages knew that there were predators around. Devereau swung away from them, leaving them in peace. But then he caught another scent – and this was one was both more familiar and more fragrant. Hmm. Interesting.

Slowing to a more sedate pace, he swung round towards the source. It was over there, beyond the park boundary. There was little more than a breath of wind in the air but it didn't escape his attention that the scent was downwind. She probably assumed that he couldn't smell her, basing her actions on years of knowledge garnered about werewolves and their abilities. She should already know better than that, however. He wasn't like the other wolves.

Devereau slunk into the copse of oak trees over to his right, keeping his body low. He weaved in and out until he had a clear line out of sight out of the park and over the road. There. She was right there.

Scarlett was alone. She was standing perfectly still, staring across at the park. He knew instinctively that she couldn't see him beneath the cover of the trees and that she didn't know he was watching her. What he didn't know was why she had come here. After one tumultuous sexy fortnight when they'd shaken the foundations of his house and christened every single room with mad, passionate bouts of heady, raw sex, she'd walked away. She told him they'd had good times together – *great* times together – but that it was time to move on. Then she'd left. Devereau had given it a few days before calling her on the phone. Scarlett didn't pick up. He'd walked into Heart, the large vampire nightclub where they'd first met, and waited for hours for her to show up - although in truth he wasn't surprised when she didn't. This was Scarlett's MO. He was hardly the first man to fall for her and then find himself dumped. If she were anyone else, he'd have given chase. At the very least he'd have demanded answers. But he knew that anything like that would simply make her less inclined to speak to him. If she was going to play it cool, then he would do the same in return. He wouldn't forget her, however. He *couldn't* forget her.

He settled back on his haunches and gazed at her. Her dark hair was pulled back into a tight ponytail. Despite the cold air, she was wearing nothing more than a lowcut bodice and tight trousers. His breath huffed out. Damn her for looking so good. *What do you want, Scarlett?* he sent out silently. *Why are you here?* And then, because he couldn't help himself, *Are you looking for me?*

After several moments, Devereau gave up on hide and seek. It wasn't his style anyway. He stood up, shook out his fur and let out a brief low howl. Scarlett's head whipped in his direction. He grinned to himself and padded out from the trees. Now all that was separating them was the old ornate fencing that circled the park, and the road. If he wanted to, he could clear both in seconds.

Scarlett's eyes met his. For one long second they stared at each other. He desperately wished he knew what she was thinking. She tilted her head, smiling slightly and revealing her single vampire fang. Then she blew him a kiss and turned away, walking quickly in the opposite direction.

Devereau felt his insides tense. Despite the laws which stated he had to remain within the park until dawn hit, the urge to leap after her gnawed at him. He doubted she would thank him for it though. Not to mention that he had a responsibility towards the motley crew of werewolves somewhere behind him. He let out a deep sigh. Then he too turned and walked away.

CHAPTER THREE

The main concourse of Heathrow's Terminal 5 was busy. Devereau's gaze swept across the crowds, from the harried looking business men and women to the tired parents and over-excited kids. He cracked his knuckles and hoped this latest venture wouldn't prove to be a test like the last one.

He used the electronic machines to check in for his flight before dropping off his bag. It was a crying shame that he was travelling economy. He'd rather hoped that MI5 would spring for a better seat. After all, he was a werewolf on a mission and he had a status to maintain. He'd suggest it to Greensmith next time. Unfortunately, Devereau hadn't yet found the key to unlocking the steely MI5 agent's cool reserve. But he promised himself that he would sooner or later.

He joined the line for the departure gates, taking up position behind a woman in a flowery dress and long overcoat. She glanced round at him. Then she blinked. His reputation clearly preceded him. Devereau smiled easily at her. He caught her gaze drifting fearfully down towards his ticket. She wanted to make sure that she wasn't going to be sharing a flight with a werewolf.

'I'm heading to Rome,' he told her. He might as well be helpful.

Relief flickered across her expression. She was travelling elsewhere then. 'Good,' she said. Then she seemed to realise she'd given too much of her true thoughts away and hastily added, 'It's lovely at this time of year. I'm sure you'll have a wonderful time.'

Devereau deliberately bared his teeth. The woman flinched. 'I'm sure I will,' he drawled.

They shuffled forward. The woman shrugged out of her coat and placed it on the conveyor belt. Devereau did the same behind her, adding his small bag, keys, wallet and passport to a grey plastic tray. He watched as she walked up to the full body scanner, submitting briefly before continuing. A moment later, the uniformed officer beckoned towards him. He strolled up, aware that a considerable number of other waiting passengers were watching him. The woman hadn't been the only person who'd recognised him.

'Step this way, sir,' the officer said blandly.

Devereau nodded and walked into the scanner, spreading his legs and raising his arms above his head. There was a swishing sound as the machine sprang into the action. It was followed by a high-pitched beep of warning. Huh. The fearful flowery woman hadn't been beeped.

'Remain where you are, sir,' the officer intoned.

The machine swished again. Again there was a beep. Out of the corner of his eye, Devereau saw three more uniformed officers marching in his direction. These ones were armed. Okaaay.

The woman ahead lifted her coat from the other end of the conveyor belt and turned to watch. She permitted herself a tiny nod of satisfaction. As long as dangerous beasts like Devereau Webb were prevented from travelling then all was well with the world. Apparently.

'Mr Webb,' one of the gun-toting officers said, 'please come with us.'

'I feel like I'm being profiled.'

The officer's eyes were stone cold. 'Are you refusing to come?'

Devereau held up his palms in submission. 'Not at all. I was merely passing comment. I know my place.'

'I doubt that,' a second officer muttered under his breath.

Devereau's wolf itched. He remained outwardly calm, however, and even managed a pleasant smile. 'Lead the way, gentlemen.'

Two of the officers flanked him while the third took up the front. He noted his bag and belongings were being gingerly scooped up and removed from the conveyor belt. Rather than let the stain of humiliation show on his face, Devereau continued to smile. He also waved enthusiastically at the flowery woman as he passed her.

'So lovely to meet you!' he trilled.

She chose not to answer. Devereau wondered whether Italians were friendlier towards supes. And whether he'd get the chance to find out either way for himself. He followed his new entourage through a heavy steel door and decided that at least he would enjoy watching the expressions of the gun loving officers when MI5 got in touch and explained what he was really doing at Heathrow.

Without ceremony, Devereau was deposited in a small room which contained nothing more than a small table and two chairs. He'd barely sat down when the door opened again and Sarah Greensmith herself appeared. Devereau couldn't mask his emotions quickly enough.

She offered him a quick smile. 'You seem surprised to see me, Mr Webb. I did tell you I'd make contact before you boarded.'

Devereau's jaw tightened. This time Greensmith had gained the upper hand on him. It wasn't something he enjoyed although she certainly appeared happy about it. 'I was expecting a phone call. Not an arrest.'

Her mouth tightened. 'Hmm. Yes, well, this wasn't my idea.' She shook herself. 'But this sort of thing is much better when it's done in person and we can't risk meeting out in the open any longer.' She waved an airy hand around. 'This way nobody beyond a select group of people will ever know that I am talking to you. Even the security officers who brought you here don't suspect what's really going on. This is what you signed up for.'

Perhaps. But meeting in public hadn't been a problem last time. 'Hauling me into a back room still seems like overkill.'

'It's for your safety, Mr Webb.'

Uh huh. 'It kills two birds with one stone too, doesn't it? That little charade you pulled out there will have proven to all those other people that their taxes are being put to good use and that supes are being kept in their place.'

Greensmith didn't bother denying it.

'You're reinforcing negative stereotypes,' he growled.

Her expression didn't alter. 'In twenty minutes' time, you'll be back out there doing duty free shopping to your heart's content. Anyone who witnessed your removal will soon know that you were briefly held and questioned and then released to continue on your journey because you have been deemed to not be a threat. It's doing the very opposite of what you allege.'

Devereau folded his arms. 'Bullshit.'

She regarded him calmly. 'Do you want to debate supe politics and perceptions or do you want to get down to business?'

He leaned back. Antagonising her wouldn't help either of them. 'Go on then,' he drawled. 'What do I need to know and who do I need to kill?'

Sarah Greensmith sighed. 'There will be no killing of any kind.'

Just as well. Devereau wouldn't hurt anyone on the British government's say-so. He'd decide for himself what was necessary before he attempted any violence. He was peculiar that way. 'Aw,' he said aloud. 'That's a shame.'

'You're not fooling either of us, Mr Webb. I wish you would stop playing the role of tough guy. At this point, when it's only the two of us, it's entirely unnecessary.'

Devereau shrugged. 'What can I say? I'm a method actor. You're sending me to Rome to do goodness knows what and I'm merely getting into character.'

'I didn't recruit you because MI5 needs a thug. Those sorts of people are two a penny.' She pulled out a file and slid it across the small table towards him. 'You already know you are heading to Rome to infiltrate a potential terrorist cell and that this is a joint operation between us and MI6. It will not be like what you did with the Wasps. Compared to this, the Wasps were a walk in the park. This operation is far more delicate and will take far more time. It's also far more dangerous.'

Good. That meant he wasn't being given another test then. This was the real thing. He murmured non-committedly and waited for her to continue.

'We've been tracking this particular cell for several years,' Greensmith told him. 'We haven't been able to officially tie them to any illegal activity but we know they have links with various well established terrorist organisations.'

'As misplaced as they may be, don't terrorists usually have specific and very particular ideologies?' Devereau asked.

'Indeed. As far as we can tell, this group's sole ideology has been that greed is good.'

'They're only interested in financial gain, you mean.'

'Up until now. They've dabbled in some arms dealing when it's been necessary, helped smuggle goods for other organisations from country to country and mopped up the messes that others have left behind.'

Devereau rubbed his chin. 'So they're like the handyman of the terrorist world.'

'That's one way of putting it.' Greensmith smiled slightly at his analogy. 'Unfortunately, however, it appears that they're now looking to make some bigger moves. We've picked up some chatter via the Dark web that they're seeking to come out from the shadows and are planning something big. We don't know if that's true or not and, in my experience, groups of this nature do tend to over-exaggerate both their accomplishments and their ambitions. We *do* know for a fact that several of them have made trips to the United Kingdom in recent months. Until now all their efforts have been focused on mainland Europe but if they're seeking to set up operations of any sort in the UK, we need to know about it. We've attempted to use agents to infiltrate them before and gotten nowhere. We haven't managed to successfully plant any listening devices at any of their known locations. The group appears to know enough about such things that any time we've tried to bug him, our tech has been discovered. Anything we've tried against so far has failed.' She pointed at him. 'But I think you might have better luck.'

'You want me to get to know them, gain their trust, and find out what they're really up to.'

She nodded. 'Essentially. As far as we can tell, they are led by a man called Christopher Solentino. He's wanted by authorities in several countries and by all accounts is a nasty piece of work. We can't simply kill him, however. Life is not as easy sanctioning murder whenever we want it. We have to find out what he's up to and what plans are in place. It could well be that someone worse will take his place if he dies. Whatever his cell is planning won't necessarily be halted by his death either. In fact, it might have the opposite effect spur them on to commit worse atrocities. You are not to harm him. Your job is to find out what he and his colleagues are up to. That is all.'

'Sounds simple enough.'

Greensmith frowned. 'It won't be simple at all. I shouldn't have to tell you that, with the advent of Brexit, relations between us and our European counterparts have become somewhat strained. The Italian government would not be impressed if they learned that we were conducting any sort of operation on their own soil, even one as low key as this one. For the purposes of both your cover and our political expediency, your presence and your work is not officially sanctioned. If you get yourself into any kind of trouble, we will not be in a position to bail you out.' She raised at her eyebrows at him and Devereau had the distinct sensation that she was expecting him to argue about being left on his own. Frankly, he couldn't imagine anything better. He didn't need MI5 or MI6 breathing down his neck at every turn. The more independence he had, the better.

'Okay.'

Greensmith appeared momentarily relieved. 'This requires a delicate touch, Mr Webb. I want finesse, not a bull in a china shop. All we need is information. The burden of evidence for that information is low. If there is anything to suggest that they really are attempting to broach our own country, then you tell us everything you can and we will take it from there. If they are not, we will pass on whatever you discover to the European authorities and let them handle matters.'

That seemed straightforward enough. 'How do I get in touch with you if I need to?'

'We have to keep contact to a minimum.' She nodded towards the file. 'Inside there, along with details about Solentino and his terrorist cell, you'll find details of an email account. Every day, whether you believe you have anything to report or not, you need to use that account to write a draft email and update me with your progress. *Every* day. If you don't write anything, I will assume the worst, order in the cavalry and blow your cover.' Her expression was stern and, all of a sudden, Devereau felt like he was seven years old and being told off for playing football in a car park. 'And this is important. Do not actually send anything, electronically or otherwise. We have no real idea as to the capabilities of Solentino and his gang so it's vital to be cautious and avoid making any digital footprints that he could trace. Leave the email in the draft folder and I will retrieve it. In the event of an emergency, call the British embassy and ask for Maximillian Jones. But that is *only* in an emergency. Otherwise, I will wait until I deem it is safe and I will contact you directly myself. Is that understood?'

Devereau gave her a disarming grin. 'Sure.'

Greensmith got to her feet. 'Good. I will leave you here to read the file and memorise the contents. You will have to leave the file here when you've finished but you'll be pleased to know that I've included details of a bank account with a small amount of funds which are at your disposal. Please do not be profligate with taxpayers' money, however, Mr Webb. I've also booked you a hotel room in the centre of Rome. It's already paid for.' She checked her watch. 'Christopher Solentino has tickets for a private auction in that very hotel this evening. We've procured a ticket for you as well. It will provide you with the opportunity to make your initial approach. Perhaps you can make yourself known to him and then invite him for a drink at the hotel bar. Or maybe he'll recognise you and make the approach himself. That would be ideal.' She shrugged. 'In any case, I'll leave it up to you. It's best to play these things by ear.' Greensmith reached for the door handle. 'When you're ready to go, knock on the door and you will be released. Your bag will be returned to you. Your flight departs in forty-five minutes so I suggest you start reading.' She flashed him a bright, brilliant smile which was completely out of character and worried him far more than anything else she'd said or done. 'Good luck, Mr Webb.'

CHAPTER FOUR

ROME WAS ENTIRELY TOO CHARMING. DEVEREAU PAID THE TAXI
driver as they drew up outside of the Hotel Condotti, stepped out
of the vehicle and gazed around. He was a London boy through
and through and this was his first visit to anywhere in Italy. Until
now, the closest he'd gotten to anything genuinely Italian had
probably been Domino's pizza. Shameful, but true. In any case,
he had to admit to himself that he was impressed. The city felt
grandiose and exciting, albeit vaguely familiar at the same time,
and the arched architecture surrounding him, along with the
blend of both ancient and modern with everything else in
between, was fascinating. It also smelled markedly different
although Devereau couldn't have put the myriad of scents into
appropriate words no matter how hard he tried. He moved out of
the path of an oncoming moped and grinned to himself. This was
the first time in several days that he'd not questioned his own
decision to work for MI5. He could certainly see himself getting
used to this sort of jet-set lifestyle very quickly.

Gulping in one last breath of heady Roman air, Devereau
turned and headed into the hotel. It was grander than he'd been
expecting. His gaze roved over the mahogany and brass fittings,

polished to within an inch of their lives, and then he strode up to the front desk.

'Ciao.'

'Good afternoon, Mr Webb,' the receptionist replied in perfect English. 'We've been expecting you.'

Devereau tried not to look too surprised. He'd expended his entire knowledge of Italian in his greeting so it was something of an embarrassing relief that the dark haired woman knew who he was and was speaking to him in his own native tongue. This was clearly a hotel that expended considerable effort on customer service. She didn't appear nervous of him. Another tick in Rome's favour. If everyone he came across over the next few days treated werewolves with this sort of relaxed attitude, he might enjoy himself. Hell, he might emigrate. 'I'm pleased to hear that.'

'Would you like to check in?'

'I would indeed.' He handed her his passport.

The receptionist gave him a professional smile and began to tap at her keyboard with her manicured nails. 'Your room is on the twelfth floor. Breakfast is served from between six and ten in the morning in the Blue Room opposite the lifts. The bar is open all day until midnight. Would you like a map of the local area?'

It wouldn't do any harm. 'Sure.'

She reached into a nearby drawer and lifted out a folded wad of glossy paper. Deftly opening it up to reveal a simple map, she pointed out the hotel. 'We are here,' she said. She moved her finger. 'The Colosseum is here. The Trevi fountain is here and St Peter's Basilica is here. And here,' she added importantly, 'is the Piazza Armerina.'

The what? 'Thank you.'

'You're welcome. Here is your key. Enjoy your stay.'

Devereau smiled, flashing his teeth. 'I certainly will.'

* * *

HE CHECKED his appearance in the mirror before he left his hotel room. Devereau wasn't typically a suit sort of man but the situation – and the environment - seemed to call for smarter attire than his usual jeans. The last time he'd worn this particular dark grey suit had been at a friend's wedding. He adjusted his cuff links and fiddled with the collar of his pristine white shirt. Then he gazed for a moment at his reflection. His dirty blond hair was just the right side of ruffled and the line of stubble around his jaw was neat enough to appear deliberate rather than lazy. He looked the part.

'So why,' he asked himself aloud, 'do you feel nervous?'

Gallingly, he already knew the answer to his question. He was in unfamiliar territory in every sense of the word. It wasn't only about Italy. For the first time in his life, he was on the side of law and order. His own country had put their trust in him. It shocked him how much he wanted to do well.

'You have nothing to prove,' he told his reflection. 'You're Devereau Webb. You've got this.' He permitted a tiny lupine growl to rumble from deep within his chest. 'You've so got this.' Devereau brushed away an invisible speck of lint from his shoulder. Then he headed out.

There was a warm buzz of chatter in the bar, and a considerable number of people milling around. They certainly couldn't all be hotel guests. Presumably they were here for the auction which was due to start shortly. Devereau caught the bartender's attention and ordered a Peroni before picking up a nearby catalogue and flicking through it. There were only nine lots and they all appeared to be jewellery. He cast a professional eye over the offerings. The fifth lot was a diamond necklace that would be easily broken down. Although the settings were elaborate, the cut of each stone was surprisingly pedestrian. Each of the separate jewels could be sold separately and no-one would be any the wiser. In fact he knew of several dealers who would give him a very good price for it and who would act quickly enough to avoid even the whisper of detection. He smiled slightly. Old habits died hard.

'You look,' murmured a female voice, 'like something has caught your eye.'

He glanced up, his eyes meeting those of a brown haired woman. She was half a foot taller than he was and had the sort of smooth complexion and alluring perfume that spoke of considerable wealth. He didn't need to touch the pearls round her neck to know that they were real and there was no doubt in his mind that the jade green dress she was wearing, and which perfectly matched the colour of her eyes, was from some sort of expensive fashion designer.

'Let's say,' he said, 'that I have a professional interest in pretty jewellery.'

The woman's mouth curved into a smile. 'I have heard that about you.' She extended her hand towards him. 'My name is Alina.'

'Devereau.'

Her smile grew. 'I know. I've seen your name in the news. You made quite the sensation when you turned into a wolf the first time. I would ask you for a demonstration but I don't think the hotel management would be very happy.'

He smiled back at her. 'Probably not. Although people here seem far more relaxed about werewolves than they do in London.'

'I imagine they are.' She nodded towards the auction catalogue. 'So will you be putting a bid in?'

'For the necklace? I doubt it. I know you won't be bidding for it either.'

Her eyebrows quirked upwards. 'What makes you say that?'

'It doesn't look like your style.' He flipped through the pages until he reached details of second last lot. 'I reckon you're here for this,' he said, displaying the well lit photo of a delicate bracelet. 'It seems much more your thing.'

Alina's eyes danced. She leaned in more closely and lowered her voice. 'Guess again,' she whispered.

Interesting. He turned to the final page. The last lot was a remarkably ugly ring. 'Don't tell me you're after this?'

'You'll have to wait and see. If that ring does what it's supposed to, it's a powerful thing indeed.' Devereau frowned. What did she mean by that? Apparently sensing his confusion, Alina gave him an amused look. 'And,' she added in a languid drawl, 'I do love power.' With that, she turned away, sauntering to the other side of the room and coiling an arm round the shoulders of a dark haired man who was in deep conversation with an older gentleman. The man looked up in his direction and Devereau felt himself tense. Well, well, well. It was Christopher Solentino. The target himself.

The blurry photos he'd perused in Sarah Greensmith's file hadn't managed to capture the essence of the man. In person, he was surprisingly squat, although his stomach was flat and his heavy shoulders and thick arms spoke of considerable power. His skin was so pale it wouldn't have looked out of place on a night-loving vampire while his crooked nose suggested numerous fights followed by poor medical assistance.

Alina said something to Solentino. Devereau strained his ears to listen but his supernatural skills couldn't extend above the hubbub of conversation to pick out her words. Solentino glanced over in his direction. Devereau noted his light blue eyes. It wasn't the colour which was remarkable, however. It was their expression. He'd seen eyes like that on several men in his time. Those eyes possessed the sort of coldness which only someone who had experience in causing the deaths of others could obtain. All the same, Devereau smiled briefly and raised his bottle of beer in acknowledgment. Then, to avoid appearing too interested, he returned his attention back to the auction catalogue. Maybe connecting with Solentino would be far easier – and far more dangerous - than he'd thought.

* * *

Devereau was onto his third beer by the time the waiting crowd were called for the auction. He drained the bottle and followed the others into a grand room filled with half a dozen rows of empty chairs, all of which faced an empty pedestal where no doubt the auctioneer would direct the evening's sales. Devereau took a seat next to the aisle and watched as the rest of the would-be bidders took their places. This was a well-heeled lot. His gaze swept over several older couples, noting the way that several of them were clutching their own catalogues with tight anticipation, and his attention hovered with vague curiosity over the row of various professional looking men and women, each of whom were holding their phones in their hands and whose clothes, while smart, did not quite possess the immaculate cut of some of the others. Christopher Solentino, with Alina still by his side, sat in the very first row. Devereau noted the faint bulge in the cut of his suit as he made himself comfortable. He was definitely carrying a weapon of some sort. Solentino was obviously a man who took few chances.

A short woman brushed past Devereau's shoulder and took the seat directly in front of him. He glanced at her before performing a double take. She was a gremlin; he'd put money on it. Then his nostrils tickled. There was a sudden faint tang of blood clinging to the air. Devereau tracked it, his eyes eventually landing on a tall male dressed in a smart cloak and holding a top hat of all things in his lap. Vampire. And sitting two rows behind the vampire were two violet haired pixies.

Devereau's skin prickled. He might not know a great deal about Italy but he was more than aware that the population of supes in Rome was similar in size to that of London's. So why were there so many congregating in this one room? What was so interesting about a small jewellery auction? He frowned. It was no wonder that so few people had stared at him or picked him out while he'd been waiting at the bar if they'd already been expecting this number of supernatural creatures. In this crowd, he was far from unique – and that little fact piqued both his interest and his wariness considerably. Then he felt the unmistakable sensation of someone watching him. He turned his head to find a pair of yellow glowing eyes burning into him with malevolence. Another werewolf. Not just another werewolf, in fact. This was a wolf who looked about ready to leap forward and sink her teeth into Devereau's neck.

He met the wolf's gaze head on. There was no other choice. Patches of angry fur sprouted across her cheekbones, causing the humans seated nearby to shuffle away in sudden alarm. Devereau growled quietly and intensified his stare. The wolf snarled once and looked away. I win, Devereau thought. But that tiny victory still didn't explain what was really going on and why so many supes were in attendance.

Before he could ponder the mystery further, there was the sharp sound of wood hitting wood. Discomfited, Devereau returned his attention to the front of the room. A smartly dressed woman was standing behind the pedestal with a gavel in her hand. She cleared her throat and began to speak in a stream of smooth Italian. A moment later, she switched to accented English.

'Ladies and gentlemen,' she intoned. 'Thank you for coming. Due to the international nature of tonight's guests, the bidding will be conducted first in Italian and second in English to ensure that everyone is able to participate. I therefore ask for your forbearance if some bids take longer than expected to complete.' She bowed slightly. 'So without further ado, let us begin.'

On cue, a muscle bound human who'd clearly spent more hours in the gym and on protein shakes laced with steroids than on real life activities appeared. In his hands, and nestled in a velvet lined case, was a sparkling set of diamond and ruby earrings.

The auctioneer smiled and launched into Italian once again before repeating her words in English. 'Our first lot is this stunning set of earrings. Everything you see tonight has been retrieved from the estate of the late Visconte Gatto, and these beautiful earrings are no exception. The platinum settings are incomparable in both their workmanship and design, while the clarity and exquisite cut of each individual stone proves their undeniable resplendence.'

Devereau blinked. Undeniable resplendence? The earrings were pretty and no doubt worth a great deal but the auctioneer's florid description was remarkably over the top. He snuck a glance around the room. The vast majority of the would-be buyers appeared patient and unruffled rather than excited. These earrings were far from the star attraction. They were barely even an amusing sideshow. The audience – including both Christopher Solentino and Alina - were obviously waiting for one of the other pieces of jewellery to come up. For reasons which weren't yet clear, it was surely the unattractive ring. It had to be listed as the final lot for a reason. Devereau flipped once again through the catalogue and gazed at the photo and description of the ring while the unenthusiastic bidding for the earrings commenced.

Cast in silver and including a large moonstone, this ring has been in the Gatto family for generations.

Huh. That was it. No overblown descriptions which waxed lyrical about the ring's supposed beauty. No mention of the quality of the silver or of the moonstone. No valuation. And a single photo which appeared to show both scratches and minor dents in the metal work. There was definitely more to this ring that met the eye. He wondered idly if Sarah Greensmith knew anything about its apparent importance and had deliberately declined to tell him. He wouldn't put it past her. Still, as intriguing as the ring was, it wasn't why he was here. He closed the glossy catalogue once more and settled back to watch the action – and in particular the dark bowed head of Christopher Solentino.

* * *

THE AUCTION PROCEEDED QUICKLY. The earrings went for a respectable nine thousand euros. The fifth lot, the very stealable diamond necklace, caused a flurry of activity and a minor bidding war between an Italian gentleman in his late sixties and an American woman who was already wearing enough heavy jewellery to sink a small fishing boat. By the time the gavel closed the bidding on the bracelet, which garnered Visconte Gatto's estate a cheery forty two thousand euros, the atmosphere in the room had ratcheted up several notches.

Solentino had been shifting around in his chair for several minutes, his agitation growing to the extent that Devereau was beginning to wonder if the man had piles. It would certainly explain the pallor of his skin. When the muscly male model appeared with the moonstone ring, however, he sat bolt upright. By his side, Alina did the same, her hand draping around Solentino's neck.

'And so, ladies and gentlemen,' the auctioneer announced, 'we come to the finale of tonight's little auction. Dubbed the Ring of All Seasons, its original provenance is unknown. The Gatto family acquired it in the late nineteenth century and it has not been seen out in public since then.' She smiled at the audience, taking a moment to savour the moment. The entire group of professionals, who were representing absent clients, raised their phones to their ears and murmured into them. The gremlin to his right made no attempt to hide his interest and actually stood up, planting his two large feet onto the seat of the chair so he could see over the heads of the others, and several audience members snapped photos of the battered ring. Then the auctioneer drew in a breath and all eyes turned to her. 'I will start the bidding,' she proclaimed, 'at two hundred thousand euros.'

Devereau's jaw dropped. Two hundred thousand? For that?

The pixie immediately raised her hand.

'I have two hundred thousand,' murmured the auctioneer.

The older man who'd won the bracelet nodded.

'Two hundred and fifty.'

A woman along from Devereau flicked her catalogue. 'Three hundred thousand.'

Devereau saw Solentino jerk. 'Five hundred,' he called out.

The auctioneer nodded in acknowledgment. Solentino's bid was quickly usurped by another and Devereau noted the spasm of rage on his face. He didn't give up, however. Within moments the bids accelerated, interest parties raising their hands and nodding from all across the room.

'One million euros,' the auctioneer intoned.

Solentino didn't miss a beat. 'One five.'

It was at that point one of the phone clutching men tipped his head towards the front. 'Five million,' he said.

There was an audible gasp around the room. Christopher Solentino began to rise out of his chair, his head whipping towards the man who'd made the bid. If looks could kill, Devereau mused, there would be blood dripping from the ceiling right about now. Alina tugged him back down again and began muttering furiously in his ear.

'Five million euros,' the auctioneer said, without a trace of a tremor in her voice, 'for the Ring of All Seasons.' She looked round. 'Going ...' She knocked her gavel. 'Gone.'

The room erupted. People pressed forward, seeking to congratulate the winner even though it was obvious that he was merely a proxy. From out of nowhere, two armed guards appeared, striding towards the male model and taking possession of the ring. Devereau didn't watch any of it, however. He kept his focus on Solentino. The man got up to his feet, took one swift glance at the ring, and spun away, marching down the aisle and towards the exit with Alina close behind him. Alina's expression was tight and, despite the smile she openly displayed, there was a cold anger lurking behind her eyes. Devereau found it fascinating. Everything about her, from her perfect make-up to her expensive clothes and her seemingly benign expression was designed to make onlookers register her exterior without delving any further to the woman beneath. Whatever else she was thinking, she really had wanted that ring. It was probably why she'd approached Devereau before the auction had begun. She'd been concerned that he was one of the many supes in attendance who'd wanted to bid on it and she'd been scoping out the competition.

Unlike his girlfriend, Solentino wasn't attempting to conceal his rage. His white cheeks were flushed with anger and his mouth was pursed tight. Even his fists were clenched. Hmmm. The last time Devereau had seen someone that upset at losing out on an object had been when Alice was three years old and she'd tried to snatch another kid's Barbie doll at the park. It was entirely befuddling that such an innocuous looking object could cause such a reaction in a grown man. Fortunately, however, it also gave Devereau the perfect opportunity to slide into Christopher Solentino's good books.

CHAPTER FIVE

Devereau didn't bother following Solentino out of the hotel. Thanks to Sarah Greensmith's file, he'd already memorised where the man lived. Whether he was going home or heading to a nearby bar to drown his sorrows with Alina didn't matter. Either way, trailing after him would be far too obvious – and therefore a complete waste of his time. Instead, Devereau ordered another beer from the bar and waited for the proxy who'd bought the enigmatic Ring Of All Seasons to complete any necessary paperwork and make his exit.

Devereau was halfway down the bottle when he sensed the approach. Turning, he recognised the female werewolf from the auction. Her shoulders were dropped and her head was tilted down, both hallmarks that she was acknowledging lupine submission. Her words, however, were far from respectful.

'When did you fucking get here?' she hissed, keeping her voice low.

Devereau allowed his mouth to curve into an easy smile. He didn't know why she was acting so overtly antagonistic but he wasn't going to rise to her bait. 'It's lovely to make your acquaintance,' he said, holding his hand out to shake hers.

She kept her eyes down but he couldn't mistake the flash of rage in her expression. 'When did you get here?' she bit out once more, ignoring his proferred handshake.

He raised an eyebrow. She was like a dog with a bone. What did matter? He considered how to answer her and then shrugged to himself and opted for the truth. Spy or not, his time of arrival was hardly a state secret. 'This afternoon,' he said. 'Not long after three.' He paused. 'So I've not had time to do any sightseeing yet but if you have any recommendations I'd be thrilled to hear them.'

The wolf glanced down at the slender gold watch on her wrist. 'You're sailing close to the wind,' she told him. 'The only sightseeing you need to be doing is Piazza Armerina.' She raised her eyes, meeting his directly for only the briefest of seconds. 'You don't have long left.' She scowled and turned on her heel, quickly marching away.

Devereau watched her go. Clearly, he was missing something. That was the second person who'd mentioned this mysterious piazza to him. Under other circumstances, he would have gone after her to find out what she had been referring to. At that very moment, however, the suited man who'd bid for the ring walked out of the auction room with the two armed men by his sides.

It was obvious from the way the men held themselves that they were professionals, likely ex-military. While Devereau was reasonably certain that in a fair fight he could take them both on and win, he knew such a move wouldn't be prudent. Werewolf or not, success here would depend on stealth and brains. Luckily for Sarah Greensmith and the rest of MI5, he wasn't always as dumb as he acted. He felt his body relax. Walking into an overtly posh auction and playing a role might have made him feel nervous and out of his depth but now he was more at home. What was about to happen was Devereau's bread and butter. Or at least it used to be.

Delving into his pocket, he withdrew the packet of cigarettes he'd purchased at the airport and ambled outside to the front of the hotel. He stepped away from the door to loiter by the ashtray helpfully provided by Hotel Condotti and slid out a single cigarette, lighting it and blowing out a single puff of smoke as a beast of a car pulled up and all three men also exited the hotel. The suited proxy was gingerly holding a small box in both hands. No doubt the little box contained the ring. The armed guards were taking no chances, their eyes sweeping from left to right and their hands hovering over their bulging guns. Neither left the proxy's side for a moment. All three of them slid into the backseat of the large car, with the two guards giving Devereau little more than a cursory glance. *That's right,* he thought. *I'm just another nicotine addict stymied by the laws on indoor smoking. There's nothing to see here.* He took another drag while the car pulled away, turning left into the narrow street. As soon as it did so, he hastily stubbed the cigarette out and ran.

By the time he reached the corner and turned, the car was already halfway down the street. At least the roads in this part of Rome weren't particularly wide. It meant that the vehicle's speed would be hampered somewhat. Devereau sent a silent prayer to whichever gods might be listening that this would only be a short journey and that the car would remain within the city limits – because he'd have no hope on any motorways or even country roads. And then he sprinted at the wall of the nearby trattoria and hauled himself up onto its roof. Thirty seconds later, as the massive car was halted by the red gleam of traffic lights at the next crossing, Devereau drew level with it, gazing down from his rooftop vantage point. The buildings around here were low rise and densely packed together and he was easily nimble enough to maintain a good speed even on slippery roof tiles. It wouldn't matter how cautious they were being, the men in the car below would have no idea that they were being followed.

The lights changed and the car turned right. Devereau followed from the rooftops, remaining level with it. He had to keep his body low in order to maintain his centre of gravity, and the exertion meant that he soon felt a slick sheen of sweat form across his skin, but the car continued to move at a slow pace and when he was forced to leap across a two metre gap between buildings, he remained apace.

They continued straight for about half a mile. There was a fair number of pedestrians on the street below and Devereau's stomach grumbled at the smells rising up from the various well lit restaurants. He promised himself a decent meal later. He would deserve it.

Up ahead the road was clearly widening out. Devereau fixed his gaze on the wider boulevard which ran perpendicular to this one and considered the options. If the car headed in any direction other than to the right, he would no longer be able to track it from the rooftops. He would have to risk dropping back down to street level. There were no taxis in sight but it was always possible that he could steal a moped or a bike and keep up with the car for at least another few miles or so if need be. Chance would be a fine thing.

He sped up, taking advantage of the flat roof ahead of him. Pulling ahead of the car, he reached the crossroad before it did, allowing him precious seconds to survey all the possibilities. The only visible parked cars and motorbikes were in a well lit area directly in front of a busy looking café. Stealing any of those vehicles was a non-starter. He hissed slightly in irritation and waited to see what the car would do.

It paused for a few beats. Then it trundled straight ahead, crossing over the wide boulevard with its bright street lamps before continuing down the opposite street. Devereau cursed silently. Still, he was nothing if not adaptable. He sucked in a breath and jumped, landing on two feet onto the pavement below. There was a jarring thud and a bolt of agony ran down his spine. He shook off the pain and forced a grin at the gaping couple who'd been wandering hand in hand down the street and who had stopped in their tracks when he'd suddenly appeared.

'Ciao!'

He didn't wait to hear if they responded. Instead he took off, sprinting across the boulevard in the same direction which the car had taken. The moment he left the bright lights of the wide road behind him, and he registered the tail lights of the heavy car disappearing down the darker street ahead of him, he tensed his muscles and called on his wolf. And even though it had barely been twenty-four hours since the full moon extravaganza had ended, it answered.

He burst out of his clothes, transforming from man to beast. It was shame about the expensive suit but he'd bill MI5 later. Right now, he was on a mission. He leapt forward, breaking into a four legged run. There were enough shadows that he could remain concealed from the view of any passersby – as long as he didn't come across anyone walking directly towards him on this side of the road. He doubted that the Italian authorities would be impressed at an English werewolf running through their quiet streets at night time so he'd simply have to cross his claws and hope that this gamble paid off.

As soon as he was less than twenty metres away from the black car, he switched tactics, abandoning the relative safety of the shadows for the more dangerous open road. He couldn't risk the car's occupants noticing any movement so, to avoid raising the faintest of suspicions, this was the safest move. He sprang into the centre of the road, angling his long, fur covered body so that it was directly behind the car itself and only just to the right of the exhaust pipe. None of the mirrors would reflect his presence if he remained in this spot. As long as he kept his muzzle within striking distance of the car's rear, the people inside wouldn't see him. Unfortunately, the drunk guy on the pavement to his right did notice him, staggering to a stop and staring at him slack-jawed. Devereau maintained his speed but couldn't prevent himself from tensing. The car didn't slow down, however, so he had to assume that neither the driver nor the other men had noticed.

They continued for several hundred feet. It wasn't difficult to keep up with the car but the further they travelled, the more concerned he became that it wouldn't be long before they hit yet another well lit road where more people would notice him. He bunched up his muscles, his tension growing, but when the car began to indicate left and began to finally slow down, he felt a burst of optimism. From his left, there was a sudden mechanical whirring sound akin to a gate or a garage being opened. Devereau breathed out. It appeared they'd reached their destination. Praise be.

Committed to this course of action, Devereau made sure to keep his body low and his nose touching against the car's bumper while it swung to the left and slowly rolled through the large heavy gates which had opened up. Together they descended into an illuminated carpark which appeared to be underground. Unfortunately Devereau was unable to make out anything from his current vantage point beyond what lay to his immediate right and left.

As soon as the ground levelled out, he detached himself from the rear of the car and sprang towards an ostentatious Bentley which was large enough to provide the cover he needed to conceal himself. He lowered his belly to the ground and waited. The driver of the car reversed it into one of the empty parking bays and turned off the engine. Devereau held his breath while the car doors opened and the men slipped out.

He tilted his head, listening. Not one of them said anything. All he could hear above their combined breath sounds were four distinct pairs of feet walking away from him. Then a door opened and everything went quiet. He waited for one long moment until he was confident that he was alone and none of the men were returning. Even the driver had vanished. He permitted himself a tiny rumble of satisfaction then rose up and looked around.

There were eight cars in total, including the large black monstrosity he'd followed in and the Bentley he'd been hiding behind. Not all of the cars were showy and expensive, however. Devereau noted a small blue Fiat and a nondescript white van, the latter of which was showing signs of rust around its wheel arches. Interesting.

He padded over to the black car and raised his head to peer inside. The windows were tinted so it was difficult to see much and, in any case, he doubted anything had been left inside. With a half shrug, he cricked his neck. Then he transformed back into human form.

Without the comfort of his fur to keep him warm, Devereau almost immediately started shivering. Unfortunately, the bonus of opposable thumbs and hands which could twist doorknobs were more useful right now than his more obvious lupine abilities. Stark naked, he walked up to the plain door set at the far end of the car park and placed his ear against it. He couldn't hear a thing. He licked his lips and, with slow deliberate movements designed to mask as much sound as possible, he opened it a fraction.

Soft light spilled out, in sharp contrast to the harsh overhead lights of the carpark. He paused for another moment, listening again. Then he opened the door wider and stepped through. At least here there was some carpet. It would allow him to proceed almost entirely silently. And, he smirked, it was much more pleasant on his bare tootsies.

He walked forward, unsure yet whether he was in a large house or a block of expensive apartments. It didn't really matter either way. He could smell the combined scents of the four men who'd not long passed this way so he knew he'd be able to track them to wherever they'd gone without too much difficulty. The only worrisome part was whether he would be noticed. If there weren't any security guards or other residents around, then there would certainly be CCTV. The expensive cars in the carpark behind him all but demanded it.

At the far end of the corridor there was another heavy door. Taking care yet again, Devereau opened it an inch and peered out. He glimpsed a single lift to the right and thought he recognised the straight back of the man who'd acted as proxy at the auction. Neither the two armed guards nor the driver were in view. Devereau glanced up and noted not merely one but three carefully positioned security cameras. Hmmm. He doubted there were any blindspots which he could sneak through undetected.

He remained where he was, watching the lift carefully. It dinged open and the proxy stepped inside. As he turned and pressed one of the floor buttons, Devereau managed to note that he was still carrying the box containing the ring in his hands. Then the lift doors smoothly closed.

Set above the lift itself was a small LED display. Devereau watched the numbers as the lift rose up through the building. Five, six, seven, eight … Then he heard footsteps approach from the other side of the lobby. Come on, come on. Eleven, twelve … thirteen. There. Unlucky number thirteen. The footsteps drew nearer. In the nick of time, Devereau hastily closed the door and darted back to the carpark. This was a lot of risky running around for one damned ugly piece of jewellery. He'd have to make sure that it would be worth it.

CHAPTER SIX

Now that he was in a position to look around, Devereau was unimpressed with the building and its immediate surroundings. The area was ringed by a high stone wall which had been coated with anti-climb paint that would make it nigh on impossible to scale even for someone of his abilities. The only way in or out was via the remote controlled gates which he'd snuck in through while hunkered behind the car. Within the walls, there was an overly ornate fountain set in one corner of the narrow landscaped gardens and a small outdoor gym that didn't look as if it received any sort of action. The grass was manicured so neatly and with such precision that it appeared sanitised to the point of ridicule. The building itself wasn't any better. He might have been charmed by the rest of Rome that he'd seen so far but this place was like a Disneyfied version. Carved sandstone that was too pristine to be anything other than wholly modern, random jutting blocks with whorls and curves which were simply too … perfect, and elaborate balconies that he supposed were meant to be romantic and inspired by Romeo and Juliet but instead looked like incongruous afterthoughts. The entire structure lacked the character of the other nearby buildings although at least the anti-climb paint didn't extend to the main structure itself. Devereau was certain the rooms inside would be large, airy and filled with ostentatious gilt features and uncomfortable furniture. He'd seen similar attempts at design in London. It was intended to inspire awe and admiration but actually ended up being both dull and cold. Whoever lived here had far more money than taste. But then he already knew that from what he'd seen of the ring.

If he hadn't been naked and it hadn't been December, he might have waited around a bit longer and spent more time working out the lay of the land. However, his teeth were starting to chatter and he was keen to get this entire operation over and done with as quickly as possible so he could get back to his hotel and get some clothes on. At least the building's design would make it easy to scale – and the physical exertion would warm him up. Heading for the side of the building, where there were no security cameras and there was less chance his mountaineering attempt would be noticed, he jumped up, using the overhanging curves of the lowest balustrade to pull himself up. He swung onto the first balcony. There was a glimmer of light from beyond the closed curtains which he completely ignored. Reminding himself not to look down, he balanced on the edge of the balcony wall before stretching up for the next section. With his muscles straining, he continued to clamber up.

'Go to Rome,' he muttered to himself. 'It'll be fun. You'll be an international super spy saving the world from the threat of an evil gang intent on wrongdoings. You'll be a hero. And you'll even get to climb up the side of an ugly building while stark bollock naked. What could be better?'

His foot landed on a jutting curl of sandstone. The moment he braced his weight on it so he could spring up to the next section, there was a loud cracking sound. It was going to give way. Cursing, he sped up, leaping upwards as the stone gave way and fell to the ground with a painfully loud crash. Oops. This stupid building was definitely not his sort of thing. Devereau hastily hauled himself up the last few metres before any security guards with big guns came to investigate the noise. The sooner he did what he'd come here to do, the better.

He planted his feet on the relative safety of the balcony belonging to the thirteenth floor and took a moment to catch his breath. Getting up here had been one thing but he doubted he'd find it quite so easy to climb back down the same way. He'd have to find an alternative route for his escape. He'd work something out. He usually did.

Devereau sidled along the wide balcony to the other side. The curtains here were also closed but the floor to ceiling glass door was open a fraction, probably to let in some fresh air. He paused for a moment, listening. There was a low murmur of voices but they were coming from further away, muffled by at least one interior wall. As satisfied as he could be that the room beyond was empty, he gripped the glass door and slid it further open so he could get inside. At least it moved soundlessly. Maybe there was something to be said for tasteless design that cost the earth after all.

Keeping his own movements slow and cautious, he planted one foot inside then the other. He held his breath and side-stepped, creating as few ripples in the heavy curtains as he possibly could. The moment he emerged from them into the large living room and expelled his breath, however, he froze. That scent. Fucking hell. *Fucking* hell.

There was a loud click as the safety was thumbed off from a gun. Then a voice barked at him from the doorway. 'Don't move.'

Devereau wasn't planning on it. He remained where he was while one of the armed guards from the auction strode towards him, the muzzle of his handgun raised.

'You've made the biggest mistake of your life, boyo,' the man said, his face twisting into a snarl.

Actually, Devereau doubted that very much. His evening was already looking up.

'Put your hands up,' he ordered.

'Either,' Devereau said, 'you want me to put my hands up or you want me not to move. You can't have it both ways.'

From the man's expression, he was quite prepared to put a bullet in Devereau's skull and smile while doing it.

'Hands up,' he repeated.

Devereau did as he was told. 'I'm clearly not a threat,' he said. 'I'm not carrying any weapon and I'm not even wearing any clothes. You're over-reacting while I stand here shivering to death. I'm shrivelling up from the cold.' He flicked his eyes down his own body. 'As you can see for yourself.'

Another voice drifted through from beyond the doorway. 'Devereau Webb. You're still a moany bastard.'

Devereau smiled. 'Hi Scarlett. Fancy meeting you here.'

There was a loud, exasperated sigh and then she stepped into the light. Her dark hair was loose, curling round her shoulders, and she was dressed casually, in a simple tunic and trousers.

'Let me deal with this, boss,' the armed guard growled. 'I'll make sure you never see this man again.'

'It's fine, Simon. I've got this.'

'But –'

Scarlett's eyes flashed and her voice turned to sharp steel. 'Get out,' she ordered.

The guard twitched. Then he did as he was told. Devereau waited until he'd gone before speaking again. 'He's no vamp.'

'How very observant of you,' Scarlett drawled.

Devereau shrugged. 'Are you branching out?'

'No. I'm merely keeping a low profile.' Her eyes narrowed. 'Not low enough, it appears.'

His smile grew and he took a step towards her. Scarlett stayed where she was. 'You were told not to move.'

He paused, pretending to be a good boy, and watched her.

'I shouldn't have to ask you this aloud,' Scarlett said, 'but it appears that I'm going to do it anyway. Why have you climbed up the outside of my building and then appeared naked in my living room?'

Devereau took another step towards her. 'It's a very ugly building, Scarlett.' He took one more step.

She folded her arms across her chest. 'I know it's an ugly building,' she said. 'I didn't design it and I don't own it. It's part of the vampires' property portfolio. We own places like this all over the world. Ugly or not, believe me, your dangling balls didn't make its exterior look any prettier and they're certainly not enhancing the appearance of this room either.'

He raised his eyebrows. 'Are you quite sure about that?'

She chose to ignore his question. 'Why did you follow me here?'

'I didn't.'

Scarlett sniffed. 'You don't seriously expect me to believe that you're here in this apartment in Rome by accident?'

'Well,' he said, with an arch grin, 'kinda.' He closed the distance between them. 'But it is good to see you, Scarlett.' His eyes dropped to her mouth.

'Whatever was between us is over, Devereau. We've been through this. We had fun for a few weeks. That's all it was. That's all it ever was.'

He raised his gaze to meet hers. 'I'm truly sorry about that,' he said softly.

'If you think that stalking me will make me change my mind …'

'I'm not stalking you,' he interrupted. 'In fact, if anyone's stalking, it's you. Why were you at Regent's Park last week?'

'I wasn't *at* Regent's Park. I was outside it.'

Devereau reached out and brushed an errant curl away from her cheek. He was inordinately pleased that she didn't pull away but he couldn't fail to spot the flicker of fearful worry in her gaze.

Disturbed by her reaction, he moved back, giving her the space she needed. He also picked up a throw from the back of one of the chairs and wrapped it round his body. 'Now you're splitting hairs.'

Scarlett's mouth tightened. 'We are done, Devereau.'

Damn it. 'I won't argue with you.' He watched her as she looked down at the floor. Huh. Maybe things between them weren't quite as clear cut as they seemed. 'I won't make any move on you. When you change your mind about us,' his eyes glittered and he took a painful gamble, 'and, Scarlett, you *will* change your mind, you'll have me to approach me yourself.'

'This lady is not for turning,' she said in a surprisingly prim tone of voice.

He tried to ignore the bitter surge of disappointment which suddenly flared deep in his chest. 'Very well.'

Scarlett opened her mouth to say something then seemed to think better of it. 'How is Martina?'

'She's well. Her dad is still an arse. And she could do with a decent female role model in her life.'

Scarlett gave him a long look. 'She has your sister. And Dr Yara. And Rachel Foster.'

'None of them are supes,' Devereau pointed out.

'I'm a vamp, not a wolf.'

'Are you suggesting,' he asked with only the faintest hint of a tease, 'that werewolves and vampires aren't capable of mixing?'

'Maybe,' Scarlett said quietly, 'I am.' She appeared downbeat for a moment. Then she tilted her chin upwards. 'You're really not here for me, are you?'

Devereau ran his tongue over his lips. 'No. I'm not. I genuinely didn't know you would be here.'

She looked away. Was she disappointed? He couldn't tell.

'That can only mean one thing then,' Scarlett said flatly. 'You're here for the ring. You were planning to steal right from under my nose.'

'Yep.' He held out his palm.

Scarlett laughed suddenly, genuinely amused. 'You don't seriously think I'm just going to hand it over?'

'All I want to do is borrow it for a few days. You'll get it back. I promise.'

She rolled her eyes. 'A few days? It won't be Winter Solstice for another two weeks.'

Devereau stared at her. 'Are you talking in code? The eagle flies at midnight. The red fox enjoys the forest.'

She hesitated. 'Devereau,' she asked slowly, 'why exactly do you want the Ring Of All Seasons?'

Er... he'd never actually disclosed to Scarlett that he'd been approached by MI5. 'There's a gang,' he hedged, 'run by a bloke called Christopher Solentino that I'm trying to infilitrate. He wants the ring and I want him.'

She watched him. 'Why do you want him?'

'Because I don't think he's a good guy. You remember Dominic Phillips,' he said quietly, referring to the horrific excuse for a human who'd enslaved Martina and who both he and Scarlett had helped to bring down.

'This Solentino is like Phillips?' Scarlett asked darkly.

'Possibly. I don't know yet. But Solentino wants the ring so I was planning to steal it and bring it to him as a way to ingratiate myself with him.'

She frowned. 'Why? Why would you involve yourself with a man such as this?'

He looked away. 'It's a long story.'

Scarlett sighed. 'With you it always is. If he's such a bad guy and you know where he is, why don't you bring him down? Why all the cloak and dagger shit?'

'He's not working alone. I need to know what his group are planning to do so that I can prevent it from happening. Solentino's death or imprisonment might not stop whatever's already in play.' Devereau paused and met her eyes. 'Anyway, why do *you* want the ring? You paid five million euros for it, Scarlett. Five *million*.'

'It's not for me,' she said absently. 'It's not my money. Lord Horvath asked me to procure it.'

'Why? I saw it at the auction. It's not pretty and it's not valuable. Not on the face of it. It's only a damned moonstone. And what does the Winter Solstice had to do with it?'

Indecision flickered across her face. Then she gave her head a minute shake, apparently coming to a decision. 'It's a supe ring,' she explained finally. 'Rooted in superstition. Legend says that if you wear it at the stroke of midnight on the night of the Summer Solstice, it will give you images from your past.'

Unease trickled through Devereau. 'And if you wear it on the Winter Solstice?'

'It will gift you with images from your future.' She held up both hands. 'I'm not saying that's what really happens but that's what legend says will happen.'

It sounded barely credible – but Devereau knew from his own experience that stranger things had happened. 'So Lord Horvath decided that the legend is believable enough to warrant the cost,' he said.

'Yes. I was sent here to get the ring and bring it back to London.'

'Why did you send a proxy to the auction then? Why didn't you go in person yourself?'

'Because,' she answered simply, 'a lot of supes from all over the world want that ring. It seemed prudent to keep our own interest secret. It makes for an easier life.' She gave him a quick, hard glare. 'Or at least it did until you involved yourself anyway.'

'Solentino is not a supe,' Devereau told her quietly. 'But I do have reason to believe he could be a very dangerous man indeed. I think he's some kind of terrorist whose ultimate agenda is financial rather than ideological. Whoever he is, he needs to be stopped. Lend me the ring. I promise you'll get it back.'

'You're Devereau Webb. You're more than capable of using your own peculiar charm to worm your way into this Solentino fellow's inner circle without that ring.'

He put his thumbs into the throw which was wrapped round his waist and posed. 'You think I'm charming then?'

'Devereau –'

'This is the fastest way to get to him, Scarlett. I don't know what he's planning or when but it has the potential to be bad.'

She gave him a searching look. Then she briefly closed her eyes. 'I can't believe I'm about to do this.'

Relief flooded through him and Devereau smiled. 'Thank you.'

'I'd better get it back.'

'You will.'

'I mean it.'

'I promise, Scarlett.'

'Five million euros isn't chump change, even to Lord Horvath. If something happens to that ring, it'll be my head on the block.'

She'd given him the perfect opening he needed without realising it. 'Well,' he demurred, 'there is a simple way to ensure that you get it back and that it's not damaged in the meantime.'

Scarlett looked at him. Then she began to shake her head. 'Oh no. Definitely not.'

'It makes sense. You already told me that you've kept your identity hidden. Nobody knows that you're the one who bought the ring. Not to mention that we worked well together last time. You'll be helping me to bring down more bad guys and maintaining the sanctity of your Lord's not inconsiderable investment.' He smiled. 'Of course, it's up to you what you decide to do but the offer is there. Work with me and win the day. It'll be fun.' He added a cheesy wink for good measure. Sarah Greensmith would be apoplectic at the thought that he was involving Scarlett but what the MI5 officer didn't know wouldn't hurt her. Besides, this wasn't just about getting to spend more time with Scarlett. She was clever and strong and resourceful -

and they really had been a great team last time they'd joined forces.

She sighed and raised her eyes heavenward. 'I was planning to spend a few days enjoying the sights of Rome before I headed home, not infiltrating some daft gang and pretending to be some idiotic hero.'

Devereau waved a hand. 'Okay. It's your call.' He could afford to be blasé; he already knew what she was going to say. He could read it in her eyes.

Scarlett muttered to herself. 'This is about protecting my Lord's investment.' She shook her head. 'Fuck it. Alright. I'll work with you. Only for a few days, however. Then I'm taking my damned ring from whoever has it and going home to London. Got that?'

Devereau nodded vigorously, trying to keep the elation off his face. 'Absolutely.'

It was all he could do not to fist pump the air and jump up and down. It had nothing to do with the ring itself. Screw the ring. His delight was because Scarlett was prepared to trust him with it - and they'd be spending more time together in close quarters. For reasons he couldn't quite articulate to himself, that meant the world.

CHAPTER SEVEN

Before she sent him packing for the night with a promise to meet him first thing in the morning and hand over the Ring Of All Seasons, Scarlett lent Devereau some clothes. He wanted to ask why she had men's clothing hanging up in her Italian wardrobe and hoped they belonged to some inconsequential vamp or one of the armed goons. He knew better to voice such questions aloud, however, and decided to be grateful that he didn't have to walk through the streets of Rome with nothing more than an embroidered throw wrapped around him. It was colder now than it had been before and fancy dress wasn't his style, whether this was the right city for a toga party or not. He was even permitted to leave via the lift and the front doors. It certainly beat climbing. Devereau declined the offer of a taxi, however. He needed the walk to clear his head.

The moon hung low in the dark sky. Devereau put his hands in his pockets and began to whistle in a bid to distract himself from his more turbulent thoughts. It didn't work. No matter how hard he tried to put her out of his mind, Scarlett sidled in again. He'd lost his head over a one fanged vampire who didn't seem to want him in return at all. Not any longer anyway. He thought of several ex-girlfriends who had frequently complained that he'd held them at arm's length, and he knew each and every one of them would piss themselves laughing at the thought that he was now a lovesick puppy. He couldn't quite pinpoint what it was about Scarlett that had him so smitten. She was beautiful – that went without saying – and she oozed sex appeal whether she was dressed in a tight leather catsuit or loose fitting loungewear. Her single fang gave her a prepossessing quirkiness and the allure of her glittering dark eyes, which always seemed to reflect some kind of special secret that she held tantalisingly out of reach, was difficult to forget. It wasn't her appearance that kept him up at night, however. He wanted her to like him and he wasn't convinced that she did, even if he was sure that part of her still lusted after him. Scarlett was intelligent and quick-witted, with the sort of confidence that took no prisoners. She knew what she wanted out of life. Unfortunately for Devereau, what he wanted was her.

He strode across the wide boulevard in the direction of his hotel, mulling over various attempts at witty repartee which he could dazzle her with when they met up again the previous morning. The restaurants and cafes looked as if they were beginning to close up for the night but he reckoned he'd still be able to order room service when he got back. A cold shower and some hot food were definitely top of his priority list.

Devereau turned down the narrow street which led away from the bright lights and tired waiters. He'd barely gone five feet when a sudden chilling howl pierced the air. He only just managed to stop his feet from stuttering along the pavement. The howl had come from somewhere over to his right. He was surprised but he certainly wasn't scared. There was, however, no doubt in his mind that the echoing call with its edge of menace was aimed at him. The full moon was scant days behind him so there was no chance it was a werewolf who'd lost control. Any and all such lupine energy would have already been expelled.

Equally, no matter how relaxed the Italian authorities were about werewolves, he didn't need to check a guidebook to know that they wouldn't usually permit supes to use intimidating behaviour in the centre of Rome. In any case, the last thing he would allow himself to do was look afraid. Werewolves he could handle.

He put his hands in his pockets and affected a nonchalant saunter. Come on then. Come at me if you dare. He slowed his steps a fraction to encourage whoever was out there to approach. If there was indeed going to be some kind of showdown, he wanted to make it snappy. He was too damned hungry to hang around here for long.

Another keening howl ripped through the night air. Interestingly, however, it was from a different wolf. There was more than one of them out there then. Devereau raised his head slightly, attempting to discern through scent alone how many werewolves he'd have to deal with. His nostrils flared as he caught several unmistakable trails. Not one werewolf. Not two either. It was difficult to say exactly but he reckoned there was a good baker's dozen of furry monsters out there. There was something oddly heartening about that. He hated it when people underestimated him. It was a pleasant surprise to be taken seriously for a change, even if it was by complete strangers who didn't appear happy by his presence.

Devereau crossed over the next street and passed under a red and white striped awning. As soon as he emerged from underneath it, he spotted a flicker of movement over to his right. Hello. Then a shadow danced somewhere to his left. Actually, make that several shadows. He looked round. This was a narrow quiet street and there were no pedestrians or passing cars. These werewolves had picked their spot with care. Devereau nodded once to himself and then strode into the centre of the road. He spread his arms out wide and turned a full 360 degrees on the spot. Now he would wait.

It didn't take long.

Two wolves appeared on the rooftops to his left. Three similarly shaggy heads emerged on the roofs to his right. He glanced over his shoulder and noted the five werewolves standing abreast across the width of the road before returning his gaze to the front. There were four at ground level up ahead.

The werewolves began to close in. Their heads and shoulders were dipped low, not in submission but in full stalking mode. In a matter of seconds, they'd dropped a net around him, making it difficult – but not impossible - to escape. Outnumbered or not, Devereau wasn't planning to run. He wanted to exactly know why his Italian counterparts had decided to make an enemy of him before he decided what he was going to do next.

He remained in place as they drew closer and closer, watching as their breaths clouded in the cold air. Not one of the approaching werewolves took their eyes away from him for so much as a moment. At least half had drawn their lips back over their teeth and he could see the raised hackles along the spine of several of them.

Devereau adjusted his cuffs and smiled. 'Good evening, ladies and gentlemen.'

The only answer he received were a few low key growls. Then, however, he heard the rumble of an approaching car. None of the werewolves reacted to the noise, indicating that it was expected. Devereau felt the brief jab of familiar, tense pain in between his shoulder blades. A moment later a brick red Ferrari that screamed ostentatious extravagance appeared from round the corner.

It rolled up towards the line of werewolves facing Devereau. Then the engine turned off and the driver's door opened. And yet, nobody appeared.

Devereau rolled his eyes. Talk about deliberately attempting a grand entrance. He made a show of yawning – and then smirked when one of the nearby werewolves also yawned. The action forced the hand of the Ferrarri's occupant and, finally, a man stepped out.

Whoever he was, he smelled, looked and acted alpha. He was taller than Devereau and possessed a more muscular build. He wasn't like the male model who'd been at the auction earlier that night, however. Regardless of the show he was putting on, the muscles belonging to this man were born for action, not Instagram. His dark hair was wavy, curling round the nape of his neck and his moustache, which would look ridiculous on anyone else, gave him a surprising air of machismo. He reminded Devereau of someone although he couldn't for the life of him think who.

As soon as he stepped forward, the werewolves facing Devereau stepped back, parting like the damned Red Sea. Devereau folded his arms and waited for the Italian alpha to come to him. When he was close enough for Devereau to see both the curls of a dark tattoo edging out from under the sleeves of his tailored blue shirt and the scars which etched across one side of his tanned face, he came to a halt. Then he raised one hand in front of him and stared hard at the heavy gold watch encircling his wrist.

'I paid twelve thousand euros for this watch,' he declared in accented English. 'It has a lifetime guarantee and it's all but brand new. And yet,' he shook his wrist, 'it already appears to be broken. Perhaps I should have purchased a Swatch instead.' He looked over at Devereau. 'Do you know why I think it's broken?'

Was this really necessary? Devereau sighed and shrugged.

'I think,' he continued, 'my expensive watch is broken because I am Nicolo Moretti. I am the alpha of Lupo. And I know with absolute certainty that as the alpha of Rome's one and only werewolf clan, any visitors to my city who claim an ethnic kinship with me will always do me the courtesy of calling on me within the first seven hours of their arrival. No wolf would dare to insult us by doing otherwise.' He raised his eyebrows at

Devereau. 'You landed at Fiumicono airport at three twenty in the afternoon. My watch tells me that it is now almost one o'clock in the morning. But that must be wrong because you would not dishonour me or my clan by waiting ten hours to come and pay your respects.' His gaze hardened. 'Would you?'

Ohhhh. As someone who used to have his own little fiefdom in London, Devereau understood the importance of both respecting someone's turf and playing by the rules. Moretti's response was heavy-handed but Devereau could grasp the reasons why. A little understanding went a long way.

'Let me guess,' he said, 'you live at Piazza Armerina?'

Moretti gesticulated expansively. 'You see?' he called out to the other werewolves. 'You see? Who was it who suggested that Signore Webb did not know us? He knows where we live. He knows who we are.' Moretti's mouth tightened and he glanced again at Devereau. 'So? Explain yourself, Signore Webb.'

Devereau dropped his shoulders by a fraction of an inch and relaxed his muscles. If appeared defensive, he would merely encourage aggression. Easy does it, Dev, he warned himself. Don't be a prick. 'I must be honest,' he said, meeting Moretti's narrowed gaze, 'I did not know of you.' Before the Italian alpha could say anything to interrupt, he continued, 'and that is on me. I should have taken the time to find out what the situation is here in Rome before I arrived. Several people mentioned Piazza Armerina. I foolishly assumed it was a tourist attraction and did not ask about it in more detail.' He swooped into a bow. 'I humbly offer my respects and apologies to the alpha of the Lupo clan.'

'Pretty words,' Moretti sneered. 'But they do not make up for the insult.'

This dance was not unfamiliar to Devereau. 'What reparations can I make that would satisfy you then?'

Moretti closed his eyes. His cheekbones sprouted fur and the shape of his mouth and jaw altered. He bared his lupine fangs at

Devereau for a fleeting moment that was designed for nothing other than intimidation. Then he returned his features to human. 'Submit to me.' He opened his eyes again and a sheen of yellow rolled across his irises. 'Submit to me and succumb to clan Lupo.'

In other words, allow himself to be forced into Moretti's clan as a wholly subservient and low ranking wolf. As if. Devereau hadn't attempted to join any of the four London clans. He certainly wouldn't join this one, no matter how delightful Rome seemed to be. 'I'm not going to do that.'

Moretti appeared unsurprised. 'Then,' he said, with an unconcerned shrug, 'you die.'

Almost immediately the circle of werewolves began to press in. Devereau hissed under his breath. 'Is this really necessary?' he asked. An instant later, one of the nearest wolves launched herself at his head. Devereau raised an arm and blocked her attack in the nick of time. She landed on the ground with a surprised whine, her legs splayed awkwardly across the tarmac.

Moretti didn't so much as look at her. 'I have heard that it took four bites to turn you, Signore Webb. I have heard that nobody has seen as werewolf of your size and power in generations.'

Devereau permitted himself a tiny smile. 'You heard right.'

'This is not London, Signore.' Moretti regarded him coolly. 'When your people were crawling out of the Thames on their bellies, Rome was being built by wolves. I am sure you have heard of Romulus and Remus. The power of the wolf is in this city's arteries. It has been this way for three thousand years. You might think you are strong. But you have not seen what the werewolves of Rome are capable of yet. In fact, you will soon learn that –'

Devereau didn't get the chance to find out what he was about to learn. Moretti was interrupted by the sudden wail of a siren. It was followed by the blue flashing lights of several police cars.

'Porco cazzo,' Moretti spat. He glared at his own werewolves in disgust. They all cowered in response. Clearly, someone hadn't done a good enough job as lookout.

'I guess,' Devereau said conversationally, 'London's not the only city where the authorities don't get on well with supes.'

Moretti glanced at him. 'They're all fucking idiots,' he said with a flash of unexpected honesty, before he turned to greet the uniformed policeman who had exited the first car and was striding towards them. 'Sostituto Commisario Venti!' he beamed. 'Come va?'

Venti launched into a stream of irritated Italian. Devereau watched Moretti's expression. Whatever the irate copper was saying, it obviously wasn't going down very well. So much for Roman authorities giving Italian supes a free pass then.

Venti turned to Devereau. 'You,' he barked. 'You are English?'

'I am.'

'This … man is threatening you?'

Devereau pursed his lips and did his best to look surprised. 'Nope. No threats here. He's giving me directions to my hotel. I'm a bit lost, you see. This gentleman here has been kind enough to help me out.' He didn't mention the dozen or so werewolves who were all lying belly down on the road with their eyes averted.

'He is giving you directions?' Venti asked, disbelievingly.

'Yep.' He looked at Moretti. 'Straight ahead, second right?'

'Third right,' Moretti corrected.

Devereau nodded. 'Ah yes. Thank you.'

Venti cursed and began yelling in Italian again. Moretti kept his mouth shut and listened. So much for the power of the wolf running through the arteries of Rome.

Devereau cleared his throat and attempted to interrupt. 'I'll be on my way then.'

Both Moretti and Venti glared at him.

Devereau held up his hands. 'Or not. I'm in no rush.' His

stomach grumbled loudly. 'Although I might pass out from hunger if this continues for too long.'

Venti rolled his eyes. 'One of my men will escort you to your hotel so that you do not get lost again.'

'That's not necessary,' Devereau began.

The policeman jabbed a finger at him. 'Yes,' he said. 'It is.' He bit out one final word in Italian at Moretti and spun on his heel, marching to his car with stiff legs. Someone ought to seriously consider yoga, Devereau thought.

'Thank you,' Moretti muttered.

'What's happening between you and me has nothing to do with them,' Devereau replied, jerking his head at the police cars.

They both watched as Venti bent his head towards the open window of one of the other cars and said something. A moment later, a younger looking police officer got out and looked towards Devereau.

Moretti was silent for a moment. 'Indeed,' he said finally. 'Listen, honest mistake or not, I can't ignore your insult. You didn't pay your respects and things need to happen because of that.'

'What do I need to do to make amends that doesn't involve either my death or my total submission?'

Moretti's yellow glazed eyes suddenly gleamed. 'I'll arrange for you to be picked up from your hotel tomorrow night. You can make it up to me then.'

Devereau frowned. 'How?'

The Italian alpha grinned. 'You'll see.'

Devereau met his eyes. 'Then I'll look forward to it.'

CHAPTER EIGHT

T HE FOLLOWING MORNING, SCARLETT FOUND HIM SLUMPED IN A
comfy chair in the lobby of the Hotel Condotti, his hands curled
round a very large cup of coffee.

'And here I was thinking, Devereau,' she said, 'that you'd be
waiting on the balls of your feet on the steps outside with a glint
of excitement in your eyes and your usual boyish verve.'

Boyish? He looked up at her with a frown. 'I had a late night.'
Not only had he been forced to contend with Moretti, but he'd
also still had to eat and write a message to Sarah Greensmith to
update her about his efforts and plans to connect with Solentino.
Naturally, he'd not mentioned Scarlett in his email. Greensmith
was on a need to know basis and where Scarlett was concerned,
the MI5 agent needed to know nothing.

'Did somebody break into your room while naked?' Scarlett
inquired without smiling. 'No? Well, then you have nothing to
complain about.'

She had a point. He sighed and got to his feet. 'Do you have
the ring?' he asked.

She reached into her pocket and dug out a small matchbox. 'I thought it would be more unobtrusive if I put it into a less showy container.'

Devereau grunted. Good idea. He moved to take it from her but she pulled it out of his reach.

'I will repeat what I said last night,' Scarlett warned. 'I am only lending you the ring. I have to get it back.'

He managed a smile. 'That's why I've invited you to tag along. Everything will be fine.' He paused. 'You know you can trust me.'

'Do I?' she asked softly. She didn't wait for an answer, however. She simply pressed the box into his outstretched palm. Devereau slipped it into his breast pocket.

'Yes,' he said. He met her eyes. 'You do.'

'How are we going to approach Solentino?'

'We will go to his apartment, knock on his door and wait for him to answer.'

Scarlett stared at him. 'That's it? That's your plan?'

'I figured you'd rather we didn't wait around. Sometimes the direct approach is best. From what I saw at the auction, numerous supes are interested in this ring. I don't want to complicate the situation by letting them know I have it. Solentino and his gang are the sole target. We don't need others getting involved.'

'How do you know where he lives?'

'I have my methods,' he said.

She tightened the belt on her knee length coat. 'You mean MI5 told you.'

It was Devereau's turn to stare.

Scarlett laughed slightly. 'Give me some credit, Devereau. You don't really think I'd believe you're here in Rome to infiltrate some kind of terrorist group off your own steam?' She tapped the side of her nose. 'Don't worry. I've not told anyone you're now a super spy.' She grinned at him and he felt his heart miss a beat. 'Did they give you a gun?'

'No.' Devereau grimaced. 'I don't even get a pen that shoots poisonous darts or a sports car with an ejector seat.'

Scarlett's smile grew. 'That's probably not a bad thing.'

'How do you really know I'm working for MI5, Scarlett? If you can find out, then others can as well and that might be a problem.'

'I told you not to worry about it. I have no reason to think anyone else knows what you're up to.'

He watched her. 'Have you been following me? Back in London?'

'You saw me at Regent's Park. You know I have been.'

'Besides that?' he pressed.

Scarlett waited for several beats before answering. 'You're an unknown quantity, Devereau,' she said finally. 'You're strong, powerful, charismatic –'

He raised an eyebrow. 'Go on.'

'You used to run a criminal gang. You have refused to join any of the werewolf clans.'

'As I recall,' Devereau pointed out, 'it was you who persuaded me not to do that.'

'Ha! You don't do anything you don't want to do.' She met his eyes. 'Let's say that you have a lot of powerful supes worried about what you're up to. The balance of peace between us and the humans is delicate and nobody wants the new kid on the block to upset things.'

Devereau's eyebrow twitched. 'So you were ordered to follow me to make sure I'm being good?'

Scarlett didn't answer.

'You weren't ordered,' he said, realisation dawning. 'You took it upon yourself to trail after me.' He couldn't stop the grin from spreading across his face. 'Don't we know each well enough already,' Devereau asked, 'that you could be sure I wouldn't do anything to harm the supe community?'

'We shagged a few times. So what? That doesn't mean you know me any more than I really know you.'

His smile dropped. 'It was more than a few rolls in the hay, Scarlett,' he growled.

'What's my greatest ambition? Or my deepest desire? Or my worst fear?'

Devereau gazed at her.

'Who's my best friend?' Scarlett's voice was light but there was something far darker in her eyes. 'What's my favourite fucking food, Devereau?'

So much for his plans for witty repartee. 'Mine is raw steak.'

She folded her arms. 'Great.'

'Scarlett –'

'Let's stop all this nonsense and get down to business, shall we? I think I've already proved my point. Now, where does Solentino live?'

Devereau gritted his teeth in frustration. 'Testaccio,' he said, naming the neighbourhood where Christopher Solentino resided.

'Then let's go.' She spun round and headed for the door.

He watched her retreating back for a moment. Scarlett thought that he didn't know the real her. The truth was that the last minute of angry chat had told him more about her than she would have ever wanted him to know.

THEY TOOK the small blue Fiat which Devereau had noted in the underground carpark of Scarlett's building. It was a far more sensible mode of transport than an expensive sports car. The battered little car made as much a statement as Solentino's bright red Ferrari had last night. It simply did so in a far less obvious manner.

'There,' he said, pointing ahead. 'There's a parking spot.'

Scarlett nodded and pulled in, nearly slotting the Fiat into the tiny space. She turned off the engine and glanced at him. They'd barely spoken five words during the entire journey. 'Are we okay?' she asked quietly.

'Always,' he told her, meaning it.

'Good.'

Devereau scanned the street. 'That must be Solentino's apartment building. The blue door. See it?'

Scarlett followed his finger. 'Gotcha.'

Unclipping his seatbelt, Devereau gave her a confident grin and reached for the matchbox. He popped it open, gazing at the ring thoughtfully. It really was a very ugly piece of jewellery.

'I appreciate that this is your gig, Devereau,' Scarlett said, 'but if you walk up there with that ring in your hand, surely Solentino will just try to take it from you by force. He might be a human but there are still such things as guns. And bad luck.'

'I make my own luck.'

Scarlett raised her eyes heavenward. 'You're so bloody cheesy.'

He flashed her a grin. 'Isn't that why you love me?'

Her expression darkened for a second.

'Come on,' he said, before the atmosphere between them soured again. 'I have a plan. Bring your phone.' Then he got out of the car and strode across the street to Solentino's door.

Scarlett followed him, watching with some bemusement as he positioned himself in front of the door.

'Is the building number visible?' Devereau asked.

She tilted her head. 'Yes.'

He picked the ring up between his thumb and forefinger and held it up next to his face. 'Could you take a photo, please?'

Her brow furrowed. 'Of you or the ring or the door?'

'All of us.'

Scarlett raised her shoulders in baffled acquiescence. 'Say cheese.' She paused. 'You should be good at that.'

Devereau smirked slightly and did as she asked. Scarlett

snapped a picture and held it up for him to see. 'Looking good.' He winked. 'Can you do a video now?'

'Devereau, what exactly are you planning?'

'Bear with me.' He met her eyes. 'Please.'

She muttered something under her breath. However, she held the phone up again. 'Okay.'

'Is it recording?'

'Yep.'

Devereau looked directly into the camera. 'I'm sure you recognise this ring, Mr Solentino. Between us, I have managed to discreetly acquire it for myself. I have no need for such an object but I know from last night's auction that you do. I'm prepared to enter into private negotiations. Let me know within the next twenty four hours if you're interested. I'm staying at the Hotel Condotti.' Then he placed the ring into his mouth and, ignoring Scarlett's look of sudden horror, swallowed it.

She immediately lowered the hand which had been holding her phone. 'What the actual fuck, Devereau?'

He gave the phone a pointed look.

Scarlett bared her single fang in a half snarl. 'I've stopped recording.'

'You wanted the ring to be kept safe. Now Solentino won't be able to get to it.' He patted his flat stomach. 'Not for a day or two anyway.'

'I have to hand that ring over to Lord Horvath!'

'Don't worry, I'll make sure it's properly sanitised once it comes out the other end.'

She made a gagging sound. 'Ugh.'

'You can't possibly be that squeamish, Scarlett. It's a normal bodily function.'

'There is nothing normal about what you just did and you know it. And what happens if Solentino decides he doesn't want to wait for it to pass through your system? What if he decides to cut you open from nipple to navel to get to it?'

'He won't.' Hopefully. 'And now he won't be able to simply snatch the ring from me either.'

Scarlett sighed heavily and passed a hand over her face. 'This time yesterday I was looking forward to seeing the sights of Rome, enjoying some fine wines and eating some fabulous food. Instead, I'll be hanging around waiting for you to take a shit.'

'You have such a lovely way with words, Scarlett.'

She folded her arms. 'I have a feeling I'm going to become far less eloquent the longer this idiocy goes on.'

'I won't hold it against you.' He crossed his fingers and held them up. 'I promise.'

Scarlett rolled her eyes. Devereau gave her his most disarming smile and then pressed the buzzer for Christopher Solentino's apartment.

CHAPTER NINE

SOLENTINO LIVED ON THE THIRD FLOOR. THE APARTMENT DIDN'T
look as large as the place Scarlett was staying in but it was
certainly well appointed. The floors were lined from wall to wall
with dusky marble, the furniture appeared antique but also
functional, and there was an arresting mural of a pretty coastal
scene on one of the lounge walls. A silk dressing gown was
draped casually over the back of a velvet covered chaise longue
and Alina's scent clung to the air. She wasn't in visible evidence,
however. The only person who seemed to be in the apartment at
the moment at all was Solentino himself – and right now, he
looked none too impressed with his unexpected visitors.

'My name is Devereau Webb. I was at the auction last night
and –'

'I know who you are, Mr Webb,' Solentino interrupted. 'And I
saw you at the auction. What I don't know is why you are here
now.' He looked over at Scarlett and his expression took on a
different slant. Devereau felt his insides tighten in irritation. 'Or
who *you* are, darling.'

Scarlett offered Solentino a tiny smile, which promised
everything and nothing all at the same time. Devereau's

annoyance increased. He sat down on a nearby chair, crossed his legs and leaned back in a bid to appear as relaxed as possible.

'My name is Scarlett,' she purred. 'Mr Webb and I are old acquaintances.'

'I didn't realise that werewolves and vampires could be friends,' Solentino said.

Scarlett laughed. 'Oh, I didn't say we were friends.'

Devereau gritted his teeth.

Christopher Solentino raised an eyebrow. Then he took Scarlett's hand and pressed his lips to it. Slimy idiot. 'I see,' he murmured. 'Well, it's a pleasure to meet you.' He sat down on the chaise longue and his face hardened. 'Now, tell me how you found my address and why you are here.'

Clearing his throat, Devereau began to explain. 'The auction was a ticketed event. It really wasn't hard to for someone of my skills to find who exactly had tickets and to track them down. I considered approaching several of the other bidders before deciding to come to you.' He gestured towards Scarlett. 'The two of us work together when it's mutually beneficial to do so. We have a shared interest in the accumulation of wealth.'

'You want money?' There was an edge of a sneer to Solentino's voice.

He smiled easily. 'It makes the world go round. Or so they say anyway. Scarlett and I offer certain ... services in return for generous payment. We seek out opportunities to help people in need. Think of us as less a small business and more as a charity.'

Solentino didn't miss a beat. 'That still doesn't explain why you're here.'

'Then I will get to the point.' Devereau linked his fingers together and placed them behind his head. 'I couldn't help notice that you were upset that you missed out on the Ring Of All Seasons at the auction.'

'Upset? I'm not a child, Mr Webb. I don't get *upset*. I wanted the ring and I didn't get it. That's all there is to it.'

Liar. 'Is it?' Devereau asked. 'Because it just so happens that I managed to track down the actual buyer of the ring after the auction.'

The muscles around Solentino's mouth tightened almost imperceptibly. 'Who?'

'The who is not important. Not any longer.' Devereau grinned. 'I divested them of their purchase. They paid five million euros for any ugly ring that they didn't even get to keep for twelve whole hours.'

'You stole it?'

'I did.' Devereau permitted himself an edge of suitably smug satisfaction. He knew it would add to his credibility.

'Hmm.' Solentino folded his arms. 'The thing is, Mr Webb, that your reputation precedes you. I was given to understand that when you turned furry, you gave up your former career in crime.'

Devereau didn't miss a beat. 'Good. That's what I wanted everyone to think.'

'Because the London werewolf clans would rip you apart if they knew you were engaging in illegal activity? What's to stop me from telling them that you're still just a common thief?'

Devereau's grin grew wider. 'I can assure you that there's nothing common about me.'

He watched the other man carefully. Solentino was deliberately avoiding asking any direct questions about the ring. He was desperate to downplay his desire to acquire it, which was exactly why he was making idle threats about blabbing to the clans. Neither Solentino's body language nor his expression were betraying him either. But it was his very avoidance of the subject that gave away his desperate interest. This was hardly Devereau's first rodeo, and he knew more than a thing or two about studied indifference.

'Anyway,' he said aloud, 'let's say that I have the Ring Of All Seasons in my possession and I am looking to sell it.' He paused. 'For the right price.'

'How do I know you're telling the truth? Let me see the ring first.'

Devereau glanced at Scarlett. She nodded and drew out her phone. 'Before I show you this, Signore Solentino,' she said, 'I feel I must inform you that this was not my idea. I would have put the ring in a safe.' She opened up first the photo of Devereau holding the ring up outside Solentino's front door. Then she showed him the video.

'You swallowed it? You *ate* the Ring of All Seasons?'

Devereau waved an unconcerned hand. 'It will pass through in a day or two. I had to ensure that it was safe. I'm sure you can understand that.'

Solentino gave him an incredulous look. 'What's to stop me from shooting you dead and cutting open your guts to retrieve it?' The way he posed his words made it clear that it wasn't a rhetorical question. Even if it weren't for his cold eyes, it was obvious he had no problem with casual murder followed by amateur butchery if the occasion suited him.

'That's what I said,' Scarlett murmured.

'I'm a werewolf,' Devereau said, with blithe unconcern. 'A very powerful werewolf. And she's a vampire. You could try to acquire the ring that way but it wouldn't help you in the long run.' He allowed the shadow of fur to emerge across his skin for the briefest moment. 'Quite the opposite, in fact.'

Solentino looked from Devereau to Scarlett and back again. 'You're fucking nuts, you know that?'

With that one statement, Devereau knew he had the other man exactly where he wanted him. It was time to turn the charm onto full blast. 'People do say that about me,' he said cheerfully. 'But I also like to think myself as resourceful. Besides, as I suggested earlier, I like helping people. And I like a challenge. You want the ring. I have the ring. Let me help you with that.'

'Don't you want to know why I bid on the ring in the first place?'

'Honestly, I don't care. I imagine it's because you think that if you put the ring on your finger on the night of the Winter Solstice, you'll see into your future. If you want to believe in that sort of guff, then I'm not going to argue with you.'

Solentino frowned. 'Guff? What is that word?'

'Nonsense,' Devereau said.

'You don't believe in the ring's powers? You turn into a beast and you are slave to the moon but you don't believe in magic?'

'Signore Solentino, I don't care what the ring can or can't do. I'm in this for the money.' Devereau splayed out his hands to emphasise his point. I'm not a threat, he sent out silently. I'm only in this for the cold hard cash. Pay me and then you can use me. Not to mention trust me. I'm at your disposal.

'How much?' Solentino asked. 'How much money do you want?'

'I'm not greedy,' Devereau told him. 'Not much anyway. You were prepared to pay one point five million last night. That's how much I want.'

'The ring went for five million. If you approached someone else, you could get more.'

'It's possible,' Devereau conceded. 'But I was charmed by your girlfriend and I'm an eggs in one basket kind of guy. One point five is enough for me.'

Scarlett coughed.

'For us,' Devereau amended.

Solentino stood up and put his hands in his pockets. Then he walked over to the window. 'I don't know you, Mr Webb. That means I don't trust you.'

Devereau pretended to consider that. 'Well,' he said finally, 'you know where the ring is.' He pointed to his stomach. 'If you're willing to pay what I ask, I'm willing to remain here until the ring is in your hands. That way, sooner or later, we will all get what we want.'

'The vamp stays too,' Solentino said.

Scarlett rolled her eyes although when Solentino turned away from the window and towards her, she smoothed her expression into a delighted smile. 'I'd be thrilled to.'

'For your information, Signorina Scarlett,' he said, 'Alina is not my girlfriend. We have sex but we are not … how do you say? Exclusive? We are not exclusive.'

Oh for fuck's sake. Devereau opened his mouth to speak but Scarlett got there before him. 'How interesting,' she said. 'How very interesting indeed.'

* * *

SOLENTINO LED them to a windowless room deeper inside his apartment and told them to stay there. He didn't bother locking the door – they all knew that such an effort would be wasted – but he made it clear that they were to remain inside. Devereau shrugged amiably, casting a glance over the sparse furniture. He didn't need to look at Scarlett to know that the scent of old blood clung to the air. Other people had been in this room before and it hadn't ended well for them. Christopher Solentino might be able to present himself as restrained but there was no denying that he also had the potential to be very dangerous indeed and that he'd happily murder the pair of them without a second thought if he decided the situation merited it.

Once the door closed behind them and they were left alone, they exchanged meaningful glances. There was a strange quality to the room. Something about the way the air sounded. No doubt the walls were soundproofed. All the better for when you needed to noisily murder someone, Devereau supposed. He strained his ears. No soundproofing could ever be one hundred percent and he was certain he would still be able to hear the hum of voices from beyond the closed door. He'd certainly never manage to pick out specific words, however. Christopher Solentino was lucky that Devereau was prepared to play along with his request to stay put. For now.

Scarlett wandered over to the far left wall and began trailing her fingers along it. 'I do hope that you've been getting your fibre lately,' she commented. 'I don't want to be here for days and days.' She knelt down by an electrical socket and gazed hard at it.

Devereau followed her lead and tilted his head up at the ceiling. There was nothing there other than a bare bulb. 'You know as well as I do,' he said, 'that it takes time to transfer that amount of money without raising any suspicions or red flags. Banks these days don't make life easy for us. A day or two here won't do us any harm. It'll be easier than obtaining the ring was.' He walked over to the light switch and flicked it on. The bulb flickered into action. He abandoned his examination of it and picked up one of the narrow chairs instead, flipping it over and running his hands along the woodwork.

'He's quite a good looking chap, isn't he?'

Devereau growled. 'If you like that sort of thing.'

There was a smile in her voice. 'I certainly wouldn't say no.'

'You can't mix business with pleasure, Scarlett.' His words came out harsher than he intended.

'Of course I can. We both know that business like this is all about pleasure for you.' She paused at a spot near the far corner and gave Devereau a quick look. He strolled over while Scarlett continued talking. 'You only do this shit because you enjoy it.'

'I don't enjoy being stuck in a tiny room while everyone waits for me to take a dump.'

'That's on you. You didn't have to swallow that stupid ring.' She sniffed. 'The part you enjoy is already over for you. You nicked the ring. The only reason we're here trying to sell it on is so you can finance your next job. You're a wolf now. You could retire from these sorts of activities if you wanted to. You simply don't want to.'

Devereau touched the spot on the wall with his fingertips. It was barely noticeable but there was definitely a faint electronic buzz coming from underneath the plaster. Both their instincts were correct. There was no sign of any camera but their words were definitely being recorded. He would have expected nothing less, especially given what Greensmith had told him about MI5's own failure to bug places like this. Solentino knew what he was doing where tech like this was concerned and was probably listening in at this very moment.

'You don't have to be here, Scarlett. You chose to come along. You want the pay-off as much as I do.'

'If I hadn't come along,' she drawled, 'then I wouldn't have met Signore Solentino. Danger is a thrill for you. Men like him are a thrill for me.'

Devereau gave her a long, irritated look. In return, Scarlett shrugged and pulled a face to indicate she found her own words as distasteful as he did.

'I'm really not all that different to you, Dev,' she said aloud. 'You like the thrill of the chase. So do I. It's simply that we both chase different things.'

'Don't forget whose side you're supposed to be on.'

'Yeah, yeah.' She made a show of dropping her voice to a whisper although any reasonable listening equipment would have no difficult still picking up her words. 'I'm not sure he trusts you, you know.'

'That's a shame,' Devereau said. 'You might be trying to make me jealous of him but he seems like a decent guy to me. You can get a good sense of someone by the way they speak to you and the manner in which they approach things. Solentino might not like or trust me but I think we could work well together.'

'Assuming he doesn't put a bullet in your head in the next couple of hours.'

'He's too smart to try something like that.'

'I hope you're right. I like Signore Solentino. I know I had my doubts about him before but now I've met him I'd like to do more business with him in the future.'

Devereau gave her a pleased nod. 'So would I.' He winked at her and she smirked. They'd set their lure and used enough amateur dramatics to please any audience. Now they'd have to see if they could reel their prey in.

CHAPTER TEN

DEVEREAU HAD ESTIMATED THAT IT WOULD TAKE SOLENTINO
around three hours to return to them. In the end it was less than
two. He'd obviously not wasted any time in finding out all he
could about his two visitors. Devereau had to trust that Scarlett
had been circumspect indeed about the reasons for her
appearance in Rome, and that there was no obvious trace of his
own involvement with MI5 despite what Scarlett herself had
managed to uncover by following him around London.

'I've been thinking,' Solentino declared, when he opened the
door to the little room and reappeared in front of them, 'that I'm
not giving you a very positive view of Italian hospitality. It's
almost lunch time. Some friends of mine have dropped by. Why
don't you come through and join us for something to eat?'

'How thoughtful of you,' Scarlett cooed. She rose elegantly
from her chair. 'I was beginning to feel a bit peckish.'

Solentino smiled at them both but it didn't quite reach his
eyes. Devereau felt a chill in the pit of his stomach. Despite the
show they'd put on earlier, they were still being tested. He hoped
Scarlett realised that.

'Then, Miss Cook,' Solentino said, using Scarlett's surname

although she'd not told him it herself, 'come with me. I'm sure you'll appreciate what I have to offer.' He stepped back and held the door open for them.

Devereau and Scarlett exchanged quick looks. Solentino was deliberately letting them know that he'd been looking deeper at both of their identities. Devereau wasn't surprised that he'd done so, but he was mildly taken aback that he was being so open about it.

They walked out, following Solentino's lead. Devereau noted a closed door behind them, at the far end of the apartment, plus what looked like two bedrooms as well as the lounge and the kitchen. Solentino bypassed them all and took them to a sunlit room towards the front of the apartment. There was a long table which was already set. Hunks of bread and a platter of various cheeses, olives and meats sat in the centre, and four unfriendly looking men were seated along the far side. Solentino indicated towards two of the vacant chairs. Scarlett and Devereau did as they were bade and sat down, just as Alina herself wafted in through another door.

'Well!' she said, clapping her hands. 'I didn't expect to see you here, Mr Webb!'

He smiled at her. 'It's good to get the opportunity to talk to you again.'

'Indeed.' Her eyes flicked to Scarlett. 'Hello.'

Solentino lifted up his chin. 'Alina,' he murmured. There was obviously some kind of unspoken command in his voice.

She nodded at him and began unbuttoning her pretty white blouse. Devereau was baffled. Was she about to strip off? Was this some kind of kinky side-show as a prelude to lunch?

Alina walked over to Scarlett's chair and knelt down, leaning her head to the side and exposing her bare neck and shoulder. 'Please.'

Identical expressions of eagerness lit the faces of the four men opposite. Devereau concealed his disgust and snuck a quick look at Solentino. He was watching Alina's every move but his expression was giving nothing away. Scarlett hesitated for a moment. Then she dipped her head towards Alina's neck.

Alina let out a tiny moan as Scarlett's single fang pierced her skin. Her hand reached out, grabbing Scarlett's wrist and encircling it, her knuckles turning pure white as she tightened her grip. The four seated men leaned forward. Devereau thought he saw a trickle of drool in the corner of the mouth of the nearest one. He tried desperately hard not to let his disgust show. After several painfully long seconds, Scarlett pulled back, her mouth stained red with Alina's blood.

'That was worth the price of admission alone, wouldn't you say?' Solentino asked.

'Absolutely,' replied the heaviest set man, a glint of lasciviousness in his gaze as he stared at Scarlett's lips. The others nodded vigorously.

Solentino picked up a white napkin and handed it to Alina. 'Tidy yourself up,' he told her. Then he walked to the head of the table and sat down as if a vampire feeding publicly on his maybe-not-girlfriend was an everyday occurrence.

Alina pressed the napkin to the tiny wound on her neck and stood up. She looked pale and shaky. Initially, Devereau thought her physical reaction was from terror but, when he saw the look on her face, he realised he was wrong. It wasn't fear she felt; it was desire.

'I enjoyed that,' she whispered.

Scarlett smiled primly. To anyone who didn't know her, they'd assume she was demurely grateful for Alina's blood. Devereau knew differently. He was well aware that inside Scarlett was seething. 'Most people find it a pleasurable experience,' she said. 'Thank you for your blood.'

'You're welcome.' Alina gazed at Scarlett with slightly glazed eyes and then stumbled over to the chair directly opposite from Solentino before she did up the buttons on her blouse.

'I know how to please a vampire,' Solentino said. 'I'm less clear about how to meet the needs of a werewolf, however.'

Devereau pointed at the artfully arranged slices of meat. 'These will do me,' he said. With any luck, Solentino wouldn't produce any live animals up for him to slaughter as the part of the second act of this bizzare luncheon.

Solentino's mouth twitched, as if he knew exactly what Devereau was thinking. 'Very well then.' He gestured magnanimously towards the table. 'Help yourselves.'

It wasn't until everyone filled their plates that Solentino spoke again. 'So Scarlett,' he drawled, 'you work for Lord Horvath in London.'

Here we go, Devereau thought.

'Yes,' Scarlett said. 'I do.' She took a sip from the wine glass in front of her. 'Fortunately, he allows me considerable leeway with other ventures as long as they don't conflict with the interest of the London vampires.'

'I see.' Solentino's eyes were intently focused on her. 'What about the vampires in Rome? Or Berlin? Or Paris? Would he care about them?'

'Not particularly. I'm loyal to my Lord but Lukas Horvath doesn't give two hoots what I do in Italy. Or in Germany. Or in France. Or indeed anywhere that's not London.'

'I see.' Solentino nodded thoughtfully. Then he turned his attention to Devereau. 'Is that why you're working in Rome rather than London, Mr Webb? Is it purely because you are attempting to remain under the radar of the London werewolves?'

'Honestly,' he said, 'the London clans can do and think whatever the fuck they want. They've not exactly welcomed me into the lupine fold with open arms. Contact them and tell them whatever you want about me. They're not my concern.'

'Interesting. I thought that loyalty to their own kind was the most valuable commodity which werewolves possessed.'

Devereau was suddenly aware that he was treading on dangerous ground. 'Oh,' he said, 'I have loyalty in spades. I will give it and I will expect it in return. But not from the London clans. Loyalty is not something which I take lightly so I'm more than a little circumspect when it comes to deciding who I pledge allegiance to.'

Something dark flared in Solentino's expression and, for a disheartening moment, Devereau thought he'd misjudged his words and had sounded too slick to be genuine. Instead, however, the Italian turned to the four men seated down the far length of the table. 'That wolf understands the value of loyalty. He knows it is not something to be taken for granted. Even the vampire has her own appreciation for it.'

The atmosphere in the sunny room suddenly dipped several degrees. Two of the men froze in mid-chew. The other two stared at Solentino. He acted as if he didn't notice. 'I've been remiss in not introducing you to my lunch guests, Mr Webb. Miss Cook.' Solentino raised his fork and jabbed it towards each of the men in turn. 'Mike Lancaster. He's from Australia originally so don't get him started on cricket. Then there's our resident Yank, Rick Moore.' Solentino glanced at Devereau. 'Don't get him started on cricket either. He doesn't understand it at all.'

'Who does?' Devereau asked in a half-hearted attempt to lighten the air.

Solentino ignored his interjection. 'The big guy next to Rick is Rospo Accetta. And you've met Alina Bonnet already, of course.' Solentino moved his fork in the direction of the last man. 'Finally we have Geraint Vissier. We call him Gee for short.'

'How fabulous to meet you all,' Scarlett said, sounding for all the world as if she meant it.

'Likewise,' Devereau added.

'I wouldn't waste time getting to know them too well,' Solentino said. 'Not all of them anyway.' He was still staring at

Vissier. He speared a cube of cheese and popped into his mouth without taking his eyes from the man even once. Vissier hadn't appeared to notice. He was carefully using a white linen handkerchief to rub at a tiny blemish on his fork. He was sat ramrod straight, with the posture of the dancer, the starched clothes of a waiter, and the obliviousness of an idiot.

'Tell us, Gee,' Solentino murmured, 'what does loyalty mean to you?'

Devereau was suddenly aware that to his left Alina was carefully placing her knife and fork down on the table and sitting back.

'Boss?' Vissier asked nervously, napkin and fork still in hand. 'You know I'm loyal.' He sounded Dutch. Or maybe South African.

'I asked you what loyalty means to you, not whether you're loyal,' Solentino said, with a dangerous glint. 'Interesting that you should think I'm questioning your personal allegiance. Do you have reason to believe I should question it? Have you been naughty, Gee?'

Vissier began to stutter. 'N – n – n – no.'

Devereau flicked his gaze towards the other men. Rospo Accetta and Rick Moore had managed to swallow their mouthfuls of food and were watching their boss with silent wariness. Despite their burly, masculine facades they both looked anxious. It was the Australian, Mike Lancaster, who caught Devereau's attention, however. His hands were twitching and his eyes kept straying to the door. He was looking for an escape route. Perhaps this little show wasn't about Vissier at all.

Solentino placed his fork onto his plate and stood up, placing his hands in his trouser pockets. If he was attempting to act casual, he was failing dramatically. He loomed over the table and held everyone's full attention. Devereau had met a lot of dangerous people in his time and they rarely impressed him - but the menace which exuded from Solentino was quite extraordinary.

'You see,' Solentino drawled, 'it's come to my attention, Gee, that somebody has been speaking to the Greeks. Stefan Avanopoulos phoned me this morning and mentioned that he'd be able to help with our German transportation issues now that Bartan is out of action. He even said that he would be able to transport materials to *any* city of my choice, be it Paris, Berlin or London. Those were his words. Not mine.' Solentino raised his thin eyebrows at Vissier. 'You know Avanopoulos, don't you, Gee?'

Vissier swallowed, his Adam's apple bobbing. 'I have met him once or twice. I don't *know* him.'

'You're not friends?'

'No!'

'You don't work together?'

'No, boss. Never.' Vissier's eyes shone with fervent denial.

'You don't pass him information from time to time? As a friendly gesture?'

'No.' Vissier's hands came together in plea. 'I would not betray you, boss. Please believe me.'

Solentino pursed his mouth. From underneath the table, Devereau felt Scarlett's knee nudge his. He dropped his hand and sought hers out, squeezing her fingers in warning. Whatever was going on here, they couldn't get involved. There was no intervention would help anyone's cause. Quite the opposite in fact. Anything they did to interrupt Solentino right now could cause irreparable and potentially life threatening damage – not to mention that there had to be a reason why he was calling out his own people right in front of them.

'You know what, Gee?' Solentino said.

'Wh – what?'

'I believe you. You're right. You are loyal.'

The air seemed to sag out of Vissier's body. 'Yes. Yes! I am loyal! Thank you, boss. Thank you. I –'

'But, *you*, Mike,' Solentino's tone was sad, '*you* are not loyal like Gee is.'

The Australian, whose eyes had been fixated on the door until that moment, began to rise out of his chair.

Solentino jerked his chin at Accetta, who turned to his companion and forced him down again. 'I've told you before that coordination between us is key. It wasn't merely the events of 9/11 alone which struck terror into the hearts of people all around the world. Or 7/7. Or the Paris attacks. It was the way in which all these events were coordinated. Chain reactions of fear,' he said grandly. 'Our plans must be coordinated and our group must be coordinated also. You, Mike, you are not coordinated. Not with me. Not with us.'

He paused for effect, while the Australian's obvious anxiety escalated. Devereau was feeling much the same. 9/11? 7/7? Paris? Was this bastard planning something as horrific as those attacks?

Solentino stared at Mike Lancaster. Everyone else stared at Solentino. 'I know you've been speaking to Avanopoulos behind my back.'

'No! I mean, I spoke to him last week but it wasn't behind your back. I wasn't doing anything wrong. I thought he might be able to help us with the project next month. He has contacts and –'

'So you did go behind my back,' Solentino said silkily. 'You just admitted it.'

'I didn't tell him anything! We've been having issues with transporting all the goods and he has access to boats that could help. All I did was approach him about maybe moving some of the boxes for us and sourcing the last few items.'

'You should know by now, Mike, that you don't speak to anyone without my permission. Not ever.' Solentino got to his feet, strolled over to the Australian's chair and stood behind him, placing both his hands on his shoulders.

'I get that now. I won't do it again. It was a mistake on my part.'

'You're sorry?'

'Very sorry.'

Solentino's hands squeezed down. It was obvious from Mike Lancaster's wince that it was painful.

'Please, boss,' he said in a strained voice.

'Do you think I will hurt you?' Solentino asked, suddenly removing his hands. 'In front of our two supernatural guests who may or may not be trustworthy? Do you really think I'd do that?'

Lancaster gasped audibly in relief. 'I –'

'Because you're right,' Solentino said, pulling out a thin wire from his right hand pocket. 'I absolutely would do that.' And in one swift movement he looped the garrotte round Lancaster's neck and pulled hard.

The Australian choked, his fingers automatically rising to his neck in a vain bid to stop the wire from strangling him. His eyes began to bulge. Underneath the table, Scarlett's fingers gripped Devereau's, clinging on tight. Solentino continued to pull on the garrotte, his own gaze lifting to meet that of Devereau's.

Hot pain jabbed in between Devereau's shoulder blades, and the animal inside him began to stir. He wanted to rush at Solentino, to rise up and attack him and stop what he was doing regardless of Sarah Greensmith's orders to the contrary. But from beneath the sounds of Mike Lancaster's hissed splutterings there was an audible click. Any normal set of ears wouldn't have picked it up but Devereau's werewolf senses had heard it and he knew exactly what it was. At least one of the other men, probably Rospo Accetta, had a gun underneath that table. Devereau would lay even money on the fact that it contained silver ammunition. Solentino had enough contacts and enough notice to obtain some. No matter how much Devereau wanted to break his cover to save a man he didn't know and wouldn't like if he did, it would end up in a bullet for either him or Scarlett. The odds were not in their favour. He was certain that Solentino would already have other contingencies in place. Both he and Scarlett had to see this through; there was no other choice.

Mike Lancaster didn't die easily. It took far longer than any of them wanted it to. When the light finally dimmed in his eyes and his body went limp, Solentino released his grip on the lethal wire and stepped back. Lancaster's head slumped forward, landing onto the plate he'd been eating from mere moments before. Alina reached down into a bag at her feet and pulled out a tiny bottle of hand sanitiser. She passed it silently over to Solentino who accepted it with a slight frown.

'I told you to get the stuff with aloe vera in. It's better for my skin.'

She licked her lips. 'I'll get some next time I'm out,' she said quietly.

'See that you do.' Solentino squeezed out a small amount and rubbed it into his palms.

'What are you going to do about the Greek?' Alina asked. 'Because we still have transport problems and he is in a position to help us with those.'

Solentino frowned. Then he turned to Vissier. 'Give Avanopoulos a call this afternoon.'

'Boss?'

'Mike was right. So's Alina. That Greek prick does have what we need to solve our current issues. See if he can meet our schedule. Now that the Ring of All Seasons is in my possession,' he glanced at Devereau, 'almost in my possession,' he amended, 'we need to step things up and make sure we don't lose any time between now and D-Day. We plan for success and then allow the ring to confirm that success for us before we proceed.'

Scarlett reached across Devereau and picked up a slice of crusty bread which sat on a platter not far from Mike Lancaster's unseeing eyes. 'It sounds as if you have something very big brewing.' She calmly spread some butter onto the slice before taking a bite. Then her eyes met Solentino's.

'We do indeed, Miss Cook. We do indeed.' He nodded at Alina and she dipped into her bag once again, taking out a narrow white cardboard box and passing it to Devereau. 'Those are for you, Mr Webb. A few laxatives should hurry things along somewhat. It's best that you finish your food first, however. It's better not to take them on an empty stomach.' He motioned towards the various plates with a vague smile. 'Eat up.'

CHAPTER ELEVEN

The rest of the meal was conducted mostly in silence.
Unsurprisingly, the corpse at the table wasn't conducive to
friendly conversation and only Solentino and Rospo seemed
inclined to continue eating with gusto. Devereau picked
unenthusiastically at some salami while Scarlett finished her slice
of bread before sitting back and watching everyone else. Gee
Vissier didn't eat a thing; he simply gazed down at his plate with
a slack expression, and Alina only sipped some wine.

Devereau was well aware that his mission was to ingratiate
himself with Solentino and insinuate himself into his little gang
but, for the moment, he was out of ideas as to how to manage it.
This didn't seem like the time for either charm or humour. In the
end, however, it was Solentino himself who provided the
opportunity.

'Rospo,' he said, once he'd finally satisfied his appetite, 'escort
the lovely Miss Cook to the red room. I would like to speak to
Mr Webb alone.'

Devereau cleared his throat. 'You know that anything you say
to me, you can also say to my colleague.'

Under the table, Scarlett's hand brushed against his thigh. *Careful.* Then she rose to her feet. 'That's quite alright. I understand how some things need to be said man to man.' She smiled at Solentino, indicating she was perfectly happy to be shut away again. But she also opened her mouth and ran the tip of her tongue across her top lip. The action was casual enough to appear unconscious – and yet also slow enough to be tantalising. Devereau didn't fail to note the spark of interest in Solentino's cold eyes. He did his best to ignore the repeated jab of familiar pain between his shoulder blades and conjured up a smile of his own.

'Be good,' he murmured to Scarlett as she was led away.

She tossed her head and winked.

Solentino's gaze followed the sway of Scarlett's hips. Then he glanced at Alina. 'You too. I want to talk to Webb alone.'

Alina didn't react with the same blithe grace. Her shoulders stiffened and her mouth twisted into a fleeting snarl. Interesting. There was still some deeply placed fury lurking inside that woman. She clearly knew her position where Solentino was concerned, however, because she too got up from the table and walked away. Vissier and Moore tagged after her. Now only Devereau, Solentino and the bulging eyes of the unfortunate Mike Lancaster remained.

'You have your hands full with that vampire,' Solentino commented.

'She keeps me entertained,' Devereau said.

'Are you and she –?' He made a gesture with his circle with his thumb and forefinger and crudely inserted his other index finger inside it.

Devereau reminded himself yet again of the role he was playing and smirked. It was important to stick as close to the truth as possible. Many a liar was undone by creating unnecessary stories that could create conflict later on. 'We have done in the past,' he said. 'But these days we don't tend to mix business and pleasure. It keeps life simpler and Scarlett isn't the type to stay with one man.'

Solentino looked intrigued. 'Does that bother you?'

'Yes,' he found himself replying. Then he looked away, annoyed with himself for the stark truth.

'Would it bother you if I approached her for myself?'

Devereau spoke truthfully again. 'Yes.' He cleared his throat. 'But I won't interfere and it won't change anything for me or for our deal. Like I said, I don't mix business with pleasure.'

Christopher Solentino tapped the arm of his chair with his fingernail. 'Hmm. I don't see why. Personally speaking, I mix business with pleasure all the time.' He smiled slowly. 'I tell you what though. I won't fuck your girl. I will, however, ask for something from you in return for not doing so.'

The man seemed convinced that Scarlett would fall into his damned bed just because he said so. Devereau forced his mouth to curve upwards and met Solentino's eyes. 'What's that?'

'That you kill her.' He reached for a fat olive and popped it into his mouth.

Devereau was halfway out of his chair before he realised what he was doing. He sat back down again and schooled his expression into a bland mask. Solentino watched him with amusement.

'She's my business partner,' he managed. 'Why would I kill her?'

Solentino steepled his fingers under his chin and leaned forward. 'I like you,' he said. 'Inasmuch as I like anyone, that is. You had balls coming here like you did. And,' he added, without a single glance or gesture towards Mike Lancaster's dead body, 'my little organisation suddenly has an opening. From what I've learnt of you so far, you're someone we can work with. From what I've learnt of Miss Cook, she's someone I can't.'

Devereau bit back the question which rose to his lips. Why? Why had he decided he couldn't work with Scarlett? What had he found out? It couldn't be her identity as the buyer of the Ring Of All Seasons. If that were the case, Solentino would be trying to kill them both. It had to be something else. 'I've worked together with Scarlett before,' he said carefully. 'She's someone who is trustworthy. And as a vampire she has considerable power.'

Solentino didn't hesitate with his reply. 'Her other loyalties indicate that she is not a good fit for us. You are a different story. Tell me, Mr Webb, how far are you really prepared to go to make decent money? I'm not talking about the sort of money that will buy you a nice holiday or a nice car. I'm not even talking about the sort of money that will pay off your mortgage. When I say decent amount of money I mean the sort that changes lives.' He raised a single meaningful eyebrow. 'For ever.'

Devereau kept his body language as relaxed and open as possible. 'Go on.'

Solentino shook his head. 'I can't say any more. Not yet. Not until I know that you can truly be one of us.' He picked up a knife from the table and toyed with it. 'Prove your worth to me and kill your little vampire friend. She's sexy and I like her but she has to go.' He paused, his fingertip on the edge of the blade. 'Unless your feelings for her are so strong that you cannot bear to end her life.' He shrugged. 'In which case, we shall part company with no hard feelings.'

It was a test. The worst kind of test. Devereau had no choice but to stall. He forced the tiniest smile to play around his mouth, giving the impression that he was truly considering Solentino's proposal. 'Am I permitted some thinking time?'

Something sparked in the other man's eyes. 'Sure. In fact, why don't you and Miss Cook take the rest of the day off? You can both leave. I will ask you to return tomorrow morning. That should be enough time for those laxatives to take effect. Give me the ring and I'll give you the money I have already agreed upon. One point five million euros. We shall shake hands and I will hope never to see you again. Alternatively, give me the ring and Miss Cook's head and the world will be yours for the taking.' Solentino ran the knife across the fleshy part of his own thumb, watching with some disinterest as beads of blood appeared. 'It's entirely your choice.'

'Very well,' Devereau said. 'I suppose that will give me the night with Scarlett to enjoy first.'

Solentino suddenly grinned. 'You are indeed a man after my own heart.'

* * *

BOTH DEVEREAU and Scarlett were ejected onto the pavement outside Solentino's apartment block. Devereau glanced towards the locking mechanism of the door as they were pushed out past it and smiled slightly to himself.

'You've not shit yourself already, have you?' Scarlett asked suspiciously. 'How strong were those laxatives?'

'Don't worry about the ring,' Devereau said cheerfully. 'It's not budged yet. Signore Solentino and I merely had a frank discussion about various matters and we've come to an understanding. There's nothing for you to worry your pretty your little head about.'

Scarlett's spine went rigid and she glared at him, rage spiking in her eyes. Then she suddenly relaxed, realising that he was concerned Solentino could still hear what they said. The windows above their heads were open. There was every reason to think their voices could drift upwards. 'I deserve a little more respect than that, Dev,' she bit out.

'Let's go to the hotel,' he said, 'and I'll show you all the respect you deserve.'

Scarlett folded her arms. 'That had better be a promise.'

He touched his heart. 'I give you my solemn vow.'

They crossed the road and wandered down to the battered Fiat. Scarlett paused beside it, examining the lock. Devereau checked the passenger side. It looked clean. Then she unlocked the door and they both got in.

'There's no sign of tampering,' she said quietly. 'They didn't peg the car as mine. We're good.'

Devereau nodded. 'Let's get out of here and I'll tell you what happened.' His tone was grim.

Scarlett put the Fiat into gear and drove off. As soon as they rounded the corner, she started to shake her limbs vigorously. 'Ugh. I'm going to need to scrub myself for hours to get rid of the taint of that man. What a fucker.'

'You have no idea,' Devereau said darkly. He glanced in the rear view mirror. There was a figure behind them on a motorbike. Their helmet was tinted so it was impossible to tell who it was. He was certain it was of one of Solentino's men, however. It might even be Alina. 'I think we're being followed. Head to the Hotel Condotti. I don't want to raise any suspicions. Solentino already knew I was staying there so the hotel room may be compromised. We'll have to be careful where we speak candidly.'

Scarlett glanced at him. 'What's going on?'

Devereau drew in a breath. 'He wants me to kill you. If I bring him your head tomorrow morning, I will get a free pass into his little gang.'

She bared her single fang and hissed. 'That fucker. I thought I'd done a good job of flirting.'

'You did.' Devereau hoped he didn't sound too bitter about it. 'It's something to do with your loyalties.'

She frowned. 'Is that what Solentino said?'

'Loyalties was the word he used.'

'I made it clear that as long as we're outside London, I am free from any constraints. I can do what I want. There's nothing in any of my history to suggest otherwise. Nothing that Christopher Solentino would be able to find anyway.'

Devereau's eyebrow twitched. 'I think,' he muttered, 'you answered the question for yourself.'

'What?' The crease in her brow deepened. Then she paled. 'You mean London. He's planning something in London.' She slowed to a stop as the next traffic lights turned red and turned to stare at him. Devereau noted the motorbike remained directly on their tail. Whoever that was behind that helmet, they weren't tried to conceal their presence.

'Keep your eyes ahead,' he advised. 'Try not to look angry.'

'Try not to look angry? What the fuck, Devereau? What are we doing by leaving Solentino back there? We should take him out right now. Done, dusted, end of problem.'

He shook his head. 'He's got more people working for him than those blokes we met just now. What if someone's waiting to take his place? What if he's not actually the guy in charge but someone else is calling the shots? We can't act until we know more.'

'When did you become so bloody cautious?'

He kept his voice even, although he wanted to slam his fists against the Fiat's flimsy dashboard as much as she did. 'When it became clear that lives are at stake. Possibly a lot of lives. Solentino has got money but he couldn't afford to come close to outbidding you for the Ring of All Seasons. He's expecting a massive payout from whatever he's planning. This is serious shit, Scarlett.'

'You don't need to tell me that,' she growled. 'I'm the one whose head he's demanded on a silver platter.' The lights changed and she took off again, narrowly missing rear-ending the smart car in front. Scarlett hissed under her breath in vexation and squared her shoulders. 'If you won't kill him, then what exactly will you do?'

'Well, I won't chop your head off, if that's what you're worried about.'

'As if you could,' she scoffed. 'I'd like to see you try.'

No. She wouldn't.

'Come on, Devereau. What's the big plan? Is MI5 going to come charging in and save the day?'

'I don't know what the plan is. I don't have one. I'll need to contact HQ and see what they think.'

'You know what they'll think. They'll order you to off me so you can continue to string Solentino along.'

'They wouldn't do that.' Then Devereau grimaced. Actually, they might say that. Sarah Greensmith might tell him to do exactly that.

'I'm a vampire. That makes me immediately expendable in the eyes of the British government.'

'Whether they order that or not, it's a moot point. Don't you get it, Scarlett? I like you. A lot. I care about you. A hell of a lot. No matter what's happened between us in the past or what's happening now, I would never ever hurt you. And I certainly wouldn't kill anyone because some tosser in Whitehall ordered it. Whether I work for them or not, I'm not their beholden to them. When they say jump, I don't say how high. I'm not that kind of person and you know that.' He drew in a breath. 'You also know somewhere deep inside you that I would kill myself before I'd ever harm a hair on your head.'

For a long moment Scarlett didn't say anything. She kept her gaze trained on the road ahead. When she finally did speak, her voice was barely audible. 'My favourite food,' she said quietly, 'is mashed potato.'

'Mashed potato?'

'With butter and cream. Sometimes with cheese melted through it. Sometimes with chives on the top. Sometimes I even go all out and add some crispy pancetta. But really, when it comes down to it, what I love is mashed potato. Even if it's lumpy.'

Devereau looked at her. 'The mashed potato I make is never lumpy.'

'Yeah, yeah.'

'It's true.'

She jabbed him in the arm. 'One day I'll make you prove that.'

Fantastic. He grinned. 'No problem.'

CHAPTER TWELVE

DEVEREAU PLUMPED UP THE PILLOWS AND CUSHIONS, MAKING
himself comfortable on the bed, while Scarlett ordered some
coffee from room service and then went out to make a call.
Greensmith's system of only writing draft emails meant that he
didn't have to worry about any lack of security within the hotel's
wifi system but, in case Solentino had indeed managed to bug his
room in the intervening hours while he'd been away, he turned
on the television, ramping up the volume to cover the sounds of
any typing. He read the email Greensmith had already left for
him, instructing him to do whatever was necessary to find out
what Solentino was up to – albeit without placing himself in any
immediate danger or crossing the Italian authorities – and told
him to update her on his progress as soon as he possibly could.
Like the good little werewolf he was, he did just that.

*CS IS PLANNING SOMETHING NASTY. Likely in London but he also
mentioned Paris and Berlin. If I commit murder for him, he'll allow me
access to his gang which so far includes Geraint Vissier and Rospo
Accetti. CS has a girlfriend called Alina Bonnet who is also involved*

somehow. There was another man called Mike Lancaster but he is deceased as of today. CS killed Lancaster in front of me.

CS IS GOING to approach a Greek named Avanopoulos who might be able to help him with some kind of transportation to Germany. From what I could gather he had someone called Bartan in the frame but he's not longer available. Don't know what kind of transport is required or what is being moved but it's likely something dodgy. I don't know how I'll proceed but I've got until tomorrow morning to decide.

DEVEREAU SCANNED HIS MESSAGE. It was short but brevity was no doubt better than any long winded descriptions. He'd deliberately left out mention of who Solentino had told him to murder. He didn't want to give Sarah Greensmith the opportunity to disappoint him. Besides, as far as his immediate MI5 boss was concerned, Scarlett was still safely tucked away in good ol' London. He hoped that his inclusion of Lancaster's murder would make Greensmith realise how dangerous both this situation and Solentino actually were. Devereau had no problem admitting that he was out of his depth. He knew how he'd deal with Solentino if the man were a werewolf or someone he came across in his old patch in London. But this sort of international intrigue, not to mention potential terrorism, was far out of Devereau's realm of experience.

Leaning against the pillows, he watched the flickering images on the television with unseeing eyes. Obviously, he wasn't going to kill Scarlett. There had to be some way to still ingratiate himself with Solentino, however, and keep Scarlett safe. Devereau's stomach grumbled loudly and he grimaced. The laxatives were already beginning to work their dubious magic. He hesitated, waiting to see if his bowels were about to empty themselves. Apparently not yet.

The laptop screen flashed and he glanced down. Huh. Greensmith had already replied. He hadn't been expecting to hear from her so soon but he supposed that not only was she carefully monitoring the email address, she was also stirred into action by the information he'd provided. There was nothing like the whisper of an impending attack on your own capital city to galvanise your security services into action.

UNDER NO CIRCUMSTANCES *are you to commit murder.*

YEAH, no shit. He snorted mildly to himself.

IT IS IMPERATIVE, *however, that you find out more about CS's plans as well as any other members of his organisation. He's not a supe. Impress him with your werewolf abilities. Talk about your time as the Shepherd. Get him to open up to you.*

SHE MADE it sound so easy.

Do you have any details on a possible time frame for the attack?

THAT WAS the one question he could answer. He quickly typed out an answer.

THE EARLIEST DATE *will be December 22nd.*

. . .

DEVEREAU WAITED a moment or two before refreshing his screen. Greensmith didn't waste any time responding.

CS TOLD YOU THAT HIMSELF?

NO. But it was could be the only reason why Solentino was so keen to get his greasy, bloodstained mitts on the Ring of All Seasons. Legend stated that anyone who wore it on the night of the Winter Solstice would get glimpses into their future. Unless he was mistaken, that was December 21st. Assuming the legend was true, it provided the perfect failsafe mechanism for anyone considering an elaborate plan of action that might involve death or life imprisonment if it went badly. Solentino wasn't planning a suicide mission. He wasn't the type. There was no doubt in Devereau's mind that Solentino wanted the ring as a rubber stamp to prove his impending action would work. If the ring showed him a future he didn't like, he could cancel everything with no harm done. Although admittedly that would also create some sort of bizarre time travel, future proofing conundrum of the type that made Devereau's head hurt if he thought about it too much. If you could see into the future, could you then change that future? Or was it already immutable? He doubted the merits of getting into that sort of discussion with Sarah Greensmith, however, and opted for a simpler answer.

I WORKED it out from other things he's said.

THERE. That ought to be enough.

. . .

THIS TIME it took Greensmith longer to answer. When she did, her instructions were terse and to the point but without any sort of helpful advice that he could actually use.

GET CS TO TRUST YOU. Find out exactly what he's planning. I'll expect another update within twenty-four hours.

DEVEREAU WAITED but nothing else was forthcoming. Eventually, he sighed audibly, massaged the back of his neck, and closed the laptop. The only good thing about any of this was that Christopher Solentino wasn't nearly as smart as he believed himself to be. Devereau certainly possessed the will to get the man to trust him. Now he only had to find the way.

* * *

BY THE TIME Scarlett finally returned, the coffee which had arrived via room service was cold. She seemed unperturbed by its temperature, downing it in several uninterrupted gulps before smacking her lips. When she caught Devereau staring at her, she shrugged.

'What? I needed something to get the taste of that woman's blood out of my mouth.'

'You didn't like how she tasted?' he asked.

'I didn't like how I was all but forced to drink from her,' Scarlett replied. 'I'm not a performing seal.'

Devereau opened his mouth to warn her against saying anything else, in case somebody really was listening in to what they were saying. Scarlett was already one step ahead of him, however. She pulled a long narrow wand device out of her bag. 'This is what took me so long.'

He raised an eyebrow. 'You were out buying a sex toy?'

She tossed her head. 'You wish.' She grinned at him easily, however, and pressed an invisible button on the side of the device. A small light glowed green and Scarlett wasted no time in waving it around the room, from one wall to another. It emitted a tiny, high-pitched whine that was annoying in the extreme. But that was all it did.

Scarlett checked the curtains, the light fittings, and under the bed. When she was finished, her expression was satisfied. 'Hotel Condotti has better security than I'd have given them credit for. Thus far anyway. The room is clear of listening devices and we can speak freely.'

Excellent. Devereau nodded towards the wand. 'Where did you get that from?'

'I'm one of Lord Horvath's most trusted vampires,' she said. 'I've got useful contacts ready to spring to my command all over the place.'

'Must be good to be you.'

'It is.' She paused. 'Mr Motorbike is still hanging around outside. Solentino is keeping a close eye on us.'

That pleased Devereau far more than it dismayed him. It meant that he wasn't being dismissed out of hand and that could only be a positive thing. 'Could you see who he was? Is it Vissier? Or Rospo?'

She shook her head. 'Nope. Could be either of them or neither of them. He's definitely male but beyond that I can't tell. Whoever our mysterious follower is, he still has the helmet on.'

He might be hiding his identity but he definitely wasn't attempting to be inconspicuous. Interesting. Devereau put aside the motorcyclist's identity for the time being and watched Scarlett silently for a moment or two. 'I've been thinking about our problem,' he said eventually.

'You mean the one where you're supposed to chop off my head in order to prove yourself as a good little wannabe terrorist?'

He shifted uncomfortably. 'Yeah, that one.'

'Did MI5 offer any useful suggestions?'

'Let's just say,' Devereau replied, 'that I left out one or two specific details when I contacted them. They don't know about your involvement.'

Scarlett looked more relieved than he'd expected her to. 'I'm pleased to hear it.' She spread her arms out wide. 'Go on then. What's the big plan?'

'You have to leave Rome. I've checked and there's still plenty of time to get to the airport and catch the last flight to London.'

Scarlett folded her arms and looked at him.

'What?' he asked, attempting to feign nonchalance.

'Are you kidding me, Dev? Are you fucking kidding me? You seriously expect me to run away?'

'I rather thought you might take a taxi and then fly. You don't have to run.'

She gave him a long look to inform him that she was wholly unimpressed by his weak humour. 'You know me well enough to know that I don't run.'

Devereau was prepared for this. 'And I thought your argument was that I don't know you at all.'

'Now you're being facetious.'

He shrugged, the very picture of angelic innocence. 'Am I?'

'Piss off, Devereau.'

He swung his legs off the bed and stood up. 'You're a hot mess of contradictions, Scarlett. I don't know you. I do know you. You want me. You don't want me.'

She flashed her single, white fang at him. 'We've been through all this.'

He splayed out his hands in a gesture of peace. 'Yeah, we have. You made a good call by ending things between us.'

Scarlett glared at him. 'Pardon?'

'We're completely different people. We have next to nothing in common. I'm independent. I like my freedom. You're wholly loyal to another man and you jump to do his bidding.' Devereau shook his head. 'I can't work like that.'

'You're referring to Lord Horvath.' Her voice was flat enough that he knew he was getting to her.

'I don't mean it as a bad thing, Scarlett. He's lucky to have you. I'm only saying that I could never be beholden to someone else like you are. It proves that at heart we're completely different kinds of people.'

Scarlett's eyes were flecked with rage. 'I'm not *beholden*,' she spat. 'It's an honour to be able to work for Lukas Horvath. There's not a vampire in London who doesn't feel that way.'

'Okay.' Devereau looked baffled. 'If you say so.'

'You jumped up furry dog! You work for a bunch of bloody humans! At least I'm with my own kind. You follow the orders of people who think that you're some kind of freak.'

'I don't follow all their orders. And I choose to work for them. Did you really choose to work for Horvath or is it just that's the way that things are done? Are you only following the crowd?'

'Following the crowd?' her voice rose. 'Following the fucking crowd? Why you … you … you …' She stopped in mid-sentence and dropped her arms. 'You stupid shit, Devereau.' She walked up to him until their noses were almost touching. 'You stupid furry shit,' she whispered. Her eyes met his. 'Did you really think that was going to work?'

Fuck. 'What?' he asked.

'You were trying to goad me into an argument. You wanted to piss me off enough that I'd storm out of here. Then you could waltz back to Solentino and tell him that you can't kill me because I'm not here.'

Devereau gazed at her. Then he sighed. 'Would that be such a bad thing?'

'You still have my ring.'

'You'll get your damned ring back. I've already promised you will.'

'I'm not the kind of coward who runs away because of one madman.'

'It's not running away,' he argued. 'It's a strategic retreat.'

Scarlett jabbed him in the chest with her index finger. 'You're the one who got me into this. You're the one who persuaded me to join forces with you.'

'I'm sorry,' he said quietly. 'I shouldn't have done that. I was wrong to involve you.'

'Too late, Devereau. *Way* too late. Now that I'm here, I'm not backing out. That's not the way I work and I definitely don't need you to protect me. I've been at this sort of thing a hell of a lot longer than you have. You might be the big bad wolf but I've still got more power than you. I'm still smarter than you.'

He wasn't going to disagree with that. He couldn't. 'I know you're smarter than me, Scarlett. I also know that the smartest thing to do here is to remove yourself from the equation so that I can work on Solentino.'

'Would you walk away if MI5 told you to, Devereau? If your spy boss, whoever they are, told you that they were putting together a crack team of specialists to take care of Solentino without your help, would you get on a plane and go home?'

He didn't immediately answer.

'Devereau?' she prodded.

He gritted his teeth. 'No,' he said. 'I wouldn't.'

'Why not?'

'Because now I know what sort of man he really is, I can't leave him be.'

She leaned forward slightly. 'Then it appears,' she murmured, 'that we're really not all that different after all.'

They stared at each other. All of a sudden, Devereau was painfully aware of her proximity. He breathed in and inhaled her scent. He could almost taste Scarlett's retreating anger in amongst the combined smells of the perfume she'd applied that morning to the coffee she'd only just finished. In fact, it wasn't only anger he could smell. There was something else there, lingering underneath her other turbulent, undefined emotions. Scarlett's eyes dropped to his mouth and her cheeks flushed a faint pink. There was no mistaking it now. That was desire.

'Scarlett,' he began.

'Shut up, Devereau.' Her hands reached for him and pulled him towards her and then her soft mouth was on his.

There was a tiny logical corner of his brain that told him to put a stop to this now. He wanted far more from Scarlett than mere sex and there was every likelihood that if they saw this encounter through to its inevitable, joyous conclusion that she would withdraw from him even more afterwards. When her hands drifted down his chest, however, and began to toy with his belt, that logic all but fled. Devereau groaned, his own hands reaching for Scarlett's curved waist. It was as if they were made for each other. Their bodies moulded together, their heat combining to create a raging inferno of hot, unbridled desire. Scarlett's fang scraped lightly against his bottom lip. In return, he dipped his head and nipped at the soft flesh on the base of her throat. Beneath his skin, his wolf growled in pure animalistic delight. This. This was what they both wanted. This was –

There was a sudden, loud insistent knock on the door.

'Mr Webb? Signore Webb?' The knock came again. 'There are several people downstairs who are waiting for you. They are … most insistent.'

Scarlett was already pulling away from him. She looked flushed – and troubled. It had taken her little more than seconds to regret making a move on him. Devereau cursed inwardly. Then he squared his shoulders and marched to the door, opening it and glaring at the unfortunate man standing on the threshold. He wasn't a lowly hotel employee, however. From the cut of his suit and his well manicured fingernails and facial hair, he looked to be somebody rather high up in the Hotel Condotti hierarchy.

'It's a pleasure to meet you, Signore Webb,' the man said, in accented English. From his expression, he was lying through his teeth. 'My name is Aldo Costa. I am the hotel manager here. As I said through the door, there are some people waiting for you in the lobby on the ground floor. They require your immediate attention.'

With his thoughts still in disarray after his encounter with Scarlett, it took Devereau a moment or two to process what Aldo Costa was saying. When he finally did, he realised why it was the manager himself who'd appeared at his door.

'Lupo,' he said. Damn it. The Italian werewolves' timing sucked arse.

Costa was too relieved that Devereau knew who he'd been talking about to register his annoyance. 'Si. Yes. As I'm sure you're aware, we are an inclusive establishment and we welcome all sorts of … people. However, this is rather a large group and they are causing some concern amongst our other guests.' He raised his eyebrows at Devereau. 'They said you were expecting them.'

'Not this early.' Moretti had said night. It was barely evening. 'But don't worry. I'll come down and see to them. I'll grab my jacket and a few things first.'

A flicker of worry crossed the hotel manager's face. 'I would appreciate it personally if you could be fast.'

Devereau gave him a stony look. 'I'll be as quick as I can.' He closed the door in the man's face.

Scarlett had already smoothed back her hair and adjusted her clothing. 'Trouble?' she asked.

Devereau pulled a face. 'An irritation.' One that he could definitely do without.

CHAPTER THIRTEEN

At least Scarlett's disbelief gave them both something else to think about beyond the near miss mutual seduction that had happened only moments ago.

'You came to Rome and you didn't check in with the Lupo clan upon your arrival?' She stared at him with the same sort of expression that she might have also worn if he'd stripped naked, placed a pineapple on top of his head and performed the macarena in front of the Trevi Fountain.

'I didn't know of the Lupo clan. How could I check in with people who I didn't know existed?'

Scarlett leaned across to press the button for the lift. He allowed himself a heart-stopping gulp of the heady scent of her hair before she continued to berate him for a fool.

'Jesus, Devereau. You're not naïve enough to think that only England has supes, right?'

He inhaled again. Damn. She smelled better than that weird shit they pumped into the atmosphere of Heart, the vamp nightclub in Soho. Then he met her eyes and remembered to focus on the conversation. 'Of course not,' he said. 'In fact, I also know that Rome was *founded* by werewolves.'

'Did Nicolo Moretti tell you that right before he beat your arse?'

'You know him?'

'I've met him once or twice.' Scarlett sighed. 'You should have done your homework, Devereau. Visiting Moretti and the rest of the Lupo clan should have been the top of your agenda. It's common courtesy. Not only that but your unannounced arrival could be seen as a genuine threat. Wolves are territorial creatures. Even you know that.'

The lift dinged as it finally arrived at their floor. 'I had other things on my mind than the werewolves of Rome, Scarlett.' They both stepped into the lift. 'But, yes, I should have considered them and done more to seek them out. I've learnt my lesson.'

The doors closed and the lift started to descend.

'However,' he added, 'Moretti didn't beat my arse.'

Scarlett sniffed. 'Not yet. But he definitely will soon.'

'I'm the most powerful werewolf that's been seen for generations. It took four separate bites to turn me,' he reminded her.

'You might be powerful, Devereau,' Scarlett said. 'But you're nothing compared to Nicolo Moretti.'

Jealousy flared deep in his chest. 'You sound like you admire him,' he growled.

She shrugged. 'I do.' She paused. 'Even if he is an ostentatious furball with an ego the size of Mount Etna.'

The lift dinged again and the doors slid open to reveal the hotel lobby. Devereau blinked. Aldo Costa hadn't been lying when he'd said there was a large group waiting for him. There had to be at least twenty werewolves standing in wait for him. Scarlett let out a low whistle. 'Yep,' she said. 'You're screwed.'

He threw her an irritated glance and strode towards them. There was no sign of Moretti himself but Devereau recognised a few faces and individual scents from the previous night's encounter. He smiled broadly in a bid to put the other werewolves at ease and then inclined his head to show a modicum of respect.

'You're earlier than I thought you would be,' Devereau said to nobody in particular. 'So I apologise for keeping you waiting.'

'You knew we were coming for you,' rumbled a dark haired male with ominous intent.

Devereau looked him up and down. The Lupo clan didn't appear to wear helpful tags indicating their ranking like the London clans did. All the same, he reckoned this fellow was a beta. He had both the age and the poise to be one of Moretti's most trusted wolves.

'I did indeed,' Devereau said cheerfully. There was no reason to antagonise the man. In fact, the more amenable and less aggressive he could appear, the faster he'd extricate himself from whatever idiocy Moretti had planned for him. The clock was ticking after all and there was the far more pressing concern of Christopher Solentino to worry about. 'My name is Devereau.'

The older wolf rolled his eyes. 'I know who you are.' Then he glanced at Scarlett and his demeanour changed instantly. 'Scarlett Cook. It's a pleasure to see you again.' He looked as if he meant it.

'Orsetto, the pleasure is all mine.' Scarlett grinned at him.

'You're not with this pezzo di merda, are you?'

Devereau wasn't sure what pezzo di merda meant but he could certainly guess. 'She's already told me off for not following the appropriate traditions,' he said.

'I'd expect nothing less.' Orsetto raised his busy eyebrows at her. 'Are you coming with us tonight?'

'That depends,' Scarlett said. 'Where are you going?'

'Il Colosseo.'

She wrinkled her nose. 'I thought you might be heading there. It wouldn't be my first choice of evening's entertainment.' She pointed at Devereau. 'But I can't afford to let this one out of my sight. If I do, he might run away when I'm not looking.'

Scarlett's words were an obvious dig at his own attempt to get her to leave the city. Orsetto didn't know that, however. His head snapped towards Devereau and his eyes narrowed, a sheen of lupine yellow lighting up his irises. 'If you run, little Englishman, we will rip the fangs from your mouth, the fur from your body and the tail from your bony arse.'

Devereau frowned. 'Bony arse? I have *some* curve appeal.' He nudged Scarlett. 'Right?'

She clicked her tongue but he was sure he could see at least some amusement flickering in her face. 'Ignore him,' she told Orsetto. Then she tilted her head and softened her voice. 'I am not apologising for Devereau Webb and I'm certainly not excusing his actions. But he is here in Rome because he must deal with a serious, time-sensitive matter. Do you think it's possible to appeal to Alpha Moretti's better nature and let him off with a warning on this occasion?'

Orsetto's response was immediate. 'No.'

Scarlett's mouth twisted. 'I thought as much. You understand I had to try.'

'Of course.'

'He's a new wolf but he's no weakling,' Scarlett said.

'So we have heard.' Orsetto's eyes gleamed. 'But that is all the more reason to ensure he understands his place.'

If there was one thing Devereau despised, it was being spoken about as if he wasn't here. 'Come on then,' he said aloud. 'Let's get this over and done with.'

'I wouldn't be in a such rush if I were you,' Orsetto smirked. He snapped his fingers and half a dozen other werewolves immediately stepped forward, encircling Devereau and separating him from Scarlett.

'I always wanted an entourage,' Devereau murmured. He smiled again, although his thoughts were in turmoil. Just what sort of shady shite was he about to find himself in?

'One question,' Scarlett said, from over to his right. 'Will you make him wear the costume?'

'If we're going to do this,' Orsetto replied, 'we should do it properly. Right?'

Devereau could hear the smile in her voice. 'Right.'

Now he had a *really* bad feeling about this.

* * *

ALTHOUGH IT WAS BARELY cocktail hour, Rome was no different to London at this chilly time of year. Sunset had been and gone and the sky was dark and cloudy. Devereau could only catch a bare glimpse of the moon as he was marched out towards one of several waiting cars.

'I trust we're not travelling far?' he inquired. He flicked a look to his right. The mysterious motorcyclist was still there, sitting on top of their bike across the road. Whether he would continue to follow them now that most of Rome's own werewolves were involved, only time would tell.

The six wolves encircling him didn't answer. Apparently Orsetto was the only one allowed to talk.

'Don't worry, Signore Webb,' he said. 'We'll be there soon enough, even with the rush hour traffic.'

'Is it closed to tourists?' Scarlett asked.

'From 4.30pm.'

Devereau's left eyebrow twitched. What was it Orsetto had said to her before? Il Colosseo?

'We're going to the Colosseum?'

This time, Orsetto elected not to answer. Devereau thought he glimpsed a smile on the face of one of the other wolves, however. Huh. Somehow he didn't think they were heading to arguably Rome's most famous tourist spot for some sightseeing. He sighed to himself and got into the backseat of the first car as directed. He'd promised Moretti he'd do this. He had to man up and take his lumps. With any luck it would all be over soon.

Despite the heavy traffic, they pulled up outside the

Colosseum within less than twenty minutes. The circular half ruins were lit up from within by warm inviting lights and, despite his attempts at maintaining a cool façade, Devereau felt himself drawing in a sharp breath. It was stunning. He would defy anyone to look up at the structure and not imagine what it must have been like during its heyday almost two thousand years ago.

The werewolf seated next to him, who hadn't uttered a single word to Devereau yet but who was communicating a great deal from the stench of his breath, turned and grinned at him. Devereau didn't know if it was caused by excitement or a deliberate attempt at intimidation, but his teeth were bared, shifting before his gaze from stubby human canines to elongated lupine fangs. 'You can run now,' he said. 'If you dare.'

'You're talking to the wrong wolf.'

'Thought you were a sheep, not a wolf.'

Don't rise to the bait, Devereau told himself. 'A wolf in sheep's clothing,' he answered.

'We'll soon see about that.'

Yeah. We will.

Devereau and the others got out of the car. Scarlett emerged from the vehicle behind. She sent him one brief wary look before curving her lips into a delighted smile. 'It's been too long since I've been here,' she cooed.

'Then we are pleased to welcome you back.'

Devereau's head turned and he spotted Moretti walking towards them. He automatically straightened his spine, drawing himself up. No, he didn't wish to antagonise the Italian alpha. And no, he wouldn't act submissive either. He wasn't beyond playing the role of dippy English tourist, however.

'We should immortalise the moment with a selfie!'

Moretti grinned. He pulled out a sleek phone and posed, taking a photo only of himself. 'Looking good, Nicolo. Looking *gooood*.' He winked at Devereau and put the phone away.

Devereau couldn't do anything but smile in return. Despite the situation and the man's propensity for grandstanding, he had to admit that, like Scarlett, he liked the man. He had a sense of humour and was quite willing to poke fun at himself. Devereau didn't think he was particularly under-handed or manipulative either, which was both unexpected and unlike the other werewolf alphas he'd come across so far. Of course, whether he would feel quite so amenable towards Moretti by the time this evening's shenanigans were over, only time would tell.

'I'm here as you demanded,' Devereau said. 'I do have a request to make of you, however.'

Moretti seemed amused. 'A request? I'm not sure you're in any position to be asking for anything, Signore Webb.'

'I have important business to take care of here in Rome,' Devereau told him. 'Life threatening business. I would appreciate it if this,' he waved a hand around, 'whatever this is, doesn't take too long.'

'That will depend on whether you still have a life to be threatened when we are finished here.' Moretti's words were ominous but there was a sparkle in his eyes which belied the gravity of what he was saying.

Devereau didn't smile. Not everything was a joke. 'It's not my life that's being threatened,' he said quietly. He'd barely finished speaking when Solentino's obedient motorcycle man appeared on foot from round the corner. He must have parked the bike somewhere nearby – and it was clear he wasn't about to give up his chase any time soon.

Moretti gazed at Devereau. 'I see.' He nodded thoughtfully while Devereau breathed out. The alpha wolf wasn't going to cause him too many problems now. He was sure of it. 'Well, we'll do our best to be finished by the witching hour but I can't make any absolute promises. Our audience won't wish to remain here all night anyway.'

Devereau's brow creased. 'Audience?'

Moretti smirked. 'They've paid good money to be here,' he said. 'They deserve value for money.'

Scarlett spoke up from the side. 'I doubt you'll have any worries on that score.' She curtsied mockingly.

In return, Moretti bowed, throwing his arm out in an unnecessary flourish. 'Ciao, Signorina Cook.'

'Ciao.' She tapped her watch. 'Shall we get started?'

'Va bene.'

CHAPTER FOURTEEN

IF DEVEREAU HAD POSSESSED ANY QUESTIONS ABOUT WHAT NICOLO Moretti was planning as a punishment for his ignorant transgressions, they were answered when they walked through to the Colosseum's interior. There was a large crowd of people above them, watching from an elevated vantage point where once upon a time no doubt ancient Roman citizens did the same. Tall, flickering candles had been placed around the various audience areas, lighting up the crowd and providing something of an eerie atmosphere, although the low-pitched murmur of conversation changed pitch when Moretti and Devereau appeared, altering from muted chatter to excited buzz. Devereau couldn't fail to notice that they were all dressed for a night out with smart suits and glowing evening dresses. This was an event for the well-heeled. He wondered if he should be irritated that Moretti and clan Lupo were going to make money out of him in this way but he decided he was actually impressed. It was certainly one method of paying the bills and keeping the locals on side. Perhaps he'd suggest something similar to the clans in London. He smiled to himself at the idea. Those sour-faced supes would turn their noses up at anything he put forward, no matter how clever or lucrative it might potentially be.

'Do the authorities know you're using the Colosseum for your own ends?'

Moretti laughed. 'They expect it. Half the city politicians are up there waiting to see what you do. They like to think that offering up such a venerated structure helps to keep us in our place. We put on a show for them and they stay off our backs for that little bit longer. Tonight, you're that show.'

'Great,' Devereau muttered.

Moretti clapped him on the back. 'Think of it as public service as well as punishment. You're following ancient footsteps here, Signore Webb. In a few years' time, there will be a retractable floor that will make this ampitheatre even better. When it's built, it will be much easier to gain a greater understanding of what the original gladiatorial experience would have been like. Until then, we have to do make do with this much smaller space.'

Devereau peered around the elevated wooden floor which stretched out in front of them. He could see the labyrinthine walls beneath and beyond that had no doubt been the underground area where the gladiators and animals had been cloistered before and after their fights.

'It's not as big as I thought it would be. The floor, I mean. Not the amphitheatre.'

'I think you'll find it will provide ample space.'

Devereau gave Moretti a long look. 'So I'm to fight? That's what this is about?'

'Seven bouts. One for each of the famous seven hills of our wonderful city.' Moretti paused. 'Well,' he amended, 'there will only be seven bouts if you manage to last that long. You can halt the proceedings at any time. If you do, however, I will demand that you swear fealty to clan Lupo instead. The same will happen if you are knocked unconscious.' The Italian shrugged expressively. 'If you die, I'll let you off the swearing part.'

Devereau folded his arms. 'Ha. Ha.'

Moretti deliberately ignored his sarcasm. 'I'm glad you are amused. Each bout will last for seven minutes.'

They were a bit too enamoured of the number seven around here. That was actually quite a long time for a fight.

Moretti seemed to know what he was thinking. 'If you incapacitate your opponents early on,' he said cheerfully, 'it'll be a very easy seven minutes.'

Yeah, yeah. Devereau grunted. This was going to be a long evening and, even with his enhanced strength and power, he suspected it would be a miracle if he made it out of the Colosseum without some broken bones and at least minor blood loss. 'Let's get started then,' he said. 'I can hardly wait.'

* * *

'You have got to be fucking kidding me.' Devereau stared down at himself. He'd been led to a small alcove out of sight of the crowd and given a new set of clothes to put on. Although calling this ridiculous costume 'clothes' was an insult to fashion.

'I think you look sexy.' Scarlett looked him up and down with mocking amusement.

'You're enjoying this far too much,' he growled. He tugged in irritation at the white tunic which only bared scraped his mid-thighs.

'You're a werewolf, Devereau. Last night you were hanging off the side of a building stark naked. You can't worry about modesty.'

'I'd rather be naked than wear this.' He glared at her. It wasn't the tunic on its own which bothered him, or the fact that he was baring a considerable amount of skin. It was the theatrics of the flimsy red cloak, the plastic moulded breastplate which he supposed was meant to look like armour but which wouldn't stop an enthusiastic mosquito, and the calf high sandals. 'I don't do fancy dress.'

Scarlett laughed. 'You do now.'

'The second I shift, the outfit will be ruined anyway. There's no point in wearing it.'

'I'm beginning to think the gentleman doth protest too much.' Her eyes danced. 'Besides, that's the very reason why it's not very good quality. It's designed to be ruined.'

'It's designed for fools.'

She was still smiling widely. 'Nicolo Moretti has an aptitude for punishment.'

Moretti himself took that moment to stride towards them. 'Did I hear my name being taken in vain?' His gaze slid from Scarlett to Devereau. 'You look wonderful. We should re-take that selfie and include you in it this time.' He waved his hand at Devereau's body. 'This is a huge improvement on your other clothes.'

Hardly. 'Is everyone I'm fighting going to be dressed up like this?'

Moretti's grin almost split his face in two. 'No,' he said. 'Just you.' He winked while a long trumpet note sounded from somewhere within the Colosseum. 'There's no time to change now. That's your cue.'

'Un-fucking-believable.'

Scarlett reached across and patted his bare arm. 'You make a very fetching gladiator. Try not to get killed, Dev. We've got real work to do later.'

He gave her his fakest smile. 'Yeah, yeah.' He rolled his eyes and stomped out to a roar of appreciation from the audience. What a farce.

Nicolo Moretti was too much of a showman to require any microphone. He strode out to the centre of the small stage ahead of Devereau and spread his arms wide. 'Ladies and gentlemen! Esteemed dignitaries! We welcome you to tonight's entertainment. Our challenger is English and therefore proceedings will be conducted in that language for his benefit. After all, he'll need all the help he can get.'

The audience tittered. Their reaction wasn't dutiful amusement. It was genuine humour. Nobody beyond himself and perhaps Scarlett expected him to do well here.

Moretti continued. 'I know you will all have heard of Devereau Webb. He is already being hailed as a legendary werewolf, bitten four times before he was turned. Apparently he is a true maverick.' Moretti paused for effect. 'But whether he can live up to his own legend or not will be determined tonight!'

This time, the crowd bellowed in anticipatory delight. They were bloodthirsty, Devereau realised. Those people watching from up there were here for brutal violence and brutal violence alone. He noted several men and women whispering and passing over wads of bank notes and he hoped for their sake that they were betting on him and not his seven opponents although from their reactions so far he doubted it. Devereau circled slowly on the spot, displaying his awful costume – and lack of fear – to everyone watching. He was from London's underbelly. He'd fought for everything he'd ever achieved and he wasn't afraid to play dirty. These Italian werewolves wouldn't know what had hit them. He scanned the crowd carefully, stiffening slightly when he spotted the lone figure wearing a motorcycle helmet behind on the second level. Solentino's man had managed somehow to gain entry then. Devereau would certainly give him full marks for tenacity.

The trumpet sang out again. Moretti stepped back, leaving him alone on the stage. Devereau's eyes sought out Scarlett for one short moment. He gestured surreptitiously towards Mr Motorcycle and hoped she noticed him. He didn't have to time to check, however, because that was when then his first opponent appeared.

It was a young male werewolf. Late teens probably, judging

from his juvenile yet muscular body. He was already in wolf form, displaying a lustrous black coat. If there were ever to be lupine shampoo adverts, this guy would be a shoo-in as the model. As Devereau watched, the young wolf spun round, enjoying his moment in the spotlight. He was the warm-up act, Devereau realised. While there was no doubt this would be an easy win, the kid had been a deliberate selection that had nothing to do with lulling Devereau into a false sense of security and everything to do with teaching the younger wolf what it was really like to fight. He approved. Rather than smack the kid down in the first blow, he'd allow him some leeway. It would do them both some good.

An older woman had taken up the microphone. 'The first challenger,' she boomed, 'is nineteen year old Arsenio. He's not yet a ranked wolf but there is no doubt that he's going to go far.'

Arsenio's shoulders rose up a fraction in response to the praise.

'The fight will begin,' the woman said, 'in uno, due, *tre*.'

The crowd screeched in delight. Arsenio, with all the hallmarks of enthusiastic youth, wasted no time. He sprang towards Devereau, his lips pulled back over his teeth and his ears flat against his head. Devereau remained where he was for a beat, waiting as Arsenio thundered towards him. Then, with impeccable timing, he leapt up into the air. Rather than collide with him as he'd expected, Arsenio met thin air. His paws skittered on the wooden boards as he tried to change direction. Devereau landed directly behind him and, while Arsenio tried to find his balance again, Devereau reached out and tweaked his tail.

Arsenio growled and spun, glaring at him with narrowed yellow eyes which were a striking highlight against his midnight black fur. He snapped forward, chomping at air. Devereau stayed put. He wasn't prepared to shift to his own wolf form yet. There were another six fights to go and he wasn't going to reveal himself and give away any advance knowledge of his abilities to his future opponents. He would, however, permit Arsenio to get a few jabs in. It was the right thing to do.

Leaning to his left and blatantly telegraphing his next move, Devereau paused. Unfortunately, when he threw his weight forward, it was clear that Arsenio had missed the advertisement. Devereau's fist connected with the side of his head. If he'd not pulled back at the last moment, he would have knocked the boy out. Arsenio was too wound up to think straight or to pay attention to what was happening. No wonder Moretti had tossed him into the ring to learn.

Devereau drew back, allowing the youngster some breathing time. Calm down, he ordered silently. Pay attention to what you're doing. Pay attention to what I'm doing too.

It seemed to work. Arsenio's chest heaved as he took a deep breath, a tiny cloud appearing as he exhaled. Devereau leaned to his left again. Watch. You'll know where I'm going if you focus.

It worked. As Devereau repeated the exact same move, Arsenio got it. He swivelled away from the blow and lunged towards Devereau's exposed flank, his teeth scraping against the daft plastic breastplate. Devereau angled himself slightly, permitting Arsenio to grab hold of the fake armour and tug. With one sharp move, he yanked it away. The plastic tumbled to the floor with a dull clatter and the crowd roared. Good, kid. Devereau thought. Good.

Emboldened by his minor success, Arsenio went for him again. Those young fangs would be painfully sharp and Devereau had no desire to bleed out because of a silly wound. All the same, he allowed Arsenio's teeth to connect with the bare flesh on his arm, scraping the skin so that beads of bright blood appeared. The kid was so delighted – and astonished – that he'd drawn first blood that he lifted his head and let out an ecstatic howl. Devereau sighed. That was too stupid to allow to pass. He reached out, cuffed Arsenio on the side of his head, and he crumpled to the ground.

The announcer allowed a moment. The crowd watching from above stared silently at Arsenio's body. He whined slightly and stirred but there was no chance he was getting back up again for more.

'Ninety-three seconds!' the woman bellowed into the microphone. 'Devereau Webb wins the first fight!'

Three runners immediately appeared, darting forward to scoop Arsenio up and take him away for medical treatment. He'd have a slight concussion but he'd be fine. And hopefully he'd learnt something in the process. Devereau gave a mocking bow to the crowd and swivelled to walk off stage and grab a drink of water.

Scarlett handed him a bottle. He unscrewed the lid and tipped the contents into his waiting mouth. He'd only just drained the bottle when Moretti appeared.

'That's not what I was expecting from you,' the Italian alpha said.

Devereau managed a grimace. 'Yeah. First blood to a kid. I'll never live that down.'

'That's not what I meant,' Moretti told him. 'As you are well aware.'

Devereau met his eyes. 'I have no idea what you're talking about.'

Moretti waved an irritated hand. 'Si, si. You have thirty minutes. Then the next fight will begin.' He walked away.

'The way you fought that kid was kind of you,' Scarlett commented quietly.

He glanced at her. 'I'm not a bad guy,' he told her. 'Not all the time anyway.'

'I never thought you were, Devereau.' She held out her hand for the empty bottle and he passed it to her.

'Thank you.' He didn't say it only for the water. 'Is this your kind of thing, Scarlett? Fighting like this? Is this what vampires do too?'

'We're a little more cerebral than your kind.' She hesitated. 'There's something to be said for having an enthusiastic crowd watching your every move though.'

'Not just an enthusiastic crowd,' Devereau said grimly, thinking of the motorcyclist who remained unwilling to peel himself away no matter what the circumstances were.

Scarlett nodded. 'I saw him. He's still up there. Judging from the way he's keeping away from the rest of the audience, he probably sneaked in here. Solentino isn't taking any chances.'

'He wants the ring.'

She wrinkled her nose. 'Don't we all.'

Devereau could only shrug. 'Maybe he wants to enjoy the show without others bellowing in his ear. Although I suspect you'd put on a better display than I did. You're more of an exhibitionist than I am.'

Scarlett grinned. 'Bullshit. You like to show off as much as I do. You just hide it better.'

'You like a show?'

'Devereau,' she drawled, 'I love a show.'

CHAPTER FIFTEEN

IF THE ONE FANGED LADY LOVED A SHOW, THEN HE'D GIVE HER A show. When it was time for his second fight, Devereau strode out onto the stage flicking his red cloak with enough melodrama to appease the surliest of onlookers. From the watching crowd above, someone screamed out his name. Devereau looked up in the direction the call had come from and blew a kiss to teenage girl. She shrieked and clutched her heart; Devereau bowed towards her.

'For the second fight of the evening,' the announcer said, 'we present to you Beatrice and Beppe.'

Devereau turned and saw the couple walking hand in hand towards him. Twins, he realised, as he looked from face to face. Well, this would be interesting. They'd elected to come out in their human forms but they wasted no time in shifting in an explosion of flying fabric and fur. Their movements were strangely synchronised and Devereau couldn't help wondering whether that was by design or because of some inexplicable bond they both as a result of their shared genetic traits. Either way, he didn't have much time to ponder the matter. The announcer was very keen to get matters underway.

'Uno,' she yelled, 'duo … tre!'

Although the twins were young, it was clear they had considerably more experience at this sort of thing than Arsenio. They took their time, separating initially to circle round Devereau's standing form. They were aiming to divide his attention – and double their chances. Devereau was well aware that he'd need to be on his guard. Until one of them made a move, he would remain exactly where he was. He had no problem with patience.

He remained still, eyeing the pair as they looped around him, again and again. He knew that they would attack when one of them was at his back. It's what he would have done in their shoes and, after six whole revolutions, that's exactly what happened. Beppe lunged at him from the front while Beatrice threw herself at his back. Devereau ducked in the nick of time, crouching down and grabbing hold of Beatrice's front legs from behind before flipping her over his head to block Beppe's attack. She howled in pain when her own twin brother's teeth latched onto her skin. Realising his mistake, Beppe released his jaws and staggered back – just in time to receive a sharp kick in his side from Devereau. As he went down, Beatrice ran at him, rage reflected in her narrowed, lupine eyes. She jumped up, claws outstretched. She was going for his neck. Devereau steeled himself, aware that this could be bad. He could block her but he would be unable to do much else. He spun, his cloak flipping through the air with him. Instead of ripping out his jugular as she'd no doubt intended, Beatrice became entangled with the cloak's snaky fabric. Devereau ripped it away from his neck as soon as he realised what was happening. Then, as Beatrice stumbled, her front paws caught up in the red fabric, Devereau took the other end of the material and wrapped it round her muzzle with deft speed. She made a good attempt at freeing herself but it wasn't good enough. In the end, she gave up and flipped onto her back. Beatrice was fierce – but she knew when she was beaten.

Devereau glanced towards her brother. 'You still want some?' he asked.

Beppe was too distraught over his inadvertent bite into his own sister's flesh. She was bleeding profusely from the wound and it was obvious that, twins or not, she was the dominant wolf. He shook his head, his fur rippling in the light Roman breeze which escaped through the many holes in the walls of the Colosseum.

Devereau shrugged. So much for fight two then. It was just as well. His stomach was gurgling again and he knew he'd to find the nearest restroom without further delay.

His bowels might feel empty but there was no sign yet of the Ring of All Seasons. That wasn't a bad thing. The longer it stayed stuck in his guts, the longer he could toy with Solentino – and maintain relations with Scarlett. She'd given him an inquiring look when he'd exited the restroom and, pleasingly, hadn't appeared too disappointed when he'd shaken his head. Laxatives could only go so far; retrieving the ring would be mostly up to Mother Nature herself.

Devereau had half expected that the third fight would follow the same pattern and that this time, he'd be forced to face three attackers. The Lupo werewolves weren't quite as predictable as that, however. His opponent was a small wiry wolf who more than made up in speed what he lacked in muscle. He gave Devereau the run around, and even landed several small but vexing nips to his arms and legs before Devereau managed to grab hold of his body and sit on top of him until the clock ran out. His fourth fight was with a female who possessed the squat bones of a naturally born werewolf but who was also surprisingly tall. She followed his lead, remaining in her human form almost until the last minute.

'Shift,' she hissed at him repeatedly. 'Show us what you really are, Englishman!'

Devereau had no intention of doing that until he absolutely had to, although when she went for his groin area he was almost forced to. It wasn't brute strength or skill which won that fight; it was merely that time ran out and he survived to continue on.

'Were you afraid to fight her because she's a woman?' Scarlett inquired, after the fight was done. 'You looked like you were holding back in the same way you did with the kid at the start. You're still too human, Devereau Webb. Maybe you'll never be a real supe.'

He gave her a long look. 'I've got enough problems with the fights out on that stage,' he told her, 'I don't need fights with you here too.'

Scarlett leaned towards his ear and lowered her voice. 'That's because if we really fought,' she whispered, 'I would win.'

That was practically a given.

'We both know,' he said aloud, 'that it's not physical pain that scares you, Scarlett, but emotional.'

Her face shuttered and she pulled back, folding her arms over her chest. Devereau immediately regretted his words. He'd hit too close to the bone and he was well aware that the truth could hurt far deeper than lies. 'Be careful with this next one,' she said coldly. 'The wolves are planning something.'

'Scarlett,' he began.

She set her chin. 'You need to be ready to shift.'

He sighed. 'I will be. I think I can hang on for at least another bout, however.'

'You're the boss,' she said, with a faintly patronising air that didn't quite mask the worried look in her eyes. She raised her wrist and pointed to her watch. 'Make it snappy though, Devereau. It's already gone eleven. And Mr Motorcycle has gone.'

Devereau stared at her. 'When?'

'Halfway through the last fight. I guess he got bored of watching your attempts to entertain. Whether he's there or not, however, we really need to get out of here and deal with Solentino before it's too late.' And she pushed him out onto the wooden stage before he could say anything else.

As soon as he walked to the centre of the staging area, he knew that Scarlett had been right. Not only was there no sign of the mysterious motorcyclist, but there was also a different atmosphere. He could sense it in the air. The audience encircling the arena also seemed to emanate hushed anticipation. There was no doubt that the fights had been getting progressively more difficult but even the last one hadn't seriously troubled him. Devereau found himself far more curious than afraid.

'Ladies and gentlemen! Signore e signori! For our fifth bout, I present to you Tatton O'Brien.'

Devereau raised an eyebrow. O'Brien? That wasn't exactly an Italian surname. Judging by the gasps from the audience, they knew exactly who this O'Brien character was – and they were impressed. Devereau frowned and glanced around him. Whoever Tatton O'Brien was, he was keeping them waiting. Maybe he'd taken one look at Devereau and had sensibly decided not to bother showing up.

Devereau raised his head. 'O'Brien? Tatton O'Brien? Come out, come out, wherever you are!'

From somewhere over to his left a disembodied voice floated over. 'I wouldn't be quite so hasty if I were ye, Mr Webb.'

Devereau gazed hard at the spot where the voice had come from. The air there was shimmering ever so slightly. He had to deal with an invisible opponent now? Seriously? Was such a thing even possible?

There was a ripple of amusement from the audience. No doubt his expression was a picture right now and he was the only one not in on the joke. He gritted his teeth. Then he closed his eyes in favour of focusing on his other senses. He was a wolf after all; there was far more to his abilities than mere eyesight.

Devereau heard a light chuckle, followed a moment later by a rush of air from his left. He instinctively raised his hands to block whatever was about to happen. Unfortunately, he was a half second too late. Something – probably Tatton O'Brien's fist – connected hard with his cheekbone. Involuntary tears of pain sprang to Devereau's eyes. Damn it.

'Aw,' came the voice. 'Is the little wolfie crying? Would you like a hankie?'

O'Brien definitely wasn't Italian. That sounded like a vaguely Irish lilt. He didn't smell like wolf either. This was entirely unexpected. Devereau wasn't going to waste his breath by replying to O'Brien's attempts at conversation. He needed to focus. His nostrils flared as he tried to pinpoint the man's position. There. Three feet away and slightly to the right. Okay. He could do this.

There was another rush of air. This time Devereau acted quicker and managed to sidestep away from the oncoming blow. O'Brien offered up a sardonic clap in return.

'Bravo, Mr Webb.' Then there was creak as his opponent moved across the wooden floorboards. Devereau spun – and was rewarded with a deft punch to his guts. He doubled over.

'Ye know, yer senses will be enhanced,' O'Brien murmured, 'if ye shift. Yer wolf has far greater abilities than yer human form.'

This guy wasn't even a wolf himself and he was explaining Devereau's own capabilities to him. There was a lesson in there somewhere. Devereau snorted mildly and straightened up. Enough already. If he didn't make his own move soon, he'd end up like mincemeat. Attack was sometimes the best form of defence. He listened carefully, pinpointing O'Brien's position.

'You're right,' Devereau said, finally engaging in conversation, 'I do have better control over my senses when I'm a wolf.' He tensed slightly and lashed out, and was immediately rewarded by a loud ooph followed by a thump as O'Brien collapsed to the floor. 'But that doesn't mean I necessarily need them.' It was only then that he finally re-opened his eyes and looked down.

Streaks of bright colour shot through the air by his feet, until they gradually coalesced together into the small figure of a man curled up in a heap. He had dark hair shot through with both silver and, unexpectedly, bright green.

'Good to meet ye, ye wee dryshite,' O'Brien croaked. He managed a smile up in Devereau's direction.

'The pleasure's all yours,' Devereau said. He reached down and offered the small man a hand up. O'Brien took it and heaved himself upwards. Then, without warning, he aimed a sharp kick at Devereau's shin. The audience gasped, as much in delight as shock.

Devereau released his grip and stepped back. 'For fuck's sake!'

'Time's not up,' O'Brien said. He nodded over towards the announcer who shrugged at them both.

Devereau stared at him. 'You've lost your only advantage. Do you seriously want to keep fighting?'

O'Brien grinned. 'Nah. Ye got me. I wanted to get in one last shot though.' He doffed an imaginary cap in Devereau's direction. 'Ye cannae blame me for that.'

Hmmm. Devereau folded his arms and eyed him. 'You're Irish?'

'Half Irish. On me mother's side. Me da' was Italian. God rest his soul.'

'And the invisibility trick? What's that all about?'

O'Brien tapped the side of his nose. 'Trade secret.'

Devereau's frown deepened but he didn't get the chance to probe any further. 'The fifth bout goes to Signore Webb!' the announcer called into her microphone. 'Things are heating up!'

Actually, it was quite the opposite. The night air had taken a turn for the worse. Not only had the temperature dropped by several degrees but some very ominous dark clouds were hovering over their heads. An icy drop fell from the sky and landed on Devereau's nose. This wasn't looking good. It wouldn't be a problem for the werewolves – obviously the various members of clan Lupo could shift and use their natural fur to shield them from the worst that nature could offer. The audience, who Devereau was certain were mostly human, wouldn't have that advantage. Fortunately, that might work in Devereau's favour. It was about time something did.

He glanced round. 'Where's Moretti?'

The announcer covered her microphone and leaned towards him. 'Is there a problem?'

'I want to talk to him for a moment.' He waved at the unforgiving sky as more icy sleet began to fall. 'I have a proposal.'

She pursed her lips. Then she turned away and spoke to one of the clan Lupo werewolves by her side. As she did so, O'Brien nudged him. 'I hope ye're not planning what I think ye are. Hasn't it occurred to ye that ye've had easy opponents so far in order to give ye a false sense of security?'

Devereau looked at him. 'You'd class yourself as an easy opponent?' he asked.

O'Brien didn't smile. 'Based on what I know is to come, yes, I would.'

Devereau certainly would not give him the satisfaction of asking what the last two fights would be. He knew he wouldn't get an answer if he did. Instead, he focused on O'Brien himself. 'What are you?' he asked. 'What manner of beastie is Tatton O'Brien?'

The small man's eyes gleamed. They really were a quite extraordinary shade of green. 'I'm only half beastie. Me mother's side.' He lifted his chin. 'Look,' he said, changing the subject, 'Nicolo Moretti is here to talk to ye. Don't do anything too stupid, Devereau Webb.' He winked and wandered off.

Devereau watched him go. Then it hit him. 'Leprechaun,' he breathed. 'That man's a bloody leprechaun.'

'Half leprechaun,' Moretti said, overhearing him. 'But even that half is rare than the pot of gold at the end of a rainbow these days.' He linked his fingers together and smiled disarmingly. 'You've been doing remarkably well, Mr Webb. Why do you want to talk to me? Have you had enough? Are you ready to submit to me and clan Lupo?'

Hardly. Devereau glanced over his shoulder and saw Scarlett watching him, her expression unreadable. 'No,' he told the Italian alpha flatly. 'But time is marching on and, as I said, I have other matters of a pressing nature to concern myself with.' He nodded towards the audience, many of whom were now clumping together for warmth. 'As excited as your ticket holders seem to be, it's late and it's cold and the weather is not conducive to comfort. This is something of an all weather arena.'

Moretti splayed his hands out. 'I cannot let you walk away now. Not after only five fights.'

'That's not what I'm suggesting.' Devereau paused. 'Combine the sixth and seventh fights together. I'll fight both at the same time. It'll halve the time and double the thrill.'

Moretti raised an eyebrow. 'These next opponents are not pushovers. The risk for you will be considerable and I cannot be seen to be giving you a free ride.'

'I'm not asking for one,' Devereau replied.

Moretti sucked air in through his teeth. 'How does the saying go? Only mad dogs and Englishmen go out in the midday sun? It might be closer to midnight but the sentiment still fits. You're playing a risky game, Signore Webb.'

Devereau could only shrug. 'These are risky times.'

The Italian hesitated before finally answering. 'Very well,' he said. 'Very well. We'll begin the last fight in ten minutes' time. Is that good enough?'

It would be if he won. Devereau nodded and turned away to prepare.

CHAPTER SIXTEEN

'THIS IS A STUPID IDEA.'

'You're the one who wanted me to hurry things along, Scarlett.'

'All I did was point out that time was running away with us. I didn't mean for you to embark on a suicide mission to beat the damned clock.'

Devereau raised an eyebrow. 'Are you worried I'll get hurt?'

She looked away. 'You're a big boy and you're capable of making your own daft decisions. But,' she glanced back, 'if something does happen to you, I'm going to have slit open your dead body to get my ring back. Do you know how difficult it is to get the congealed blood from a corpse out of your fingernails? Not to mention that I'd feel obliged to tackle Christopher fucking Solentino on my own as well.' She glared at him as if all this were his fault. Then again, he supposed it actually was.

Devereau felt his mouth tug upwards of its own volition. 'You really *are* worried that I'll get hurt.'

Scarlett folded her arms across her chest. 'You have my ring. Of course I'm worried.'

'It's not the ring that concerns you. You don't want to see me bleed.'

'I'm not a sadist, Devereau. Just because we're no longer sleeping together doesn't mean that I want you to get injured. Or worse. I'm not that bloodthirsty.'

He shook his head. Her concern was more than that of a mere good-hearted bystander; he was certain of it. He'd already skated close enough to danger with Scarlett once tonight, however. He wasn't willing to risk pushing her further on the topic of their non-existent relationship. Yet.

'It will be fine,' he declared. 'In less than twenty minutes we'll be walking out of here and heading off to deal with Solentino.'

'Is that a promise?'

He extended his pinky towards her. 'Absolutely.'

Scarlett sighed. She did, however, hook her own little finger round his. 'Don't lose any limbs, Devereau.'

He grinned at her. Then he ambled out towards the wooden stage for the last time.

'Signore e signori!' the announcer said over the roar of the crowd, 'we know it is late and that the weather is against us. So for you and only you, we are offering something unheard of that will spice things up and make this truly a night to remember.' She paused. 'There will only be one more fight –' Boos of dismay echoed round the ancient Roman edifice. '-but,' she continued, 'that is because Signore Webb has elected to fight both opponents from the final two rounds together.'

Devereau grinned broadly. To his surprise, however, the vast majority of the audience didn't cheer. They simply stared at him, slack-jawed. He blinked. Was such a thing really so strange? He gazed at them, wondering if he were indeed making a rash mistake. It was too late to back out now, however. And when one of the bookies began calling out in Italian what he presumed were revised odds, lots of people sprang into action to make their final bets.

Devereau cracked his knuckles. Five fights in and he was feeling pretty damned good. There were a few aches and pains and he had the odd scratch or two but he'd acquitted himself well and his injuries were very minor. In seven more minutes he'd be done here – and he'd have proved an important point to the Italian werewolves which would hopefully reach the furry ears of the London clans as well. Devereau Webb paid his dues but he wasn't to be messed with. Not by anyone. And not even when he was in fancy dress.

The announcer tapped her microphone and the crowd immediately ceased their flurries of desperate gambling and hushed. Two fights for the price of one. He wasn't the only one in the Colosseum eager for this.

'Ladies and gentlemen, signore y signori, as I already said, Signore Webb genuinely thinks he is strong enough to take on two opponents at the same time.' There was a ripple of laughter from the watchers and the announcer permitted herself a smile. 'Typical English arrogance.' The laughter increased.

Devereau felt a stab of irritated pain at the familiar point between his shoulder blades although he knew that the announcer's words were designed to piss him off and therefore encourage him to take risks and make mistakes.

'The first contender, from what would have been the sixth fight, is Vincent Orsetto!'

The crowd clapped their hands, and cheered. A moment later, Orsetto strutted out onto the stage, halting mere metres away. Devereau stared at him. Hang on a minute. Hang on a *fucking* minute.

'He's got a sword,' Devereau protested. 'How's that fair? Why don't I get a sword?'

'Did you ask for a sword?' Orsetto inquired.

'Of course not!'

The Italian shrugged. 'Well, then. Nobody ever said that

weapons were disallowed.' He ran the tip of his finger along the edge of the gleaming blade.

Devereau's eyebrow twitched. 'May I have a sword?' he asked through gritted teeth.

'Can you use a sword? Have you even picked one up before?'

He folded his arms. 'Fine. I'll take a gun then. Give me a damned gun with silver bullets in it and then we'll see what kind of fight this becomes.'

Orsetto smirked. 'You have to bring your own weapons to your own fight, Signore Webb. And silver of any kind is forbidden. Besides, you should be pleased. Either I use the sword or I shift to my wolf. I cannot do both. My advantage is not so strong as you imagine.'

Yeah, yeah. Devereau bit out a curse. 'Fine. Where's the other guy?'

Orsetto's eyes gleamed. 'Wait,' he said. 'And watch.'

All around the ancient arena, the audience began to stamp their feet. The sound reverberated through the air, slow at first until the crowd picked up speed, moving their feet in unison. Then there was a crackle and the stirring opening of Nessun Dorma could be heard, followed by Luciano Pavarotti's deep voice. Devereau glanced at the announcer. She was holding her mobile phone up to the microphone with one hand. Her other hand was clutching her heart.

'Usually we have an opera singer here in person,' Orsetto said confidentially, 'but this was rather short notice and even with an old recording the effect is much the same, wouldn't you say?'

Devereau was English. He understood a little something about the allure of pomp and circumstance. He was also unwilling to do nothing more than stand on the spot and scowl so, yielding to the situation, he closed his eyes and raised his right hand to his own heart too. If you can't beat'em, join'em.

When the music finally faded away, and Devereau re-opened his eyes, Orsetto gave him an approving, albeit surprised, nod.

Then the announcer spoke again. 'And, naturally, the final contender to enter the arena is Dark Hair.'

Dark Hair? What kind of daft name was that? Devereau turned to where Orsetto had appeared from. Nobody was there. Not a soul strode forward. Then, however, he heard a loud snort. From the darkness beyond, first one paw appeared, followed by another. Devereau's nostrils flared. The scent of power and strength was palpable. Whoever this seventh opponent was, whether he'd already shifted to his wolf form or not, he exuded formidable authority. It was Moretti himself. It had to be.

Devereau squinted as the wolf revealed more of himself. He was large, almost as tall as Devereau was when he was in wolf form. His fur was glossy and dark and his yellow eyes were focused intently on Devereau, who felt the inexplicable urge to dip his shoulders and admit submission before he'd even begun. He held his ground, however. Barely.

The audience were now completely silent and Devereau didn't need to glance upwards to know that every single person was leaning forward and holding their breath. He'd never seen anyone command attention in this way before. It was nigh on impossible to look away.

The enormous wolf padded silently forward. It wasn't until his entire body was visible that Devereau's jaw fell open. It couldn't be Moretti. There was no way. Because while the magnetic, authoritative wolf in front of him acted like the Italian alpha, his physical form suggested otherwise. Instead of four legs, he only possessed three.

His gait was slightly awkward. There was a visible shoulder roll as he moved, which would have been out of place on anyone else, although he didn't actually walk as if he were hampered in any way. Quite the opposite. In fact, from the way his lean muscles curved and bulged beneath his smooth fur, it was clear he was incredibly strong. He looked as if he were capable of achieving greater speeds on three paws than Devereau could manage on four. Underestimating this opponent would be at his own peril.

The announcer spoke into her microphone with undisguised glee. 'Seven minutes,' she said. 'And may the victors be swathed in glory.'

Victors. Not victor. Nobody was expecting him to win here. Devereau wanted to glance over at Scarlett to see her expression but he didn't dare take his eyes away from Orsetto and Dark Hair.

'Uno, due …' she paused for dramatic effect, ' … *tre.*'

There was no time for niceties. Orsetto deftly jabbed his sword forward, immediately piercing the skin on Devereau's bare thigh. It was a minor flesh wound but the point had been made. Never mind seven minutes. These two had the potential to take him down in seven seconds. Dark Hair proved just that by following up Orsetto's move by leaping straight at Devereau's head. He tried to dodge and raised his hands to deflect the worst of the blow but he still staggered backwards, falling to his arse. The wooden floorboards of the temporary Colosseum stage creaked their complaint; the crowd roared their joy.

There was no point remaining as he was. This wasn't a fight he could win in his human form. From his fallen position, Devereau initiated the change, before springing upwards and twisting to land upright as his body transformed from ordinary human to massive wolf. The cheap Roman costume burst off and there was a satisfying gasp from around the ancient walled arena when his werewolf was finally revealed. Neither Orsetto nor Dark Hair so much as flinched.

Swinging his sword again, Orsetto clipped the edge of Devereau's ear. He snarled in response but, at least this time, he managed to avoid Dark Hair's follow up attempt at a blow. Although he knew instinctively that Dark Hair was the more dangerous opponent of the two, he decided to focus on disarming Orsetto first. The reach of that blade, not to mention its lethally sharp edge, was too much of an immediate danger.

He backed up to allow himself a few precious seconds to analyse the best form of attack. Then he feinted right towards Dark Hair. Orsetto lunged, the tip of the sword slicing towards Devereau's fur covered neck. Devereau was ready for that, however. He dipped down at precisely the right moment. Orsetto's attempt went wide – and Devereau wasted no time in positioning himself before he leapt or Orsetto's sword arm. In one deft move, his teeth clamped down. Orsetto howled in sudden pain and dropped the sword then, while Devereau's teeth were still attached to his forearm he shifted. Dark Hair barrelled into Devereau's flank in a bid to shake him off his friend but he'd expected that. He let go of Orsetto and backed away once again, panting. Now he was facing two wolves rather than one – but at least the threat of the weapon had been neutralised. He'd take it.

It clearly wasn't the first time these two had fought together. With easily synchronised movements, they came at Devereau again, determined not to allow him any opportunity to catch his breath. Dark Hair went for his right and Orsetto aimed for his left. If he wanted to avoid being pinned between the two of them, Devereau had no choice but to sprint forward towards the edge of the staging area.

He ran. Orsetto clipped his front leg. Dark Hair's teeth scraped his flank. He was swift enough to avoid serious injury, however. Rather than come to a screeching halt at the edge of the stage and be forced to face the two of them again, Devereau took the only sensible option left to him and leapt forward into the air, exiting it entirely. There had been no mention of any rules regarding weapons – and there had been no mention of any rules regarding remaining on the stage. Devereau landed beneath it, all four paws hitting the lower level. Now he was in the maze of masonry underneath what would have been the entire stage. It was dark and it was narrow, and his odds had increased magnificently.

Dark Hari came after him first. He could tell it was him because of the way he landed behind him, his three paws making less of an impact on the hard stone floor than four would have. Devereau darted forward, weaving his way towards the other side of the Colosseum. The further he went, the darker it became and the crowd above voiced their disapproval. They were here for a show and right now they couldn't see a thing beyond flickering shadows.

Mindful of his role in this entire event which had been designed for entertainment as much as punishment, Devereau spun right then left then right again. He could feel Dark Hair on his tail. As soon as he reached another narrow crossroads, he scrabbled up the wall, returning to the surface. He ran along the edge of the uneven masonry, stumbling slightly. Then he spotted Orsetto, still poised at the edge of the stage. Excellent.

Devereau made a beeline straight for him. By the time Orsetto realised what he was planning it was far too late. Devereau smacked into his side and sent him tumbling headfirst down to the underground maze he'd just exited. Orsetto landed badly, whining with a plaintive sound that suggested he was out for the rest of the fight. Devereau certainly hoped so. Unfortunately he didn't have time to celebrate. Dark Hair was already on him.

They tumbled together, rolling across the floorboards in an almost cartoonish flurry of snarls and spinning bodies. Devereau hissed as Dark Hair ripped a decent sized chunk of fur clean from his skin. In response, he managed to angle himself so he could kick at his opponent's vulnerable belly. Then they were both back up on their paws, circling round each other with bared teeth and narrowed eyes, first one way and then the other.

They'd completed two whole circuits when Dark Hair came at him again. Devereau leapt up, intending to tumble round in the air and land behind Dark Hair before he went for his throat and forced him down into submission. The black furred werewolf was too clever for that, however. He raised himself up on his one single hind leg in a contortion that appeared both balletic and impossible. Then he opened his jaws, grabbed hold of Devereau's tail and brought him down the floor with a heavy thump. In the blink of an eye, Dark Hair had him pinned.

Devereau writhed, twisting left and right and a bid to break free. He knew he was stronger than Dark Hair. But he didn't have the same skilled technique. Dark Hair towered over him, his three limbs pressing down on Devereau's four in such a way that it was impossible for him to free himself without receiving a nasty swipe from either Dark Hair's sharp teeth or pointed claws. Then Dark Hair's muzzle loomed forward. Shit. Devereau jerked forward, headbutting the other wolf. There was a loud crack as their skulls connected. Dark Hair collapsed to one side while Devereau fell backwards, his long spine banging painfully against the floor.

He grunted. He had to get up again but his limbs wouldn't obey. If he didn't move soon, however, he would be wolf food. He dimly heard a similar groan from Dark Hair, and the throbbing cheers of the crowd beyond. Get up, he ordered himself. Get up. Get. The. Fuck. Up. And the floor shook as a high pitched trumpet note sounded. Praise be. It was over.

* * *

Neither he nor Dark Hair moved for some time, despite the fact the clock had run out and the audience were on their feet. Devereau's entire body screamed in pain. He had a huge lump appearing on his forehead and a line of bruises down his spine, and he was bleeding from several small wounds. It was only when he heard the click of heels across the wooden floor that he opened his eyes. The audience were on their feet, yelling, cheering and waving their hands. Scarlett was crouched beside him.

'Time to change, darling,' Scarlett said softly.

Darling? Did she just call him darling or did he imagine it? He swallowed and blinked several times. Then he did as she'd ordered, his tired body barely managing the shift. He staggered up to his bare feet, wrapping the robe she handed him round his body. He looked across and realised that Dark Hair had also shifted back to human. It *was* Moretti after all.

'Dark Hair?' he asked.

Moretti's eyes met his, crinkling at the corners as he smiled. 'It's a direct translation. My Jewish forebears chose the name Moretti to fit in to their new home when they moved to Rome hundreds of years ago. We all do what we can to adapt to new situations.'

'I guess we do.' And in more ways than one. Devereau glanced downwards. Moretti's right leg was cut off at the knee. As if on cue, one of the other Lupo werewolves appeared and passed over an artificial limb. Moretti grinned at Devereau and bent down to strap it on to his stump while Scarlett moved back, allowing them a moment alone.

'Is that a war wound?' Devereau asked, wondering if he was being impolite for asking.

The alpha shook his head. 'Motorbike accident. I was young and foolish.' He shrugged. 'But it could have been worse. I've adapted pretty well.'

Pretty well? In his human form and fully clothed, there had been no indication whatsoever. In his wolf form he was the most powerful supe that Devereau had ever come across.

'You have indeed,' Devereau told him, inclining his head in a show of respect and adding a wry smile.

'That was a good showing, Signore Webb,' Moretti told him. 'And more than enough to keep the authorities off our backs for some months to come. They'll be talking about this fight for a long time.'

'I'm glad I could be of service,' Devereau replied drily. His head throbbed and his limbs were aching all over. Even with his extended healing powers, he knew he would be limping for a few days at least.

'You've been a good sport,' Moretti said. 'You're the first werewolf who's beaten me in many years.'

'I didn't beat you.'

'You lasted the course. That's a win for you as far as I'm concerned.' Moretti smiled again. 'See? I can be gracious when the situation calls for it.'

Devereau couldn't stop himself from smiling back. 'You know,' he said, 'you remind me of someone. I've only now realised who it is.'

Moretti nodded. 'Christiano Ronaldo. I get that a lot.'

Devereau managed not to laugh. 'That's not who I was thinking of.'

The Italian quirked an eyebrow. 'Who then?'

'Lady Sullivan,' Devereau told him. 'She's one of the four clan alphas in London. She –'

Moretti frowned. 'I know of this woman. She has a reputation as …' he waved his hands around as he searched for the right word. Then he glanced at one of werewolves on his right, barking something in Italian. The wolf blinked slowly before answering.

'Ball breaker,' he offered.

Moretti pulled a face.

'Dragon lady?' the wolf suggested.

He stroked his chin. 'That is better. Yes. Dragon lady. A strong woman who takes no shit.'

'What can I say?' Devereau said. 'You remind me of her.'

He grinned. 'Okay,' he said. 'I can accept that. This Lady Sullivan. Is she single?'

Uh … that was not what he'd been expecting Moretti to say. 'I believe so. She's quite a bit older than you though.'

'She's a woman, right? Not a cheese? Not a fine wine?'

Devereau scratched his head. 'Yeah.'

'Then, my man,' Moretti said, clapping him on the shoulder, 'it's all good. Next time I am in London you will introduce us.'

Devereau could do nothing more than smile weakly and hope that the Italian government revoked Moretti's passport before too long. Frankly he could think of nothing worse than Lady Sullivan believing that he was trying to set her up with an Italian werewolf thirty years her junior. The Sullivan alpha already disliked him enough as it was and Devereau was certainly no cupid. He couldn't even get his own love life to where he wanted it to be. Not to mention that the thought of Moretti and Sullivan joining forces was enough to make the strongest of supes blanch. Those two together would be unstoppable.

'We should take our leave,' he said, inclining his head to indicate that both he and Scarlett had to go. 'I would like to stay but we really do have other serious business to attend to.'

'I understand.' Moretti's eyes grew serious. 'This … situation you are in. The lives that are being threatened. If you require assistance, I am here to help. You did not show respect to clan Lupo when you arrived but you have more than made up for it now.' He handed Devereau a business card. 'I will be a friend to you, Signore Webb. I suspect you don't have many of those.'

'You're right,' Devereau told him, slipping the card into his wallet, and displaying genuine honesty. 'I don't. Thank you.'

Moretti looked over at Scarlett. 'She only takes her eyes off you when she knows you are looking at her,' he murmured. He lowered his voice. 'Stick with her. She will be worth the effort.'

Devereau nodded. 'Of that,' he replied, 'I have no doubt.'

CHAPTER SEVENTEEN

AFTER HASTILY GETTING DRESSED IN HIS NORMAL CLOTHES AGAIN, Devereau exited the Colosseum with Scarlett, making it out before the crowds who were no doubt still squaring up their bets. Scarlett marched ahead, her hips swaying. Devereau limped.

'Come on,' she called over her shoulder. 'We have to hurry. I've got a car waiting.' She glanced back and noted his shuffling gait. 'Men,' she said. 'You're all the same. A few scrapes and you'd think you'd been through a real war. Next you'll be getting a sniffle and telling me you've got pneumonia.'

'I've just endured six fights!' Devereau protested.

'And,' Scarlett said, 'if you'd been at all smart, you'd have avoided this entirely and endured none. You're absolutely fine.'

So much for her softly spoken darling endearment then. 'I wasn't complaining,' he pointed out.

'Just as well.' She sniffed. Then she hesitated. 'Are you alright?'

'As you said yourself. I'm absolutely fine.'

'Good. Let's get a move on then and deal with Christopher Solentino.' She smiled at him humourlessly. 'While you were running around play fighting, I came up with a plan.'

'Play fighting? It was hardly …' He sighed and shook his head. Never mind. 'What's the plan?'

Scarlett smirked at him. Belatedly, he realised she'd been goading him in much the same way as he'd done to her earlier that evening in a bid to take his mind off his aches and pains. 'Well,' she said, 'it doesn't involve you chopping off my head.' She gave him an arch smile. 'The end goal here is to find out what that slimy wanker and his gang of wannabe terrorists are up to, right?'

'Right.' Devereau put his hands in his pockets and gave her a wary look.

'Okay then.' She bobbed her head with enthusiasm. 'Solentino sent his own man to follow you here. Based on how the evening's entertainment was supposed to go, you're not due to finish up for another half an hour. Mr Motorcycle left long before the decision was taken to only have six fights rather than seven.' She motioned towards the Colosseum. 'We're still supposed to be there.'

'Solentino must think I'm still busy fighting.'

'Indeed.' Scarlett began walking quickly again. Devereau caught up with her, doing his best to ignore the stabbing pains from his injuries and remain stoic. 'The last thing he's expecting is for us to show up at his door again right now. We have a tiny window of opportunity to find out what he's up to while he believes we're elsewhere.'

'You think we should sneak into his place while he's unaware and see what we can find out?' Devereau frowned. 'If he catches us, the game is up.'

'You sneaked into my place,' she pointed out.

'And I got caught. I wasn't injured then either.'

'That's why,' Scarlett said with a grin, 'you wait outside while I do all the sneaking. In the best case scenario, I find the information you're looking for. In the worst case scenario, if

Solentino catches me, I say that I'm working alone because I no longer trust you and think you're plotting behind my back. I'm looking for proof that you and Solentino are in cahoots. You can claim ignorance and play the part of the poor betrayed werewolf.'

He shook his head. 'That's far too dangerous, Scarlett. I've got years of experience at this sort of thing and I'm not convinced I could pull it off. But you …'

She smiled serenely. 'I have a secret weapon.'

Devereau looked at her. 'What?'

She winked and jabbed her thumb over at the car waiting by the kerb, its engine ticking over. 'He's waiting in the car.'

* * *

DEVEREAU HADN'T BEEN sure what to expect when he'd clambered into the back of the car. When he saw who was sitting there however, with his nose all but pressed up against his smart phone, he understood.

'Oh,' Devereau said. 'It's you.'

Tatton O'Brien didn't answer. Devereau glanced at the screen of the leprechaun's phone. Candy Crush. Really?

'Give him a moment,' Scarlett said, sliding into the driver's seat.

'Where did the car come from?' Devereau asked.

'Simon delivered it.'

Devereau's eyes narrowed. Simon? 'You mean your goon for hire? The idiot who tried to confront me at your place?'

'I mean,' Scarlett said, 'the hero who tried to stop a would-be burglar in his tracks.'

Devereau did his best to keep his tone casual. 'He's an employee, right? I mean, he's not a vampire so -'

'Simon,' she said, 'is not any of your business.'

Devereau's left eyebrow twitched.

156

'Bastard!' Tatton hissed.

Both Devereau and Scarlett looked at him. He jabbed furiously at his phone, his attention entirely caught up in the game.

'Simon,' she said softly, 'works for the security firm that take care of our overseas properties. That's all. You have no reason to be jealous.' She paused. 'And no right to be jealous either.'

Devereau drew in a breath, biting back the automatic denial which rose to his lips. It would have been a lie – and they both deserved the truth. 'But I am jealous,' he said. 'I know I don't have a right to that emotion. I know you never made me any promises. The thing is, Scarlett, I can't help the way that I feel. Jealousy is a natural feeling that arises out of the fear of loss. I can't stop myself from feeling that way. It's how a person acts on those feelings that matters and I told you already that I won't act.' His mind flashed to what had happened between them in the hotel room before Moretti had shown up. 'Unless,' he amended, 'you want me to.'

Scarlett's eyes briefly met his. 'Sometimes, Devereau Webb, you're too honest for your own good.'

'I know it scares you. I know emotions scare you. But sometimes it's good to be scared. Fear pushes you to be your best.'

'Not always.'

No. Not always. He ran a frustrated hand through his hair. He was trying to be truthful and it wasn't doing any good.

'Are we leaving or not?' Tatton asked, without looking up from his game. 'Because all this fecking relationship stuff is *not* what I signed up for.'

Scarlett returned her gaze to the front and turned on the engine. She didn't say anything else – and neither did Devereau.

* * *

THEY TRUNDLED through the streets in silence for several minutes until finally Tatton scowled at his phone and switched it off.

'Stupid game,' he muttered. 'I'd have won if I could see the screen properly. I left me glasses at the hotel. I didn't think I'd need them.' Then he flicked a look at Devereau, properly acknowledging him for the first time. 'Good to see ye again so soon, dryshite. I'm impressed with how ye did back there.' He nodded approvingly. 'Ye've got smarts as well as strength. There's slight hope for ye yet.'

'Thank you.' Devereau wasn't actually convinced that thanks were in order given the little man's last statement but he knew when to be polite. 'So you're a leprechaun?'

'*Half* leprechaun.' He peered at Devereau. 'Go on. Ask it.'

'Ask what?'

Tatton sighed. 'Ye know what. Let's get it out of the way so we can move on.'

Devereau considered pretending he didn't know what he was on about. But he actually was curious. 'Do you have a pot of gold at the end of a rainbow?'

Tatton snapped his fingers. 'There it is.' He shook his head in weary dismay. 'I have no gold and no rainbows. I never wear the colour green and I bloody hate St Patrick's Day and silly hats.'

'What about Guinness?' Devereau asked.

Tatton pulled a disgusted face. 'Yuck. Never touch the stuff. Is that it? Or are ye finished with the daft questions? Do you have any questions about potatoes?'

'No,' Devereau said. 'But I'm not finished. Because while you might not fall into those stereotypes, you *do* turn invisible.' He gave Scarlett a quick look. 'And that, presumably, is why you're here now.'

Tatton gave him a wink. 'Aye, it is. That and the fact that I'm an all round good guy who can't resist the chance to help a wee wolfie in need.'

Scarlett coughed delicately.

'Plus,' Tatton added, 'she's paying me to be here.'

'I'll expect to be reimbursed by your lot later,' Scarlett said to Devereau. At least she wasn't naming MI5 out loud and some secrets would remain hidden.

'I'm sure we can work something out,' Devereau murmured. 'So how is this going to work?'

'Can you deal with the main door?' Scarlett asked. 'Pick the lock without anyone hearing you?'

Devereau pursed his lips. Probably. Such operations were never wholly silent but it was late at night by now so most people who lived in Solentino's building would likely be sleeping. From what he could remember from their first visit, the lock looked easy enough to navigate.

'Good,' Scarlett said, interpreting his expression. 'If you can open the door, then Tatton and I will head inside and attempt to gain access to the apartment itself. I'll piggy back onto his invisibility and, unless we're very unlucky, neither Solentino nor anyone else will know we're inside.'

Devereau's brow creased. 'What do you mean, piggyback? How does that work and why can't I do it instead of you?'

Tatton snorted. 'Because you weigh twice as much as she does.'

'It's a literal piggyback,' Scarlett said with a smile. 'Once I'm on Tatton's shoulders, I'll be as invisible as he is. It won't last long so we have to move fast but it should be more than enough for us to look around the rest of Solentino's apartment and find the incriminating information that you need.'

Devereau's frown deepened. 'You'll make a lot more noise that way.'

'Which is why it has to be her and not you.' Tatton flashed him a crooked grin. 'I can only sustain it for around five minutes, especially with a passenger on board. We'll have to be both fast and quiet. From what she's already told me, however, it's worth the risk.'

'I've been thinking about the layout of the apartment,' Scarlett said. 'We already saw several of the rooms. There was one closed door towards the back. I reckon that's where the secrets will be kept. We nip in and nip out and bob's your uncle.'

'I don't like it,' Devereau growled.

She shrugged. 'Then you shouldn't have gotten me involved. This is the best plan we have and you know it.'

Unfortunately, he couldn't disagree with that. And there was no doubt in Devereau's mind that Christopher Solentino was both highly dangerous and slightly unhinged so they had to find out what he was really up to. Fuck it. 'Okay,' he said with a brief sigh. 'Okay.'

* * *

THEY SLIPPED through the silent Roman streets with speed and ease, arriving near Solentino's street within minutes. Scarlett parked the car round the corner from the apartment, tucking it safely out of sight. It wasn't a legal parking spot but at this hour they'd be in nobody's way and it would allow for a quick exit should circumstances demand it. In the event this little escapade went tits up, they'd have to be prepared to skedaddle if they needed to. Devereau prayed it wouldn't come to that.

The three of them stepped out of the car. Devereau immediately began casting around on the ground, searching for the tool he needed. It didn't take long for his eyes to alight on the empty water bottle nestled in a small pile of old sweet wrappers and curling dead leaves. He bent down and scooped it up, using the edge of his fingernails to rip off a square of plastic. He felt both Tatton and Scarlett watching him with curiosity so, in a bid to ward off his own gnawing feeling of foreboding, he held the translucent scrap up and winked.

'You don't need a lockpick,' he said in a low voice, 'when you've got plastic.'

'I prefer the sort of plastic that gives ye credit,' Tatton replied.

'Ah, but this plastic doesn't charge interest.' Devereau smiled and picked up speed, swerving round onto the street they needed and double checking that there were no late night pedestrians out for a walk. Then he marched forward to Solentino's front door.

'Car,' Scarlett hissed.

Devereau nodded and paused, hoping it looked like he was merely searching for his house key. The swooping headlights didn't pause. Tatton audibly exhaled and Devereau wasted no further time, hunching down and deftly inserting the plastic square between the lock and the door frame.

'Is this going to take long?' the leprechaun asked in a whisper.

Devereau stood up and grinned, while the door clicked open. 'Nope.'

Even Scarlett's jaw dropped. 'I thought the credit card thing was a myth.'

'Nope. The lock mechanism was incorrectly inserted. It happens more often than you'd think.' He nodded at the door. 'Especially on old doors like this one.'

'I'll have to review me home security,' Tatton muttered. He gestured to Scarlett. 'Alright then, lovie. Let's get on with this.'

Scarlett looped her arms round his neck and hopped up, her legs wrapping round his midriff. Tatton grunted slightly. 'Which floor is it?'

'Third.'

His nose wrinkled. 'Now you tell me. Alright, let's do this.' His eyes rolled back into his head and the air around him took on a faint shimmer.

Devereau's head jerked up. 'Stop.'

Both Scarlett and Tatton glanced at him.

'Dev,' Scarlett said, 'we've been through this. It's the best –'

She stopped in mid-sentence and dropped down from Tatton, whose green eyes squinted at her.

'What? What is it?'

Scarlett and Devereau exchanged glances. 'Blood,' she whispered.

Devereau nodded grimly. 'A lot of it.'

CHAPTER EIGHTEEN

Tatton was already backing up, his hands in the air. 'Nuh uh,' he said. 'No fecking way. Ye said this fecker was a murderer but I didn't think I'd have to witness the evidence of that with me own eyes.'

Devereau's nostrils flared. It wasn't blood from Mike Lancaster, the Australian who Solentino had casually killed earlier, that he was smelling. It was too fresh and there was too much of it for that. With his toe, he nudged the door open further – and both he and Scarlett took a step back.

'Jesus.' Her face was pale. She shook her head. 'Jesus.'

Devereau forced down the sudden rise of nausea and sniffed again. 'I'm getting different blood types.' He glanced at Scarlett. 'Can you tell how many victims there are?'

She swallowed. 'Four. Wait, no.' She hesitated. 'Five, I think. Maybe even six.'

There was jab of sharp pain between Devereau's shoulder blades. 'It doesn't seem likely that Solentino killed six people inside his own damned apartment. He's a psychopath but he's intelligent. A massacre is not a smart move, not for someone

163

who's got to stay beneath the radar of the police. It doesn't make sense.'

Scarlett's voice was grim. 'No,' she replied. 'It doesn't.'

He motioned towards Tatton, who was by now several metres away. 'Head back to the car,' he said. 'If we're not there in ten minutes' time, call the police.'

The leprechaun's expression was darkly relieved. 'Noted.' He spun round and took off at high speed.

Devereau looked at Scarlett. 'You can join him if you want.'

She threw him a scornful glance. 'No chance. Let's see what horrors are up there.'

With slow, wary steps, Devereau stepped across the threshold. Even from the ground floor, which was some distance away from Solentino's apartment, the smell of blood was strong. Devereau marvelled quietly that the stench hadn't woken up the other residents and then headed for the stairs. He strained his ears, noting the few snuffling sounds which had to be from people slumbering in other nearby apartments. There was nothing else to be heard and so, with Scarlett on his heels, he ascended the staircase.

The closer they got, the more the sickly iron rich scent filled the air. When they reached the second floor, Scarlett hissed his name. He turned and she gestured towards a dark smear on the banister. Blood. Devereau examined it carefully, making sure not to touch it directly with his own fingertips. It looked fresh. Very fresh. He steeled himself and nodded at her before continuing on upwards.

He wasn't sure what he'd been expecting to see when Solentino's own front door came into view. If they went by sight alone, it would appear that nothing was amiss. The door was closed and there were no obvious signs of violence other than the now overpowering reek of spilled blood. His tongue wet his lips. Then he walked over to the door and carefully opened it.

It wasn't locked. Instead it swung open at his first touch,

creaking faintly as if in mild protest. Devereau inhaled – and then gagged. It wasn't just blood he was smelling now. It was faeces and fear and anger and, if he wasn't mistaken, intestines.

Scarlett touched his arm. *Careful,* she mouthed.

He nodded grimly before walking inside.

The first room they came to was the kitchen. It was devoid of either bodies or blood. Devereau moved past it and glanced in at the equally empty lounge before walking quietly into the dining room where Solentino had slit Mike Lancaster's throat. The Australian's corpse had gone – but there were three others. He and Scarlett moved swiftly from one to the other, checking for any signs of life. There were none. Devereau only recognised one of the unfortunate souls. It was Rick Moore, the American man who worked for Solentino. His eyes were wide and staring and he was sprawled on the floor with his head at an awkward angle. From the way he'd fallen, it appeared that he'd been trying to run. He hadn't gotten very far. Devereau knelt down and gazed at his shattered skull. Moore had been shot once in the head. One bullet was all it had taken.

The other two bodies were also men of a similar age and build to Rick Moore. Devereau took out his phone and quickly snapped photos of each of their faces. Then he followed Scarlett out of the dining room and into the first bedroom.

There were three pairs of narrow bunkbeds, along with various suitcases in different stages of disarray. Scarlett was already kneeling by the only body. She glanced round at Devereau and shook her head to indicate that he'd already gone. 'Rospo Accetta,' she said quietly. 'It looks as if he was fast asleep when it happened.'

Devereau nodded briefly. It was bloody carnage. 'Gunshot?'

'Yep.'

He ran a hand through his hair and turned. There were more rooms – and no doubt more bodies – yet to go. The second bedroom was grander than the first, and included an ensuite bathroom. Judging by the lingering perfume and the strewn clothes, this was where Alina and Solentino slept. There was, however, no sign of either of them.

Scarlett tapped her fingernails against the next door. 'This is the soundproofed room where we were kept.'

Devereau felt his stomach tighten and exchanged a glance with her. There had to be a reason why this particular door was closed. She bit her lip and turned the doorknob, revealing the scene inside.

Christopher Solentino was on his back on the middle of the floor. His arms and legs were spreadeagled and his lifeless eyes were tilted up towards the ceiling. They didn't need to check his pulse. There was a blade sticking out of his chest, pinning him in place and his stomach had been slit open, revealing his guts. Devereau pushed away his nausea andedged over to examined the weapon. 'Zombie knife,' he said. A blade with a serrated edge that was designed not just to kill but to cause as much excruciating pain as possible.

'Look at his fingers,' Scarlett said softly.

Devereau glanced down. Every digit on his right hand had been sawn off. He swallowed.

'The others were shot by someone who knew what they were doing and who wanted to kill quickly. They had to have used a silencer or the entire block would have been woken up. Solentino, however, was taken to the one room where his screams wouldn't have been heard. And then he was tortured.'

Scarlett bobbed her head in grim agreement. She pointed towards the far wall, where the listening equipment was housed. 'You see the blood there?' she said. 'It's not his.' She strode up to the arcing splatter that was gruesomely reminiscent of a Jackson Pollock painting and touched a dribble with the tip of her index finger before licking it delicately. 'Alina Bonnet,' she told him. 'I've still got the taste of her in my mouth from earlier.'

Devereau's jaw clenched. 'No sign of her body,' he said.

Scarlett shook her head. 'Not yet.'

They both edged out of the room. Scarlett gestured towards the final door, where they'd both already surmised Solentino's best secrets were hidden. Devereau tensed his body and took point, striding forward. He pushed open the door, revealing a small room lined with bookshelves and two desks. One wall had an empty pinboard, although there were scraps of torn paper still clinging to various drawing pins. It looked as if it had been cleared in a hurry. Devereau reached across and picked off one of the scraps. There were four letters scrawled across it. R. B. P. L. He squinted. The acronym meant nothing to him whatsoever.

A computer lay on the floor beside the nearest desk. Its screen was cracked. Devereau knelt down and squinted at the debris of the modem. He was no IT expert but he doubted if would ever yield any information. He ground his teeth. The eavesdropping bugs housed into the walls of the room where Solentino had met his end had probably been tied to this machine. Whatever had happened in there would remain a mystery because the computer looked completely destroyed, with shards of plastic and the telltale green of a smashed motherboard buried beneath the keyboard. Damn it all to hell.

The drawers of the second desk had been yanked open and obviously rifled through. 'What's the bet,' he said, his voice vibrating with pent up rage, 'that everything of value and every bit of information about what Solentino was planning has been taken?'

Scarlett folded her arms across her chest and swivelled slowly round the room, her dark eyes taking in every detail. 'It certainly looks that way. I'm not sorry that man is dead but, Devereau, we have no idea who did this. Or why. If someone is muscling in on Solentino's plans, whatever they are, this could be bad.'

A chill descended down Devereau's spine. It wasn't merely the devastating bloodbath and the trail of corpses which caused the sensation. They'd known that Solentino had been planning something terrible but at least they'd also known who their enemy was. Now they could only guess.

'There's no sign of Geraint Vissier,' he said, referring to the Dutchman who'd also met with Solentino's disfavour earlier that day. Maybe he'd decided after the lunchtime dramatics today that Solentino had to be stopped and had done what he could to stop the man in his tracks and therefore prevent any international atrocities from occurring. Unfortunately, the manner of Solentino's death, not to mention the ransacked room, suggested such muted optimism could well be misplaced. It seemed likely that this was a coup rather than a conclusion.

'Do we think that Mr Motorcycle was Vissier?'

Devereau's mouth flattened. 'There's no telling. We obviously didn't meet all of Solentino's team earlier today. There could be other players we still don't know about.'

'The motorcyclist isn't here,' Scarlett pointed out. 'He was wearing full leathers and none of the corpses match his body shape. In fact –'

There was a sudden noise from out in the hallway. Both Devereau and Scarlett froze. It had sounded like the front door.

Motioning to Scarlett to remain where she was, Devereau turned and moved swiftly to the wall. He pressed his back against it and then craned his neck to catch a glimpse of who was out there.

A shadowed figure stood stockstill, framed by the outer doorway. Mr Motorcycle. The man himself. Devereau held his breath, watching as he took a step forward. He was still wearing the helmet but his visor had been raised. His features weren't clear and Devereau couldn't yet tell who it was. A surge of adrenaline zipped through his veins. All wasn't lost. They still had someone they could question.

Mr Motorcycle's shoes squeaked as he edged further along the marbled floor. He turned his head and glanced in at the dining room. Then he made a muttered hiss. Devereau sniffed the air. Whoever the man was, he reeked of terror. That was hardly surprising. Devereau looked at Scarlett and raised his eyebrows. She nodded once. A second later, he threw himself out of the room and down the hallway towards the helmeted figure.

The motorcyclist had lightning speed reactions. A split second after Devereau had begun to move towards him, he twisted and pelted for the front door, escaping through it and slamming it closed behind him. Devereau was forced to fumble with doorknob to wrench it open again. The action cost him vital seconds. By the time the apartment's front door was open again and Devereau sprinted out with Scarlett right behind him, Mr Motorcycle had already reached the first floor.

Devereau's feet skidded as he swerved and leapt down the first flight of stairs. His target was one step ahead of him, however, vaulting over the banister itself and landing on the floor of the small lobby. He groaned but picked himself up quickly enough. Devereau threw himself after the man and, a breath later, felt a rush of air as Scarlett darted past him, her own speed overtaking his own. She reached the lobby before he did, ducking her head down and yelling as she ran out onto the street. But Devereau could already hear the roar of an engine. As he passed through the front door, he initiated the transformation from man to wolf then, as the motorbike screeched away in a cloud of choking white smoke, he bounded after it on all fours hoping that Scarlett make her way to the car where Tatton was waiting. On two feet she was faster than him but she couldn't match the speed of a wolf without mechanical aid – and Devereau wasn't going to let Mr Motorcycle get away. He couldn't.

His muscles bunched up as he focused on releasing all his remaining energy. The streets in this part of Rome were narrow and twisting, and it was far easier for an animal on all fours to navigate them at speed than it was for even a motorbike. When the bike reached the first corner and was forced to slow down,

Devereau sped up, his claws clattering against the hard cobbles. He threw everything he had at sustaining his momentum. Until the motorcyclist reached one of the wider roads, Devereau had the edge.

He ignored the dirty water that splashed into his eyes when his front paw landed in the centre of a muddy puddle and strained himself to catch up. Faster. Further. He was less than three metres behind the motorbike's tail-light. One jump and he might manage to grab the rider and haul him off. But adrenaline only takes you so far and Devereau had already fought hard this night. He'd pushed the past the pain of his earlier injuries but it didn't take long for the searing jabs of agony to attack his hind legs. When the road beneath his paws changed from smooth tarmac to uneven cobbles and he lost traction, he knew deep down that he wouldn't catch up. He still tried – he wasn't a quitter – but the motorbike pulled away spluttering fumes in its wake. Devereau gritted his teeth, biting back the pain, and limped after it. Alas, it did no good. In less than twenty seconds the bike had rounded another corner and disappeared.

Under normal circumstances, Devereau was gallingly aware that he could have caught up to the bastard. He had it in him. Usually. He blinked away involuntary tears of pain. The after-effects of his six fights in the Colosseum were simply too much. He snarled to himself and felt his hind legs give away. He'd pushed his body too hard. It appeared that even a werewolf could only take so much.

CHAPTER NINETEEN

'IT'S FORTUNATE YOU CALLED ME, SCARLETT,' MORETTI SAID,
peering at Devereau. 'He's in a bad way.' He clicked his tongue.
'What did you think you were doing, man? You can't push your
body to such extremes so much in a short space of time. Not
without giving yourself a break in between. No wolf can do that.'
He paused. 'Well, *I* can but I'm special.'

Devereau grunted. 'It was an emergency.'

'Mmm. I take it the murders you discovered are related to the
dire situation you mentioned earlier?'

Scarlett tipped her head. 'Yes. Things have taken a turn for the
unexpected.'

'In a good way? Should we be pleased that these people are
dead? Does it mean your concerns are over?'

Her mouth tightened. 'Unfortunately not.'

Moretti sighed. 'You English. You always like to complicate
matters.' He handed Devereau a plate piled high with meat. 'Here.
Eat this. It will help you recover.' He sniffed. 'Although what you
really need is rest and lots of it.'

Devereau nodded his thanks and began to eat. It was only
when the first mouthful hit his stomach that he realised how

truly ravenous he was. He blotted out Scarlett and Moretti's voice and turned his whole attention to devouring the food. He barely noticed when there was a polite knock at the door and Arsenio, the kid he'd beaten in the first fight, appeared and murmured something to Moretti.

He finished the entire plate in less than five minutes. The meaty sustenance was already working wonders and he was beginning to feel strength surge into his limbs. The fact that Vissier had managed to escape was still galling but he supposed that at least he now knew what the limits of his endurance were. And that he had limits. Devereau might be a supe but he wasn't invincible. Far from it.

'You had me worried there for a moment,' Scarlett murmured. 'Don't do that again.'

Devereau's eyes darted to hers. She smiled at him lightly and he felt his heart flip. The night's physical exertions might have sapped his strength but he knew that Scarlett had the ability to do the same to his emotions with little more than an uplift of the corners of her mouth.

'Where did Tatton go?' Devereau asked, in a bid to appear slightly less pathetic and on top of matters.

'One of Moretti's crew took him home after they brought you here to Piazza Armerina,' Scarlett said. 'There didn't seem much point in keeping him around and he certainly had no desire to stick around. I think he prefers to stay out of bloody massacres if he can.'

Fair enough. Devereau would prefer to stay out of them too.

Moretti gestured to Arsenio, sending him away, before folding his arms. 'I hate to add fuel to the fire,' the Italian alpha said, 'but you have another problem now.'

Both Scarlett and Devereau looked at him.

'The police are searching for you. Apparently you made quite the ruckus when you left that apartment. You also left the door open. One of the neighbours looked out their window and saw you leaving. They got suspicious enough to investigate and came across the bodies. You two,' he wagged his fingers, 'are now the number one suspects in the gruesome murder of five people.'

Devereau cursed under his breath. That was all they needed.

Scarlett appeared less concerned. 'Three hundred people saw us at the Colosseum. That's got to be more than enough of an alibi for the police.'

'Eventually,' Moretti agreed. 'But that doesn't mean they won't haul you in for questioning for several hours first. You'll be expected to explain why you were at the crime scene in the middle of the night.' He looked at them both. 'I doubt you'll want to tell them the reasons why.'

Scarlett raised her eyebrows questioningly at Devereau. He shook his head. Sarah Greensmith had made it very clear that he was in Rome without appropriate jurisdiction. There was no explanation that he could offer up to the Italian authorities that they would accept.

'You're foreigners,' Moretti reminded them. 'And supe foreigners at that. You might spend days in a police cell before you're cleared.'

Devereau growled. 'We don't have that kind of time to spare.' He rubbed the back of his neck. Spy or not, this was not the sort of situation he'd expected to find himself in.

'My offer of friendship before was genuine,' Moretti said. 'What can clan Lupo do to help you?'

Devereau considered the Italian's words and stood up, his bones cracking. His whole body felt stiff and unyielding, pain seeping in through every pore despite the meal he'd just eaten. 'Some clothes would be good,' he admitted. 'Preferably not a gladiatorial costume this time.' Moretti smiled faintly while Devereau looked at Scarlett. 'Vissier is Mr Motorcycle. Where do you think he was before he showed up at Solentino's place?' he asked her. 'He only escaped a bullet in his skull because he wasn't there.' He had a theory but he wanted to hear her confirm it.

She raised her shoulders in a shrug. 'Vissier followed us first to the hotel and then to the Colosseum. He left halfway through the fights. If he didn't head straight to Solentino at that point then I reckon he went to Hotel Condotti to nosey around your room while you were obviously otherwise occupied. Solentino was probably dotting his Is and crossing his Ts and doing what he could to check that you would be trustworthy even if you did do as he requested and chop off my head.'

Moretti's eyes widened slightly. 'Goodness,' he murmured. 'How dramatic. What exactly have you gotten yourselves entangled in?'

'A mess,' Devereau said shortly. 'Do the Italian police have our names yet?'

He shook his head. 'Not yet. It's only a matter of time though.'

He grimaced. It wouldn't help that his phone was now lying amidst the debris of his scattered clothing at Solentino's apartment. 'We should have time to get to Hotel Condotti then,' Devereau said. 'We can check to see if there's any evidence that Vissier did break into my room and I can also grab what I need.'

'Then what?' Scarlett inquired.

Devereau passed a hand over his forehead. In theory he should write another draft email for Greensmith so she was appraised of the situation. But it was now four o'clock in the morning in Rome and three o'clock in London. No matter how diligent the MI5 agent was, she'd surely be sleeping. Devereau didn't want to have to wait around until she woke up. Until they knew who had killed Solentino and his men and why, they couldn't afford to rest. No matter how shitty he was feeling.

'We'll go to the embassy,' he said finally. 'There's someone there we can talk to.'

'We?' she asked.

'You're now implicated as much as I am,' he said. 'There's no other choice.'

'If you're in as much of a hurry as I think you are,' Moretti said, 'let me send some of my people to the hotel to look around and pick up your things. In the event that the police do identify you quickly, that will be the best option for all of us. In the meantime, you can go straight to the British embassy and we can meet later.' He paused. 'If it's possible to do so.' He wagged his finger at Devereau. 'I wasn't lying before, however. You really do need considerable rest. You might end up doing yourself permanent damage if you keep pushing.'

'I'll be fine.'

'You don't look fine,' Scarlett said, almost sternly.

'Let's worry about me later,' he told her. 'Let's focus on who might have killed Solentino and nicked his plans for terrorism first.'

For the first time, Moretti looked genuinely concerned. 'Terrorism? Things are that serious?'

Devereau recalled Solentino's grim allusions to other terrible and tragic attacks. 'Yes,' he said. 'I think they are.'

* * *

THE BRITISH EMBASSY was a large squat building located on Via XX Settembre, smack bang in the centre of the city. The gates were firmly closed and, while the wall surrounding the building looked easy enough to climb, Devereau didn't relish the thought of attempting any sort of minor acrobatics in his current state. Not to mention that any guards patrolling inside would be likely to shoot first and ask questions later. The last thing either he or Scarlett needed right now was to be peppered with damned bullets. Officially, the building didn't open for another four hours. This was, however, an emergency.

'Call the emergency embassy number on the website,' he told Scarlett, 'and ask for Maximillian Jones.'

She nodded and did as he asked. He watched while she waded through various recorded messages before finally managing to get hold of a real person. He wasn't the only one who'd been suffering from their long night. Scarlett's skin was far paler than normal and he knew she was feeling the same level of anxiety that he was. More lives could be resting on both their shoulders right now. It wasn't a pleasant thought.

'Someone is coming to meet us,' she finally said, hanging up and tucking the phone into her pocket. 'Whoever this Maximillian fellow is, he must be someone important. As soon as I mentioned his name, I was told we'd be admitted straight away.'

Almost on cue, the embassy gates began to swing open. It gave Devereau some hope that he was not only going to be taken seriously but that someone was already waking Sarah Greensmith up in London. 'Go MI5,' he murmured.

A young man with ruffled hair and an open shirt appeared at the embassy's front door with a tablet in his hands. He was accompanied by two blank faced security guards holding large guns. The man beckoned them forward. Scarlett and Devereau wasted no time, slipping through the open gates and up the few steps.

'I'm Devereau Webb.'

Scarlett inclined her head. 'Scarlett Cook.'

The man said nothing. Instead he looked down at the screen of his tablet and looked up again. 'Do you have your passports?'

'No.'

'You should have them on you at all times for identification.' The man sighed as if this were all terribly inconvenient. Devereau bit his lip and tried to avoid snapping that he was supposed to be a fucking spy. He didn't want to be identified at all times. 'But very well,' the young man continued. 'Follow me.'

The two guards immediately moved, flanking Scarlett and Devereau as if they were dangerous criminals. 'We have silver bullets,' one of them said for no other reason than pointless intimidation. Devereau rolled his eyes. Even now, bruised, limping and serving his own damned country, he had to put up with the same old anti-supe bullshit.

'Silver bullets?' Scarlett cooed. 'How exciting! Are they pretty? And shiny? I like shiny things.' Her eyes drifted to the guard's neck. 'And blood. I like blood too. Especially from men in uniform.'

The guard couldn't stop himself from recoiling. Devereau suppressed a grin.

'Alright,' the younger man with the tablet snapped. 'Enough of that.'

Scarlett pouted. 'He started it.'

Devereau pretended not to notice that the second security guard was eyeing Scarlett with lascivious interest. His buddy might not enjoy the thought of being fed upon by a vampire but he was clearly game. 'Let's get a move on,' he said. He squared his shoulders, ignored the renewed flash of hot pain that rippled down his body, and strode inside the building.

They trailed through various wide corridors which were well appointed, clean, contained some interesting art work but still maintained the definite whiff of strict adherence to bureaucracy. Eventually, when it seemed as if they were deep in the very bowels of the embassy, they were deposited in a small room with a keypad entry. There was nobody inside. But there was an open laptop sitting atop a narrow aluminium desk with Sarah Greensmith's face blinking blearily on the screen. She'd clearly been roused directly from her bed. Her eyes were heavy-lidded and, instead of her usual smart suit, she was wearing a terry cloth bathrobe. Still, as soon as Devereau came into view, she straightened up, her expression altering to its default business-like facade.

'Mr Webb.'

Devereau nodded at her. 'I was expecting Maximillian Jones.'

'He doesn't exist. His name is merely a code word for action stations. We are MI5, Mr Webb. We do like our little secretive games.' She permitted herself a tiny smile. Then her gaze hardened. 'The vampire has to wait outside.'

'The vampire,' he replied coolly, 'already knows everything.'

Scarlett moved into view and waved enthusiastically. 'It's true. I do.'

Greensmith did not look pleased. 'Nobody,' she snapped, 'is supposed to know what you're doing or who you work for, Mr Webb. That's been made to clear to you on several occasions.'

'She worked out that I'm with MI5 all on her own,' Devereau said, 'which is a shortcoming on your part, not mine. But if you want to scold me instead of finding out what the real problem is, then knock yourself out. For my part, I think we've got bigger problems than protocol.'

Greensmith scowled. From her expression, she wanted to pursue the matter of Scarlett's involvement further and Devereau was certain it was a conversation he'd have to deal with later. Fortunately for all of them, however, she also knew when to prioritise. 'Tell me,' she said. 'Go on then. What's the problem and why is it an emergency?'

Devereau drew in a breath. Then he explained what had happened to Solentino and what they'd seen at his apartment, leaving out no details.

Sarah Greensmith listened, her face giving away none of her thoughts. It was only when Devereau finished speaking that she spoke. 'Do you think this Geraint Vissier is the one responsible?'

'I don't think so. Not from the way he acted when he entered the apartment. He was as shocked as we were.'

'In fact,' Scarlett added, 'he probably thinks that *we're* the ones responsible. He certainly ran fast enough to indicate that he believed his own life was in danger.'

Greensmith sucked on her bottom lip. 'And there was definitely no sign of Alina Bonnet's body?'

'Nope. It was her blood on the wall, however. If she's still alive, I doubt she's in good shape.'

'Why take her and leave the others?' she mused.

Devereau knew that Greensmith wasn't expecting an answer from him. It was just as well. He didn't have any answers to give.

'Maybe whoever is responsible wanted to keep her alive because she has information about Solentino's plans that they still want,' Scarlett suggested. 'Or maybe there's more to Alina Bonnet than we realised and we're underestimating her involvement. Or maybe the killer was simply squeamish because she's female. Who the fuck knows?'

'Hmm.' Greensmith tapped her mouth thoughtfully. 'Regardless of the outcome of Ms Bonnet's disappearance, we have no way of knowing whether any of these developments will prove to be a good thing or a bad thing.'

Given the killer's lack of compunction, not to mention the manner of Solentino's death, Devereau strongly suspected the latter. He was the novice at all this stuff, however. He was prepared to defer to her, at least for now.

'Give me five minutes,' Greensmith told them. 'I need to pass this up the chain of command. Don't go anywhere.' She glared at them both through the screen. 'And don't do anything stupid.'

'A thank you would have been nice,' Scarlett murmured, as the laptop screen went momentarily blank.

Devereau sat down heavily on a nearby chair and closed his eyes. His head was pounding and his legs were feeling shaky again.

'R.B.P.L.'

'Pardon?' Scarlett asked.

'The letters we found on that piece of paper. R. B. P. L. What could they mean?'

There was a pause. Devereau opened one eye and squinted at Scarlett. She waved her phone at him. 'Google says Risk Based Profit and Loss.'

Huh. 'Lots or risk,' he muttered. 'And so far, not very much profit.'

'Indeed.'

A spasm of sharp pain assailed Devereau's gut. He winced.

'What is it?'

He rubbed his stomach. 'Those damned laxatives.'

Scarlett pulled a face. 'Still no sign of the ring?'

'Not yet.' He sighed. 'I'm sorry.'

'Hey, at least we know where it is.'

'I wasn't referring to the ring.' Devereau shifted on the chair. 'Well, I am sorry about the ring but I what I really meant was that I'm sorry for getting you involved in all this. I shouldn't have done it.'

Scarlett snorted. 'You didn't force me, Devereau. I am the master of my own fate, and perfectly capable of making my own decisions. I chose to come along and help out. I didn't have to.' She paused. 'Although I did kind of think that being a spy meant more time hanging around casinos and jumping out of planes to ski down mountains.'

'I know, right? I've not had a single Martini yet. Neither have I been given an Aston Martin to drive.'

Scarlett winked at him. 'You do have a femme fatale by your side.'

'You're telling me,' Devereau said.

The smile dropped from Scarlett's face. For one long, outstretched moment, they both stared at each other. 'Dev,' she said. 'Listen, I ...'

'Mr Webb?' Sarah Greensmith's tinny voice broke in. 'Are you there?'

Damn it. Scarlett and he seemed fated to endure eternal interruptions. He stood up and returned to the laptop. 'I'm here.'

Greensmith gazed out at them. She didn't look remotely happy. 'Okay, Mr Webb. I have booked you onto the next available flight out of Rome.'

Devereau stiffened. That was not what he'd been expecting.

'Miss Cook,' she continued, 'will have to make her own

arrangements.' Greensmith's eyes were flinty. 'But we would appreciate it if she is included in the debrief when you return to London.'

'This isn't over,' Devereau said. 'We don't know who murdered Solentino. We don't know what's happening with his terrorism plans.'

'You also don't know what those plans were, Mr Webb. You were tasked with infiltrating Solentino's gang. With his death, alongside the deaths of the other known members of his cell, your role is now over. Other sections of MI5 will take up the baton from here. Those murders have escalated the situation and this is no longer merely about information gathering. We will liaise with the Italian security forces and then decide how to proceed.' She paused. 'But thank you for your efforts thus far. For your first assignment you did an excellent job.'

Devereau clenched his jaw. 'I thought this was my second assignment,' he said pointedly. 'I dealt with the blackmail situation involving Alexander Carruthers, remember?'

Greensmith didn't miss a beat. 'I meant international assignment. Someone from the embassy there will transport you to the airport and somebody else will collect your things from your hotel room and ensure they are forwarded to your home address in London. In the meantime, I will send a car to pick you up at Heathrow and then we shall meet after that. Understood?'

He understood alright. 'You're shutting me out.'

Greensmith sighed. 'That's not what's happening at all.' Her expression, however, told otherwise.

'I have a good grasp of the situation here in Rome,' he lied. It was as good a grasp as anyone else had anyway. 'I've met Solentino. I know how the man worked. I'm best placed to look into who killed him and what's going to happen next.'

'We have other agents and you're very inexperienced, Mr Webb.'

'I'm already here on the ground. Returning to London is

stupid when things could already be in motion to put Solentino's plans into action. Whoever killed him could already be making their move.'

'You told me it would be after December 21st.'

'That was when Solentino was in charge. Now that he's gone, the time line may well have changed.' Devereau could feel his frustration growing.

'We are aware of that and will factor it into what we do next,' Greensmith told him. 'I appreciate that you think of yourself as a lone wolf but MI5 is a large organisation. We require different services now and there are other people more suited to them. Not to mention that your new status as potential suspect for the murders makes it difficult for you to continue.' She softened her voice. 'It's not a snub or any kind of rebuke, Devereau. Don't treat it as such. You've provided us with great information so far. You remember you mentioned Bartan? The one who Avanopoulos was supposedly going to replace?'

'Yes.'

'We tracked him to Berlin. He was found dead two weeks ago. His throat was slit. There are no suspects and it appears that the German police aren't looking very hard. Bartan was well known to them and had his own ties with various minor terrorist organisations. That information cements our concerns about what Solentino was up to. What you've done is provide us with the confirmation we need to proceed. You should feel pleased with what you've accomplished.'

Maybe. But it wasn't enough. He counted to five in his head then bit out a nod. 'Very well.'

'I'll see you in person soon,' Greensmith said. 'Take care.' Then the screen went blank.

Devereau ground his teeth. He was invested now. Personally. It wasn't easy to follow orders and take a step back.

'So,' Scarlett said, 'it appears my career as a spy is over before it's even really begun. And,' she added, 'my head remains thankfully on my shoulders.' Then she glanced at him and murmured sotto voce, 'you didn't tell her that your belongings will no longer be at the hotel.'

Devereau flicked her a look. 'No,' he said, 'I didn't.' He paused. 'But then I didn't get the chance.'

'Uh huh.'

He shrugged at her, ignoring the brief ripple of pain which ran through his body as a result of that simple action.

Scarlett smiled slightly. 'I'll get Simon to pack my own things and send them to London. I might as well come to the airport with you now. I'm sure I can nab another seat on that same flight.' Their eyes met. Devereau knew instantly that they were on the same page.

'Sure,' he said. 'No problem.'

CHAPTER TWENTY

THE YOUNG MAN WITH THE TABLET WAS TASKED WITH ESCORTING them to Fiumicino airport. It was likely his last task before he went home to sleep for the day.

'This really would be easier,' he muttered, from the middle seat in the back seat of the embassy car, 'if you had your passports with you. It's bad enough that we have to side-step the police. You'll have to go through the diplomatic channels. It's being arranged already with Roman immigration but it's really not supposed to happen this way.'

Devereau had the sense that the man was mostly annoyed about the paperwork he'd be forced to do as a result of their supposedly illegal, albeit MI5 sanctioned, travel. Not to mention their sudden disappearance when they were both wanted for questioning by the Italian police. 'What's your name?' he asked. He might as well butter the poor fellow up.

'Mark.'

'Well, Mark,' Devereau said. 'I appreciate all that you're doing to help us. Your country called and you answered.' Out of the corner of his eye, he noted Scarlett's mouth twitch.

'Devereau is right,' she agreed. 'You're performing a vital

service and we will ensure you are rewarded. I don't imagine this sort of thing usually happens on the night shift.'

Mark's cheeks had taken on a faint flush. It was clear the praise was making him both uncomfortable and pleased all at the same time. 'Not normally, no. Most of my work,' he said grudgingly, 'involves drunk tourists who are banged by the Roma polis. It's not very glamorous.'

'I bet your parents are proud though,' Scarlett said. 'Mine would be.'

He looked down. 'Yeah. They're impressed. I'm just another civil servant as far the government is concerned but my mum and dad are thrilled.'

'As they should be.'

'Mark,' Devereau said, 'does the acronym RBPL mean anything to you?'

He pursed his lips and thought about it. 'The Royal Borough of Parks in London?' he guessed.

'Is that a thing?'

'Not that I know of. It could be though.' His fingers twitched at the shiny material of his trousers. Then he fell silent and didn't say anything until the car pulled up outside Terminal 3. 'Wait here. I'll go and find our escort through immigration.' He exited the car although the driver remained in the front seat. And as soon as Mark had left, there was a click as the car doors were locked. Hmm.

'Did you text Moretti?' Devereau asked casually.

'Yep.' She looked him up and down. 'How are you feeling now?'

'Sore,' Devereau admitted. 'But I'm getting better.'

'Better enough to go for a run?'

'I suppose,' he said. 'If it was a short one.'

Scarlett leaned back against her seat. 'That's good to know. You must be on the mend.'

A minute or two passed. Then the passenger door opened

from the outside. 'Okay,' Mark said. 'We're all sorted. If you want to step out and come with me, I'll take you right up to the gate.' He pointed at a gruff looking official standing to the side. 'This is Antonio Scalzi. He'll be coming with us.'

MI5 weren't taking any chances. Sarah Greensmith – or by extension her bosses – were desperate to get both Devereau and Scarlett out of Rome and apparently he wasn't to be trusted to leave without his own babysitters. He'd gone from being a genuine help to a vexing hindrance. MI5 should get used to it; Devereau often had this effect on people.

'Sure,' he said easily. He stepped out, followed by Scarlett. Then he took a moment to pause and stretch. Man, that felt good.

'It looks like it'll be a pretty sunrise,' Scarlett commented. She turned to look at the horizon, squinting over the top of a nearby airport carpark.

'They often are in Rome,' Mark agreed.

Devereau reached across and clapped him on the shoulder. 'You're a good guy,' he said, 'doing a thankless job. I'll make sure the higher-ups know that none of this was your fault.'

Mark's forehead creased. 'What do you mean?'

Scalzi, the Italian official, took a step towards them. Devereau smiled. And then a split second he pivoted round and both he and Scarlett were running away from the terminal building and towards the car park she'd been gazing at.

'Hey!' Mark yelled. 'Wait! What are you doing?'

'We really better not be going far,' Devereau said to Scarlett. The burning pain in his legs was swiftly making a comeback and, by the sound of the heavy footsteps behind them, Scalzi had already taken up pursuit.

'We're not,' she told him. 'I promise.' She darted down a flight of stairs and threw open the heavy car park door and beckoning him ahead. 'Straight ahead. There should be a black BMW at the far end.'

Devereau nodded and did his best to sprint. It wasn't easy. It was, however, enough. While Scarlett stayed by the door, slamming the heel of her hand into Scalzi's nose when he appeared, he continued forward. Moments later, the BMW appeared, its tires squealing as it sped down the car park. It halted right in front of Devereau and the back door swung open.

'In you get,' Moretti grinned.

Devereau didn't need told twice.

Scarlett appeared from behind and joined them. 'I just assaulted a Roman official,' she grunted. 'This hero complex shite better be worth the effort.'

Tell me about it, Devereau thought. 'I hate leaving a job unfinished,' he said, reaching down to massage his calf.

'Amen,' she said. 'Amen to that.'

* * *

THEY MADE it out of the car park and away from the airport with ease. Devereau imagined that young Mark was having to make a difficult phone call right about now. He'd do what he could to smooth things over for him later. It wasn't the kid's fault. Right now, however, they had far bigger worries.

'Your things are in the boot,' Moretti told him. 'We've arranged to pick up your bag as well,' he said to Scarlett. 'Although your presence in Rome was not heavily advertised, it's best if you don't go back to that same building.'

She nodded. 'Agreed.' Then she glanced at Devereau. 'So what's the plan? Presumably, we need to find out who killed Solentino and what they're going to do next.'

'Indeed. It's possible our killer won't be a threat and their sole purpose was to put Solentino and his gang out of action. It's also possible that they wanted to steal Solentino's plans and put them into action on their own. We need to be prepared for both possibilities.'

Scarlett gestured towards Devereau's stomach. 'Solentino wanted the Ring of All Seasons. I wonder if that's still in play.'

He shrugged. 'Maybe. I doubt it, however. I think it was supposed to be Solentino's own insurance policy. It's not going to be vital to whoever else might be taking up the reins.' Alina Bonnet's face flashed into his mind. She'd desperately wanted the ring. Unfortunately it wouldn't do her any good now, wherever she was. He rubbed his chin, his fingertips rasping against the dark line of stubble across his jawline.

'We have three lines of inquiry,' he said. 'We have to find Geraint Vissier. He'll be able to tell us exactly what Solentino was planning, and he might have an idea about who betrayed him.'

'I might be able to help with that,' Moretti said. 'The police are looking out for him as well so he's no doubt gone to ground. But my wolves can reach the corners that the authorities can't. I'll put out an alert and see what turns up.'

Devereau indicated his thanks. 'Good,' he said. 'We also need to see if we can locate Stefan Avanopoulos.'

Scarlett's expression brightened. 'The Greek. Solentino wanted his help with transport issues.'

'Mmmhmm.' Devereau dropped his hands to his lap. 'If he heard about Solentino's plan from either Geraint Vissier or Rick Moore, he might have decided that he wanted the action all to himself. Avanopoulos might be our killer.'

'I'm on good terms with one of the alpha werewolves in Athens,' Moretti said. 'I'll contact her and see if she's heard of this man.'

'What's the third thing?' Scarlett asked. 'That's only two lines of inquiry. You said there were three.'

Devereau opened his mouth to answer. Then he closed it again.

'What?' she asked. 'What is it?'

He drew in a breath. 'I'd been going to say RBPL. But we might already know what that refers to.'

Scarlett stilled. 'What?'

'That embassy kid said it himself. Royal Borough of Parks in London.'

'But that doesn't mean anything. There's no such thing.'

'*London*,' Devereau said quietly. 'Remember Solentino's reasons for wanting me to kill you? He wanted to know if Horvarth would have any issue with you working for your own interests in Rome. Or Berlin. Or Paris.'

Scarlett stared at him. 'And I effectively told him that as long as it wasn't London, it would be fine. Rome. Berlin. Paris.' She paused for a beat. 'London.'

'RBPL.'

'Shit.' She let out a low whistle. 'So we think something was planned for those four cities?'

Devereau felt a twitch between his shoulder blades. 'It looks that way. Greensmith herself said that Solentino's old contact called Bartan was killed in Berlin. He had terrorist links.'

'Fuck.'

Moretti's face darkened. 'Something terrorist is planned? Here? In Rome?'

'Potentially.'

'Why?'

'Not for any cause or ideology.' Devereau rubbed his thumb and forefingers together. 'Solentino was all about the money.'

Moretti's hands were clenched into tight fists. 'Terrorism doesn't strike me as a particularly lucrative line of work.'

'Unless,' Scarlett mused, 'you're planning to use it as a threat to hold cities to ransom.'

'He wanted Avanopoulos involved because of transport issues. Solentino said himself that the Greek was amenable to transporting goods to Paris, Berlin and London and sourcing some materials that he still required.'

'Explosive materials, no doubt,' Moretti growled.

Devereau's stomach twisted. Fuck. Oh, fuck. 'I need to contact Greensmith again.'

'You also need to rest,' Scarlett chided, 'or you'll be no good to anyone.'

'I'll search for Vissier and Avanopoulos. You won't be much help with that anyway,' Moretti said. 'In the meantime you call this Green lady and get some sleep.' His features twisted into a snarl. 'And then we bring all these fuckers down.'

All three of them looked at each other. 'That sounds,' Devereau said grimly, 'like a damned good plan.'

CHAPTER TWENTY ONE

Sarah Greensmith hadn't yelled at him. Yelling wasn't her style. She had, however, been icy cold and demanded that he get his arse to the airport and onto a plane to London without any further delay. She hadn't appeared particularly impressed with his theories about RBPL either.

'You're basing this off what? A scrap of paper and a brief conversation with a crazed wannabe terrorist?'

'It fits,' Devereau had insisted. 'Not only that but Solentino made a point of mentioning coordination in relation to terrorist attacks.'

'Chrisopher Solentino is dead.'

'But his ideas might not be.'

She had gone silent then. But not for long. 'MI5 will consider this further. You will return to London.'

'Not yet, I won't.'

'Goddamnit, Devereau!'

He'd hung up after that and destroyed the burner phone which Moretti had given him for the very purpose of calling her. There was no point continuing the conversation further and he'd told her everything he knew. He crossed his fingers and hoped that MI5 would take his theory seriously. But he was ready even if they didn't. Devereau Webb, Nicolo Moretti and Scarlett Cook might be an unlikely trio to save the world. They'd do it if necessary, however. With that thought, he tumbled into the bed in one of Moretti's lesser known properties and crashed out.

When he woke up five hours later, he felt like a new man. Or wolf. Whichever. Six fights and a chase through the streets of Rome might have pushed him to his physical limits and, unlike a human, his inevitable collapse had been far more dramatic, but at least his lycanthropic blood allowed him to recover quickly. It was just as well. Devereau was well aware that there was a considerable amount to do.

He found his suitcase, thoughtfully left at the foot of his bed, and quickly dressed before heading in out search of Scarlett. She'd clearly taken advantage of the hiatus to get some sleep herself and also looked considerably refreshed. Even better, she also had a pot of coffee on the go.

'It's good to be Nicolo Moretti,' she said, passing him a steaming cup.

'And it's good to be one of his friends,' Devereau agreed. The Italian alpha might possess a gargantuan ego – but both the size of his heart and his willingness to help matched it.

'You've timed your sleep well. He just phoned,' Scarlett informed him, 'and by the sounds of things, he's managed to dredge up some useful information although he wouldn't say what over the phone.'

Excellent. Devereau nodded and took a sip of the coffee. He had faith that Moretti would come good and that it wouldn't be long before they'd catch up with Vissier, Avanopoulos, and whoever the fuck had murdered Solentino and the rest of the crew.

'How's your stomach doing?' Scarlett asked.

'Better,' he said.

She raised an eyebrow. 'And my ring?'

Devereau scratched his chin. 'No sign of it yet. It's proving more stubborn than I'd have expected. In fact -'

Scarlett held up her hands. 'You know,' she said, 'on a need to know basis, I've decided I don't need to know. You can keep your bowel movements to yourself. Give me the ring when it finally appears.'

Devereau grinned at her although, secretly, he was regretting swallowing the damned thing at all. It had seemed like a good idea at the time and it helped to get them in with Solentino. It had been a rash move, however, and wasn't something he'd be tempted to try again. He also realised that discussing his toilet needs wasn't the way to appear to be the suave, sophisticated man that Scarlett deserved.

'What is it you look for in a partner?' he asked suddenly.

Scarlett flicked him a side look. 'I take it,' she said, with a sudden cool note, 'that you're referring to a romantic partner?'

Devereau bobbed his head. 'I'm not asking because I'm fishing. I'm genuinely curious. You had a fling with that young copper in Supe Squad.'

'Fred, you mean.'

'Yep. He seems like a nice kid.' Devereau pursed his mouth. 'If you like that kind of thing.' He paused. 'But he and I have nothing in common. Do you have a type, Scarlett? Or you more of a pick and mix kind of woman?'

'Perhaps,' she said, 'I simply like a buffet.'

'Uh huh. I'm more of an a la carte kind of man.'

Scarlett snorted. 'I bet you are.' She met his eyes. 'What are we talking about any more? I'm getting confused.'

Devereau kept his tone soft and non-combative. 'Stop trying to change the subject.'

'I'm not,' she said. 'I like who I like at the time and that's all there is to it.' She turned away and busied herself with washing up the coffee pot.

Devereau gazed at her rigid back. Unfortunately, he knew

exactly what he had in common with Police Constable Fred Hackert. Hackert was a bright-eyed, bushy tailed human male who would likely end up with a sweet wife, two point four chubby cheeked children and a house in the suburbs. Devereau was a growly, ex-criminal werewolf who worked best on his own. Neither of them were the sort of men who would be expected to want to settle down with a vampire. They were safe – as far as Scarlett was concerned – because in theory neither of them would want a long term relationship with someone like her. Theories were all very well, however. In practice, Devereau wanted to wake up next to Scarlett every day in his foreseeable future. From what he knew of Fred Hackert, the young policeman had wanted the same before she'd gently pushed him to the side. The trouble with Scarlett was that she under-estimated herself far too much. And for reasons known only to herself, she was terrified of commitment. She didn't want to be caged by a man. But Devereau didn't want to trap her. Neither did he want to put her on a pedestal. She wasn't perfect and neither was he. He was convinced, however, that they were perfect for each other. What he wanted more than anything was to run wild with Scarlett by his side. He let out a long sigh. It didn't appear a particularly likely outcome right now. More's the tragic, heart-rending, stomach-churning pity.

The sound of the front door opening broke into his reverie. A few moments later, Nicolo Moretti appeared, striding through to greet them with an intensely satisfied expression on his face. Devereau felt automatically buoyed. It was clear he'd made headway. This was good. This was what they all needed.

'All right!' Moretti rubbed his palms together. 'All right! I have news and you're going to like it!' He pointed to himself. 'Who's the man? Who *is* the man?' He gazed at them both expectantly.

Devereau couldn't help smiling. 'You,' he said drily. 'You are the man.'

Moretti nodded with excited vigour. 'I am the man.' He beamed from ear to ear.

Both Devereau and Scarlett looked at him.

'What?' he asked blankly.

Scarlett raised an eyebrow. 'What is the news then?'

Moretti jumped up onto the kitchen counter, his legs swinging in the air like a small child's. 'We've located Geraint Vissier. I've got eyes on his motorbike as we speak and I know which building he's cowering in. He's not far away.'

Devereau was already moving towards the door. 'Where? Where is he?'

'Holed up in a house on the edge of the city. The sort of place frequented by drug users and those wishing to keep away from the prying view of the Roman authorities. The police won't know about it yet. These people do not usually talk. They are not snitches.' Moretti bared his sharp teeth in satisfaction. 'But I am not the police. They talk to me. Or at least some of them do.' He looked at Devereau. 'And before you go marching off at high speed, I also have information on the Greek.'

Devereau paused. 'Go on.'

'The Athens clans all know of him.' Moretti took a piece of paper out of his pocket and passed it over. It was a photo of a dark haired man who certainly looked the part. He was muscular, heavily tattooed and his face was twisted into an ugly snarl. 'Apparently,' Moretti continued, 'he is a particularly nasty piece of work although one of the Athens alphas told me they'd met him and didn't think much of him. What is your British expression? A few sandwiches short of a picnic? The people I spoke to said that sums up what they know of Stefan Avanopoulos. Dangerously malleable. Their words, not mine.' He shrugged. 'In any case, I have called in a few favours and the Greek wolves are searching for him as we speak. They know how to track someone down. We'll have him pinpointed by the end of the day. I am sure of it.'

'We're getting somewhere,' Scarlett said. Her voice was quiet but there was a hard smile on her lips.

Devereau met her eyes. 'Yes,' he agreed. 'We are.'

* * *

IT TOOK LONGER to reach the house than Devereau would have wanted. Moretti was relaxed and joking the entire way, reassuring both him and Scarlett that Vissier wasn't going anywhere and that there were werewolves from clan Lupo watching the place. Until he was looking the slimy Dutchman in the eye, however, Devereau wouldn't be confident. They had to get to him and they had to find out everything he knew.

The afternoon sunlight was insipid by the time they got to the right street. The impressive buildings and architecture of the city centre had been replaced by uninspiring office blocks and apartment buildings. This wasn't the sort of area that tourists frequented. Devereau instantly felt more comfortable. He knew places like this; he'd spent most of his life in them.

'The house we want,' Moretti murmured, 'is over there.' He gestured towards a ramshackle building. Half of its roof appeared to be missing. There was an old chimney stack, veering to an angle that even the Tower of Pisa would have balked at. All the windows, which were firmly closed, were lined with grime. Even if they had been sparkling clean, however, it would have been impossible to see inside. Most of them were covered from the inside with old newspaper. Devereau noted the young woman hanging around outside. She had thin arms and a pinched face, although she couldn't have been more than twenty years old. The ravages of drugs like heroin and spice weren't confined to London. He glanced past her and spotted the motorbike parked by the side of the pavement. Excellent.

Scarlett looked the building over. 'It's three storeys,' she said, 'and stretches quite far back. There must be a lot of rooms. I don't suppose your intelligence includes where exactly Vissier is?'

Moretti shook his head. 'Once it was established he was inside, I told my people to leave the place alone. I didn't want to alert him in any way. Our best chance of grabbing him unharmed is to catch him by surprise. If you wanted him dead, it would be easy but I expect you'd like to talk to him first.' Moretti cracked his knuckles. 'But do not think that I will allow him to stroll away from here no matter what answers he provides. This bastard is threatening *my* city. Nobody does that and gets away with it.'

Devereau knew exactly how he felt. 'We can't become executioners and we can't hurt him,' he said nonetheless. 'We need to know what he knows. All of it.'

'Have no fear on that score,' Moretti told him. 'By the time we are done with Geraint Vissier, we will know everything.' There was a steely ice behind the Italian's eyes that Devereau hadn't seen before, even when they'd first met. He nodded once and stepped out of the car. Vissier was within striking distance. They were practically breathing the same air,

Nicolo Moretti might indeed be well connected enough to get information about the current occupants of this place but there was no doubt in Devereau's mind that Vissier also had to have close contacts. When they'd met over that gruesome lunch, there had been nothing about the Dutchman that had indicated he was a drug addict, or that he dabbled in such things. He obviously wasn't a native to this city either. Someone had told him about this place. Vissier still had friends – and that meant he still had avenues of escape which were open to him. They would have to tread very carefully indeed.

A young werewolf bounded up to Moretti with her ponytail swinging. She muttered to him in a stream of low Italian. Then Moretti translated.

'We have the house surrounded on all sides. If Vissier makes a run for it, he won't get far. Besides, the man is a human, no? We are all supes. And I am the best supe of them all. He will not get away.'

'You are wrong, Nicolo,' Scarlett said. 'You are a werewolf. Vampires are superior to werewolves in every way. You are not the best supe.'

'I am.'

'You are not. You may be the best wolf but I will not allow that you are the best supe.'

Moretti allowed his cheekbones to momentarily sprout fur. 'Can you do this?' he taunted.

'Why would I want to?' she replied.

Devereau hissed in irritation. He knew the light hearted banter was Scarlet and Moretti's way to diffuse the tension of the situation and to convey their confidence that Vissier would soon be in their custody. But it still annoyed him. As childish as it was, he wanted to be the only damned supe that teased Scarlett like that.

'Aw. The English wolf wants us to think he's the best supe.' Moretti reached across and chucked him under the chin.

Devereau gave him a hard frown. 'Let's focus, shall we?' He marched ahead until he was level with the front door. The young woman loitering outside glanced at him with vague disinterest, dismissing him quickly when she decided he wasn't someone who could help with her particular needs. Devereau noted the bruises and track marks on her arms and felt a wave of empathy that he knew she wouldn't appreciate. She sniffed and turned away, starting to walk down the street and away from him with a curiously bow-legged gait. Devereau watched her retreat for a moment or two. Then he turned to the house.

'Ready?' Moretti asked, walking up with Scarlett.

He nodded. 'I only want Vissier. Nobody else is to be hurt.'

'Not a problem.' Moretti whistled, raising one hand and circling the air with his index finger to indicate to his waiting wolves that they were ready. 'Let's go get'im.'

'No.' He set his jaw. 'I should go in alone.'

'You want to play sole hero, Englishman?' Moretti asked.

'It's not about that.' Devereau glanced at Scarlett's scowl. 'I know places like this,' he said. 'I know how to act in a manner which will not draw trouble or attention. The two of you, not to mention all those other werewolves, will stick out like a sore thumb. You're more likely to cause problems rather than solve them. You don't belong somewhere like here. I do.' He smiled faintly. 'Or at least I belong more than you do. We need Vissier to talk. We don't need him injured.'

A muscle throbbed in Moretti's jaw. 'My werewolves would not hurt him unless I told them to.'

'I know that,' Devereau said calmly. 'But Vissier might injure himself in an attempt to escape. There are others inside that building too. I can conduct myself in a way that won't draw either their suspicion or their ire. Those people will be closer to me and my kind than they ever will be to you and yours. It'd be better if you stay out here in case Vissier does decide to run. In that case, it's open season. But let me make the initial approach on my own.' He met Moretti's eyes. Both men knew he wasn't asking but instructing. Fortunately, for once, the Italian didn't let his own ego get in the way.

'Very well,' he bit out.

Scarlett folded her arms. 'I don't like it.'

'But you know this is the best way.'

Her mouth tightened. 'I still don't like it.'

Devereau grinned at her. 'Thank you, Scarlett.'

She rolled her eyes. 'Just don't fuck this up.'

CHAPTER TWENTY-TWO

The stench that assailed Devereau's nostrils as soon as he pushed open the door and crossed into the all-but derelict building was quite something. Stale body odour combined with the pervasive smell of damp, potent alcoholic beverages and vomit. Underlying it were the odours of both desperate desire and depressed resignation. Yeah. Devereau knew this smell. It wasn't any different to a hundred different places he'd been to in London in his previous life as a human. When you reached the dark bottom of a bottomless pit, this was the kind of place you ended up. It was an easier situation to fall into than most people realised. But Devereau was also aware that there was a camaraderie amongst those who'd dropped through the holes in the fabric of society that people on the outside wouldn't recognise. They wouldn't take well to threats against one of their own, no matter who that person was or whether he truly belonged there. That was one of the reasons why he was better doing this alone.

As if he'd flicked a switch, his demeanour altered dramatically now that he was inside. His shoulders dropped and, while his facial expression remained unchanged, his body language exuded menace and fear all at the same time. One emotion fed the other but being able to put on a front that included both was something that the most skilled actor would struggle with. You had to understand the emotions to be able to present them effectively. And Devereau understood. It didn't matter that he didn't speak Italian. His aura would do all of the talking.

Side-stepping a pile of stained blankets, Devereau walked into the first room. There was a couple huddled together on a dirty sofa and a man humming to himself from a rug on the floor. All three of them glanced up at him before their eyes slid away less out of intimidation and more out of recognition as a kindred spirit. He grunted an acknowledgment. No Vissier here then.

Devereau turned, ignoring the heavy creak of the floorboards, and headed for the narrow staircase. He toed aside some of the strewn litter blocking his path and then ascended. Tinny dance music was throbbing from one of the rooms on the first floor. Devereau looked in at the half dozen or so people dancing inside. Half of them were moving to the beat of the music. The other half seemed to be in a world of their own, their bodies swaying to a rhythm all of their own.

A young woman barged past him, her body brushing against his shoulder. She glared at him for getting in her way as she was trying to leave. Devereau gave her a wide smile in return but made sure not to allow it to touch his eyes. She recoiled slightly and continued on her way. Devereau elected to go towards the direction from which she'd come.

The further he went, the darker the house seemed to become. There were a lot of nooks and crannies were someone could hide. It made sense that Geraint Vissier would choose to come somewhere like this. Nobody would think to look for him here without a solid tip-off like the one Moretti had received. And yet Devereau doubted that the Dutchman was comfortable here. From what little he'd gleaned of the man during Solentino's lunch, he was a nervy sort of fellow as well as fastidious. He'd be used to far more sanitary conditions than here. Devereau considered the matter before tipping his head upwards. Vissier would want to keep himself to himself and away from the taint of the decrepit house. He was a penthouse kind of a man.

With that thought in his mind, Devereau abandoned his attempts to search every single room and instead quickly continued upwards to the top of the house. The higher he went, the more draughty the building became. The debris on the stairs became harder to navigate and it appeared that a large amount of the roof which had caved in had fallen inside. With the remnants of old roof slates and chunks of brick, it was impossible to attempt to move silently so Devereau didn't bother trying to be quiet. He simply ensured that his steps were unhurried so that anyone listening in from above wouldn't be threatened by a sense of approaching urgency.

He passed a few more people, marvelling at how many were actually inside the house in total and glad that he'd come alone. There was no doubt in his mind that at least several of the current residents were armed with knives at the very least and that any sort of incursion by a large group of werewolves on the hunt would only have resulted in unnecessary bloodshed and pain. It wasn't the wolves he was protecting; it was the sorry human beings who'd ended up here. They deserved better than this. Everyone did.

By the time he was on the final flight of stairs, Devereau could see the darkening sky from above through the gaping hole in the roof. He could also hear steady breathing from someone who was above him. When he rounded the last corner, and his eyes fell on the huddled shape wrapped in a blanket on the broken landing on the top floor, he knew he'd found Vissier.

'You,' the Dutchman gasped. 'You. How did you find me?' Vissier fumbled underneath the blanket and, a moment later, produced a gun. He wasted no time in pointing it directly at Devereau's head.

'I'm not responsible for what happened to Christopher Solentino,' Devereau said calmly. 'No matter what you think you saw. I arrived at the apartment only minutes before you did. You know I was at the Colosseum. You know I wouldn't have had the time to kill all those people.'

He wasn't sure that Vissier had heard him. The man's hands were shaking, causing the muzzle of the gun to jerk. 'I've got silver bullets,' he quavered. 'And I will shoot.'

Devereau splayed his hands out to show he was unarmed. 'If you had silver bullets, you'd have already pulled the trigger.' He gazed at the gun without a flicker of fear. 'Do you have *any* bullets in that thing?'

Vissier raised his voice. 'Get away from me! Get the fuck away!'

Devereau crouched down until he was eye level with him. 'Geraint,' he said. 'Or would you prefer Gee? You need to relax. You knew this was inevitable. You knew you wouldn't get away.'

The Dutchman stared at him wide-eyed.

'The house is almost completely surrounded. You won't get away. There are werewolves from clan Lupo all around this place.' He paused for a moment to allow the information to sink into Vissier's thick skull. 'But luckily, they're not here to hurt you. Nobody is. All I need is for you to talk. Tell me everything you know and I'll let you walk away from here.'

Vissier waved the gun at him. 'I don't know anything! All I know is that you murdered all my friends! You're a madman. A fucking madman!'

That was rich coming from someone who was a terrorist. Wisely, Devereau didn't say that. 'First of all,' he said, 'I didn't murder anyone. Even if I'd wanted to, I didn't have time – a fact that you should be well aware of. Second of all,' he continued, 'I don't believe those people were your friends. I was there yesterday, remember? I saw how Solentino treated you. Nobody stood up for you then and I saw what he did to Mike Lancaster afterwards. There might be honour amongst thieves but there was certainly no honour amongst your little group.'

From the way Vissier twitched, Devereau could tell that his words were striking a chord.

'I thought you killed him and the others,' Vissier said, almost spitting the words out. 'So if you didn't then I don't know who did. I can't help you.'

He'd already suspected as much. 'You know you'd be dead too,' Devereau told him, 'if you'd not been following Scarlett and I.'

Vissier's face spasmed into an ugly twist. 'So you're claiming that it's because of you that I'm still alive?'

'I'm here now,' Devereau said quietly, 'and you're still breathing. Right?'

Vissier's eyes shifted, darting from side to side.

'Why were you following us?'

'Alina wanted me to make sure we could trust you. She was sure you were too attached to the vampire to do what Solentino wanted and she made Solentino send me after you to be sure. So I waited until I knew you were out of the way and I could get into your hotel room to take a look around and plant a few bugs to listen in to what you were up to. Clearly, the bitch was right and there's not a single trustworthy bone in your body.'

'Or maybe,' Devereau returned, 'I'm not as keen to murder my own colleagues as your supposed friends are.'

A shadow crossed Vissier's face. He didn't drop the gun but his voice did alter slightly. 'If I talk to you,' he said, 'if I tell you everything I know, you'll let me go?'

'Absolutely.'

The Dutchman drew in a shaky breath as he weighed up his options. Truthfully, from the moment Devereau had entered this building, he had none – and he knew it. 'Fine,' he snapped. 'What is it you want to know?'

'Whoever killed your boss and the others also hurt Alina. But her body wasn't at the apartment. Either she was taken by the killers or she ran. Given the amount of her blood we found at the scene, it's more likely the killers took her. Why would they have done that?'

Despite his precarious situation, Vissier still stared at Devereau with complete incredulity. 'How would I know?'

'What would Alina have known about your activities that the others didn't?'

'How to suck Solentino's damned dick. She thinks she's smart but she's nothing more than an airhead with a pretty face. Eye candy. Who gives a fuck about Alina?'

Clearly not Geraint Vissier. Regardless, Devereau persisted. 'Is there any reason at all why she wasn't killed like the others?'

'Not that I know of. She's a woman,' Vissier scoffed. 'And a stupid woman at that even if she did have Solentino wrapped around her little finger.'

Devereau tilted his head. Curious. Even for a unstilting misogynist, Vissier was dismissing her far too quickly. 'Was there something between you two?'

He didn't answer.

'Did you try it on with Alina Bonnet and she turned you down?'

Vissier recoiled. 'No! She was mine! It was Solentino who took her from me. Before he came along, Alina and I had a good thing going. Then she decided he was the better option,' he said bitterly. 'Fucking bitch.'

Huh. Devereau scratched his chin. That was interesting. No wonder Vissier was so bitter about her. Switching tack for now, he dropped his voice. 'You know,' he said, 'Solentino was tortured.'

Vissier jerked.

'And,' Devereau continued, 'the room at the back where I presume you kept all the details of your upcoming plan was completely ransacked. Almost everything was either destroyed or taken.'

Vissier's brow creased as he considered the ramifications of that particular titbit. 'They wanted them,' he said. 'They wanted the plans for themselves. Everything was set up and ready to go. If Bartan hadn't gotten himself killed and if Solentino hadn't listened to fucking Alina and been so determined to get that ring to see into the future,' Vissier rolled his eyes, 'then we'd could have started at any moment. Instead, he wanted us to wait till he could get the ring even though everything was already in place.'

'What?' Devereau prompted. 'What was in place? What were the plans?'

He snorted. 'To make money. What else is there?'

'Go on.'

Vissier allowed himself a tiny smile. Pride, Devereau realised. He was proud of whatever shit they'd cooked up together. 'We start in Rome,' he said. 'We contact the government. We tell them that either they pay us what we demand or we blow something up.'

'And what?' Devereau asked baffled. 'Surely you wouldn't expect them to give you money based on a threat like that.'

Vissier tossed the gun to one side. 'You were right,' he said, 'it isn't loaded.' He gesticulated towards Devereau. 'And of course they wouldn't give us anything. We didn't expect they would.'

'So?'

A smile spread across Vissier's face. 'So we blow something up.'

Devereau stared at him. Vissier laughed.

'You're looking at me like I'm some kind of bloodthirsty maniac. I'm no psychopath, Mr Webb. None of us are.' His mouth downturned. 'None of us were. Not even Solentino, although he had his moments. We had a shortlist of targets ready to go. They were carefully selected to create maximum impact. But because we're not monsters, we wanted minimum bloodshed.' He shrugged with cold-hearted pragmatism. 'Some innocents would inevitably die. But not many.'

'What do you mean?'

Vissier smiled nastily. 'You saw what happened with Notre Dame, right?'

Devereau squinted. 'You mean the fire?'

'The fire. The outpouring of grief that an old building could be placed in such mortal danger. The money that was raised to save it.' Vissier waved around him. 'This is an old building. You don't see anyone rushing to return it to its former glory. But it's not in the right place and doesn't attract the right people. And this is Rome. There are no shortage of beautiful old buildings.'

'Like the Colosseum.'

Vissier nodded. 'It made our shortlist. But it's already in ruins. There were other candidates. The Trevi Fountain. St Peter's Basilica. The Sistine Chapel. All were viable. We blow one up. And then we move on.'

Devereau already knew where they were planning to move on to but he was unwilling to reveal to Vissier what he'd already worked out. 'To where?'

'Berlin. There we repeat what we already started. We contact the authorities. We make our demands. And if those demands are not met, we blow something up. Solentino reckoned it was fifty fifty that we'd make any money from the Germans. By the time we moved onto Paris, however,' his smile broadened, 'well, by then not only would our threats be believed but we would be taken very, very seriously. Maybe we'd choose Notre Dame. Maybe somewhere else. The Eiffel Tower perhaps. Or the Louvre.' His eyes danced with cold amusement. 'Imagine all those works of art,' he snapped his fingers, 'gone forever.' Vissier smiled to himself. 'And then when we got to London it would be a fait accompli. The British government would fall over themselves to pay up whatever we demanded.'

It was a bone chillingly clever plan. It wasn't as foolproof as

Vissier imagined, however. 'Those governments don't negotiate with terrorists.'

Vissier smirked. 'That's a myth. Governments negotiate with terrorists all the time. They pretend they don't but they absolutely do. Sometimes they go out of their way for such negotiations and make the first approach. *Here,*' he mimicked, '*take these weapons that I will give you for free. Just make sure you only use them to kill people we don't like.*'

'You don't really think you'd be able to get away with all this though?'

Vissier dismissed his doubts with a flick of his wrist. 'Solentino had all the details worked out. He knew a lot of people who could help with the plans and the set-up. And he wanted the ring you have in your belly to double check that everything would go ahead as it should. From the moment the first button was pressed here in Rome it would have been plain sailing.' He snarled suddenly. 'Until Solentino was murdered himself that was.'

Devereau tried to control his breathing. 'You had a shortlist of specific targets for each city? But you don't know what the final decision was and what actual buildings are going to be attacked?'

'We had to remain flexible. After all, who knows what last minute security procedures might be put into place? We are talking about rich cities. But rich cities with a lot of history and a lot of potential places to target.' He raised his shoulders. 'And who knows? Maybe it would end up being a positive thing when people around Europe realise that their governments are more willing to spend millions to save mere bricks and mortar than put money into helping save their own people from poverty and ill health.'

Devereau watched him with expressionless eyes. 'You're all heart. You have no idea who might have killed Solentino and taken all the plans? Can't you speculate?'

Vissier pursed his lips. 'If it definitely wasn't you, then there's only one obvious choice. It always seemed a bit suspect that Bartan died when he did. He was integral to a lot of our movements between each country. Avanopoulos appeared very eager to step in and fill his shoes.' His eyes narrowed. 'Too eager. Before now I didn't think he would be smart enough to pull something like this off. But I was wrong. Solentino was right to be worried about him.'

'Perhaps. Devereau gazed at him for a moment or two. 'I hope you've not left anything out,' he said finally. 'I found you here. That means I can find you anywhere. If I discover that there's anything you're not telling me, it won't go well for you. I can promise you that.'

Vissier glared at him. 'I've told you all I know. Will you let me go?'

Devereau didn't smile. 'Let's walk out of here together.'

* * *

THE OTHER INHABITANTS of the building paid them no attention as they walked out. Devereau pocketed the gun rather than leave it for someone else to find and took up position behind Vissier.

'I still have to hide,' Vissier said. 'Just because you didn't kill Solentino doesn't mean that whoever did isn't still after me.'

'I wouldn't worry about that,' Devereau murmured. He gave him a nudge out onto the street. There were already a dozen werewolves waiting there, including Moretti. Devereau glanced in Scarlett's direction. She was watching him but her face was giving nothing away. He gave her a quick nod to indicate that Vissier had told them what they needed. Then Moretti stepped forward.

Vissier glanced to the side, frowning. 'I left my bike here. Where has it gone?'

'You won't be needing it,' Moretti said.

Vissier tensed. 'What is this?' He swung his head towards

Devereau. 'You told me I'd be safe! You told me that you'd let me go!'

Devereau took a step back, crossing his arms over his chest. He didn't feel an ounce of sympathy or so much as a whisker of guilt. 'You might be right,' he said aloud, 'that governments are willing to negotiate with terrorists. But I am not. Yes, I told you that I'd let you go. Unfortunately for you, however, I lied.'

Vissier launched himself at Devereau, fists raised. He didn't get very far. In a split second, a wolf landed on his back. Vissier was sent sprawling to the ground. Within mere moments, he was surrounded by a ring of snarling werewolves.

'You fucking bastard, Webb! You fucking bastard!'

Devereau shrugged. He'd been called worse. He looked at Moretti. 'I know the plan,' he said. 'And now I know it, we can stop it, no matter who had decided to fill Solentino's shoes.'

He'd barely finished his sentence when a strange rumble tore through the air. The cracked tarmac underneath Devereau's feet began to shake. From the distance, somewhere towards the other side of the city, a sudden plume of smoke and fire shot up into the night sky. Oh no. Oh hell no. There were shouts of alarm and panicked screams from both near and far away.

From the ground Geraint Vissier began to laugh. 'That came from the city centre,' he said. 'It's already started. You're already far too late to stop anything.'

CHAPTER TWENTY-THREE

It wasn't easy getting through the streets of Rome. For one thing, virtually every emergency vehicle and all available personnel, from police to paramedics to firefighters, had been called to the scene. Not to mention the vast numbers of media hordes who were also descending on the area. The Roman authorities had wasted no time in setting up checkpoints which barricaded access to the disaster zone in a bid to stop people who might get in the way from getting close – and people who might be responsible for the attack from getting away. Frankly, if it weren't for Moretti, they wouldn't have gotten within three miles of the blast site. It took him three phone calls to reach the Dirigente Generale, the Inspector General of the Italian police, and five precious minutes to persuade him to allow clan Lupo to access the site of the blast and help the immediate recovery attempts.

'It's the Pantheon,' Moretti said through gritted teeth. 'Those fuckers have blown up the Pantheon. It has stood for two thousand years and now it's little more than a pile of rubble.'

Devereau sucked in a breath. 'Was anyone inside?'

'It's December. It might be late evening and already closed for

211

the night to tourists but Christmas isn't far away. There were out of hours rehearsals going on for the upcoming Noel services. There's no word on numbers yet but the Dirigente expects there will be multiple casualties.' Moretti's skin was pale and he held himself tightly, his rigid muscles belying the tension and anxiety they all felt. 'I should have been the first person he contacted. As wolves we can quickly reach places that would take humans hours to safely get to. And our enhanced sense of smell permits us to locate survivors far faster. We are frequently called upon when earthquakes cause local buildings to collapse.'

'This is no earthquake,' Scarlett muttered.

'No,' he agreed. 'And that is all the more reason to ask for our help. It is obvious an act of terrorism like this was committed by humans. Supes don't blow up their own fucking cities.'

Devereau massaged the back of his neck. The familiar pain between his shoulder blades – the one which only jabbed at him when he was tense and worried – felt less like an irritation and more as if someone had rammed a hatchet into his flesh. 'Well,' he said, in a voice as dark as midnight, 'one of our questions has been answered.' He bared his teeth and let out a low snarl. 'Solentino's killers weren't attempting to stop him from committing atrocious acts. They were stealing those acts for themselves.'

Scarlett turned her head and glanced out of the car window. The streets were lined with people. A few were crying. Some were hugging both themselves and others close to them. And all of them looked terrified. 'Sometimes,' she said softly, 'I wonder what has happened to our world and where it can possibly be going.' She shook her head. 'The capacity which humankind has to destroy itself is unbelievable.'

'It's not all humans,' Devereau said.

'Perhaps not. But it's enough of them.'

He reached for her hand, his fingers entwining with hers. For once she didn't pull away but instead leaned into him while

Moretti's car pulled up behind a bank of waiting ambulances. They all knew this would be a horrifically long night. Devereau closed his eyes for a few seconds, using one brief moment of calm to centre himself and mentally prepare. Then he and Scarlett followed Moretti out of the car and into the screaming hell that awaited them.

Two soldiers, with stoically blank faces that couldn't mask their horrorstruck eyes, directed them to a narrow side street, shouting something at Moretti over the shouts and yells and wails of various sirens and alarms. Devereau didn't understand the words but he caught the gist from their hand signals. The rest of clan Lupo was waiting for their alpha. And Devereau knew they would all do whatever he and their city required of them.

He looked round, his stomach clenching as he tried to catch a glimpse of the Pantheon itself – or at least what was left of it. It was impossible to see anything, however. There were too many other buildings and people in the way, not to mention the thick acrid smoke which had filled the cool night air. Devereau gave up trying to see and marched after Moretti with Scarlett by his side and, when they turned the next corner and he saw the large group of waiting werewolves, something inside him eased. There was comfort in his own kind, even under the direst of circumstances. Moretti broke away to speak to an official looking human who seemed to have been waiting for his arrival. Devereau clenched and unclenched his fists, watching the discussion that took place but unable to hear a word of it. This wasn't his city and he wasn't in charge. But, man, it was hard to stand by and wait for instructions from someone else.

Scarlett seemed to sense what he was thinking. 'Once we are done here,' she murmured, 'we should go back, retrieve Geraint Vissier from wherever those other Lupo werewolves took him, and,' she licked her lips delicately, 'beat the shit out of him. It won't change a damned thing but it'll make me feel a hell of a lot better.'

Devereau offered her a ghost of a smile. 'I have a feeling I know who's behind all of this,' he told her. 'This attack and Solentino's murder. I don't think it's the Greek.'

Scarlett's eyes flew to his. Before he could say anything else, however, Moretti pivoted and began to speak in Italian, bellowing at the top of his voice so that all the assembled werewolves could hear him. Devereau watched, his frustration growing at his inability to understand another language.

'My Italian isn't great,' Scarlett admitted, 'but I can understand enough. He's saying that the priority is to find survivors. Some parts of the building are still standing and others have collapsed completely but the entire place is unsafe. The Lupo wolves need to tread carefully and use their noses to find any and all who might still be breathing. There are people in there who are counting on them to find them.' She paused, her mouth flattening. 'He says that the city needs them.'

Every single werewolf in front of Moretti nodded. Nobody looked eager but there was no mistaking the sense of grim anticipation at their upcoming task. Then Moretti continued.

'They're going to split up into teams,' Scarlett translated. 'If anyone locates any signs of anyone still alive under there, they have to howl once and wait for search and rescue to reach them. They have the technology to do the heavy lifting.'

Moretti pointed to five separate people. Scarlett squinted.

'Each beta wolf will lead a team. Everyone is to follow their lead at all times and do nothing which might risk further building collapse or their own safety,' she told Devereau.

He nodded. 'Noted.'

The first group of wolves took off, sprinting in the direction of the destroyed Pantheon. Devereau began to head after them but Scarlett grabbed his arm. 'Wait,' she said. 'Are you sure you're up to this?'

'Of course I am,' he growled.

'You collapsed only yesterday, Dev. If something like that

happens again and you need rescuing yourself, you will cause more harm than good.'

'I've rested and eaten since then,' he snapped. 'I'm fine.' Then he scowled at himself. Damn it. 'Sorry. I shouldn't have spoken like that to you.'

Scarlett's expression was understanding. 'I get it. I feel the same way you do and you don't have to apologise. But you do have to be sure that you're well enough for this.'

'I am,' he said simply. 'I promise. You should stay back, however. You don't have the nose of a wolf, Scarlett. It's better if you keep out of the way.'

'Devereau,' she murmured, 'with all due respect, you can fuck off.'

They gazed at each other for a moment with perfect understanding. 'Okay then,' he said finally. 'Let's go together and help our hosts as best as we can.' He half closed his eyes, allowing his animal to come to the fore. The wolf inside him was bursting to be released. 'I'll give you a ride,' Devereau told her. 'It'll get us there faster.'

Scarlett blinked but gave him a tiny nod. Then Devereau's human body yielded entirely to the beast.

Scarlett moved quickly, straddling his body with her fingers curling tightly into his fur so she didn't fall off. He waited until she seemed comfortable and then he took off, bounding after the Lupo werewolves, all of whom were heading into the fire and destruction rather than away from it. They all had to do this. There was simply no choice.

Even without the chaos, Devereau wouldn't have known where he was or where he was going. He kept his head down and followed the trail of the other werewolves. As it was, he almost on top of the Pantheon before he realised. He came to a skidding halt and blinked through the clouds of dark smoke which billowed up from various spots. Jesus.

They'd come at the Pantheon from its eastern side. At least

half of the massive structure seemed to have been pulverised in one stroke. The domed ceiling had completely caved in and small fires were dotted everywhere, springing from goodness knows what. Devereau had never been in the army but it certainly looked like a warzone to his eyes. He swallowed hard and felt Scarlett tug on his left ear, indicating that she wanted him to move. He padded in that direction, spotting the famous Pantheon façade. Only two columns remained standing – and it was doubtful that they would remain that way for much longer judging by the taut, disturbed expressions of the hard-hatted engineers who were cautiously examining them and the first section of the building which was still upright just beyond.

A single sharp howl pierced through the chaos. Moretti's wolves had already found someone. Devereau breathed out and looked round, noting the low shapes of the werewolves as they clambered gingerly across what was left of the once magnificent building. Scarlett slid off his back and he turned his gaze towards hers. She nodded once and then together they took off, aiming for the nearest pile of collapsed stone.

He'd been expecting that his vision would be hampered by the smoke and the fire and he'd known that progress up and over the ruined building would be slow. What he hadn't anticipated was how hot the jagged stones would be under his massive paws. He growled, forced to scamper quickly and not remain in one place for too long. It was easier said than done. The debris shifted and groaned under his weight. He had to be both nimble and careful.

Although she was wearing knee high boots which should have been entirely unsuited to this sort of task, Scarlett was fast on her feet. She leapt away from a sudden flare of flame before locating an undamaged section that she able to run up. Then she paused and looked down from her vantage point, her figure silhouetted against the terrible orange glow of the fires around them.

Devereau spun to follow her lead, while another howl ripped through the air. As soon as he reached her side, she pointed down. 'There's a space down there,' she told him. 'Can you scent anything?'

Devereau turned his head and gazed at the gaping black hole by their feet. They were at least thirty feet above ground level and it was impossible to see anything in the space below. He lowered his muzzle towards it and inhaled. It was incredibly difficult to distinguish between the different smells the collapse of the building offered up. He focused all his energy and attention, blotting out the rest of the sights, sounds and smells around him. There. There was something down that dark chasm of pantheonic destruction that smelled of human and pain and terror. He tilted his head and listened. That was a moan. He was sure of it.

Devereau yipped, indicating to Scarlett, and then took the plunge without thinking. He leapt long before he looked, stretching his front paws forward to prepare for the landing. It came sooner than expected and he tumbled forward, knocking the left flank of his fur covered body against something. He whined briefly and pulled himself upright again, as another thump came from behind him.

'For fuck's sake, you're supposed to howl and let Search and Rescue know someone's here. You're not supposed to throw yourself into a space that might collapse on top of you at any second,' Scarlett hissed.

Devereau turned his head and gave her hand a tiny nudge with his nose. He wasn't the only one standing down here. Scarlett huffed, her annoyance easily audible now that the sounds of the chaos from outside were muffled. Then she shrugged at him, delved into her pocket and drew out her phone, flicking on its torchlight to get a better look at their surroundings.

There was a stone column to their right. Ominous cracks were displayed along its length but it was still standing and was obviously the reason why this pocket of space remained, despite the devastation around them. Devereau pawed at the floor. It was covered in a layer of thick soot and ash but it appeared to be marble.

'We must be in part of the main atrium,' Scarlett said. 'Most of it seems to have collapsed when the domed ceiling caved in but this section appears alright.' She gestured to the right. 'There's a gap there. It might be enough of a crawl space to get through and investigate further.'

Devereau dipped his head in a lupine nod and lowered his body, sniffing the bitter air. The moaning, which had ceased briefly, had started up again and seemed to be coming from that direction. So did the human scent.

'Out of the way,' Scarlett ordered. 'I'm smaller than you. You'll have trouble fitting through that gap in that body.'

Devereau's eyes narrowed. He could make it – if he breathed in and sucked in his stomach. Scarlett had already pushed past him, however, and was wiggling her way through.

'Shit,' he heard her say. Then, with more urgency, '*shit.*'

He didn't bother wasting time. Transforming back into his human form so he could slide through after her, Devereau crouched down and ducked. When he saw what she'd found, he could repeat Scarlett's own words. 'Shit.'

There were two bodies, both of young boys. The nearest boy seemed almost completely unharmed – apart from his dull, staring eyes that was. His only visible injury was a trickle of congealed blood at his temple. He was definitely dead, unlike his companion who was covered in blood and whose legs were at such an angle that they had to be broken. That boy was still alive. His breath was shallow and if he didn't receive medical attention, he wouldn't last. But right now he was clinging on.

'Choir boys probably,' Scarlett muttered. 'Doing nothing more than rehearsing an angelic chorus for Christmas.' She cursed. 'We have to get him out of here without causing further injury.'

Devereau stared at the boy's young, innocent face. Beyond the dirt and the blood and the pain was a child who'd done no wrong. And next to him was his dead companion. Probably his friend. If Devereau had acted faster against Solentino, if he'd made different choices or done things in a different way, then this might not have happened. For one stark, horrible moment, it felt like his fault. It *was* his fault. Guilt and rage rampaged through him. He'd not been good enough or strong enough to prevent this from happening.

'Devereau?' Scarlett questioned.

'Yeah.' His voice sounded as if it were coming from a great distance. 'I'll take his head and shoulders. You take his feet. We can slip him through the hole and then I'll transform and howl for help.' He reached down with one hand and smoothed back the boy's dark hair. 'You'll make this, kid. I promise you. You'll make it.'

CHAPTER TWENTY-FOUR

Dawn, when it finally came, felt like an affront. Despite the cold winter weather, the sun was determined to shine upon all of Rome. Instead of lifting moods, however, the contrast merely made everything appear worse – and in daylight the devastation caused by the explosion at the Pantheon was even more horrific.

Devereau sat on the edge of a pavement, gazing at the scene. One of the paramedics had sourced a space blanket for him, which helped to preserve his modesty – such as it was – given his clothes had been destroyed yet again in his sudden transformation, and keep him warm. What the blanket couldn't do, of course, was make him feel any better on the inside.

'Here.' Scarlett handed him a hip flask. 'I pilfered this from one of the journalists hanging around by the cordon. It's good stuff.'

Devereau chose not to pass comment on her thievery and instead took a long draught. Scarlett was right - the whiskey was mellow and tasted of spicy peat and considerable expense. It still burned his throat as it went down, however. He gave the flask a morose glance and took another swig.

'How many?' he asked. 'Do you know the total?'

Scarlett sighed and sat down next to him. 'Including the three we found? Twenty-six alive. Thirty-eight dead. It could have been worse.'

Devereau looked at the smoking ruins. 'Not for those thirty eight people and their families,' he said quietly.

Scarlett lowered her head. 'No, not for them,' she agreed. She sighed. 'It looks like the choirboy might make it.'

The heaviness around Devereau's soul didn't lift. 'That's something.'

'Yeah. It is something.' She bit her lip. 'And clan Lupo are being hailed as heroes. It'll help with the anti-supe sentiment that exists here as well as everywhere else even if it's not usually as blatant in Rome as in London.'

Devereau nodded distractedly.

Scarlett continued, unwilling to allow him to mire himself in his own misery. 'You said before that you know who's behind all this.'

He ran a hand through his blond hair. It was caked with ash and dirt and goodness knew what else. It was better not to think about it. 'Not for certain,' he answered. 'But I have strong suspicions.' He passed the flask back to her and realised she'd lifted her head and was looking straight at him. Scarlett was in as much of a mess as he was and he longed to reach over and wipe away the smudges on her face. Despite the grime, her eyes still sparked. That was the definite gleam of intelligence and energy that he associated with her – but now it included something else. Retribution, he realised. Her eyes glinted with her own personal vow of retribution against whoever had caused this to happen.

Devereau drew in a breath. 'Vissier told me a few things about Alina Bonnet when we had our little chat together. Such as how she had suggested Solentino get hold of the Ring Of All Seasons.'

Scarlett stilled. 'Okay,' she said slowly.

'At the auction, she'd seemed desperately keen to get hold of the ring. But we all know that if it does allow the wearer to see into the future, it only works on the Winter Solstice and that's still more than a week away. Maybe she wanted a reason for Solentino to delay his operation to blow shit up so she had time to get rid of him and take his place.'

Scarlett looked dubious. 'It seems a stretch. We might not have found her body but there was a lot of her blood at the scene.'

'True,' Devereau conceded, 'but the only reason we know it was Alina's blood at all is because you drank from her. That's incredibly convenient, don't you think?'

'Solentino forced her into that situation.'

'Did he though? It seemed that way at the time but Vissier said Alina had him wrapped around her little finger. I had the impression from the Dutchman that there were a lot of other things she persuaded Solentino to do.' He paused. 'And get this - before Alina was with Solentino, she was shacked up with Vissier. It was Alina who wanted Vissier to follow us. When he left the Colosseum, he headed to my hotel room to check it out. It might be a coincidence that it meant he was absent from the massacre at Solentino's apartment and therefore didn't die. Or it might be that she still had feelings for him and wanted to spare him by waiting until he was safely out of the way. Not to mention that leaving him alive means there was somebody left to point the finger at Avanopoulos. A man who's already been described as *dangerously malleable*.'

Scarlett considered what he'd said. 'That's a lot of ifs. Avanopoulos can't be ignored. He has to be a serious contender.'

'I'm not discounting him,' Devereau said. 'But he came into the game late and he seems too … convenient. There may well be other players involved who we haven't met yet. But my gut is telling me that Alina Bonnet is looking like the most likely candidate for terrorist of the year. There was something about her. Something in her eyes.' He sighed. 'There's no real proof. It's only speculation and we don't know where she is or how to find her though so we can't do much about it anyway. Berlin is next and Avanopoulos is involved in at least some regard. Despite my theories about Alina, we have a better chance of finding him and –' He broke off in mid-sentence.

'What is it?'

The hairs on the back of Devereau's neck were standing up. 'That fucking embassy guy. The young one. Mark something. He's over there.'

Scarlett followed his gaze, stiffening when she saw him flanked by two security guards. He marched up to one of the more senior police officers who was directing the continuing operation to secure the disaster site and make it safe. From the way he began to gesticulate, it looked as if he was asking a question.

'He's looking for you,' Scarlett commented.

'And you,' Devereau replied.

They both watched for another moment. 'It's the million pound question,' Scarlett said softly. 'Now that Solentino's operation is underway, do we fall into line and let the real professionals take over?'

'The circumstances might have changed but my answer hasn't. I'm not stepping back. I can't.'

'In that case,' she said, as the police officer glanced round, searching for them to point out to Mark, 'we'd better move.'

'We have to speak to Moretti before we go.'

She waved her phone at him. 'I'll call him and get him to meet us somewhere safely away from here.'

They both got to their feet. In the distance, Devereau saw Mark look over in their direction. He shouted towards them and began striding over, with the guards also moving at double speed by his side. Devereau flashed Scarlett a quick, humourless grin. And then they both turned and quickly walked off in the opposite direction. Sarah Greensmith would be incandescent, Devereau thought. He shrugged. Oh well.

* * *

NICOLO MORETTI no longer looked like the suave, arrogant alpha of clan Lupo with designer clothes and an unruffled façade. It wasn't only his now ragged and dirty attire. There was a weariness behind his eyes and considerable pain etched into the lines on his face.

'I am sorry for what has happened,' Devereau said.

Moretti's jaw tightened. 'Do not be sorry,' he hissed in an undertone that was far more intimidating than shouting would have been. 'Be furious.' He drew himself up. 'I am.'

'We will find the people responsible for this, Nicolo,' Scarlett said. 'All of them.'

'I know you will. But can you find them before they repeat this in Berlin? In Paris? In London?'

'We will do our best.'

Moretti's gaze was hard. 'Do better than that.' He folded his arms across his chest. 'I had a phone call from Athens twenty minutes ago. Avanopoulos left on a private flight for Berlin ten minutes after the Pantheon exploded.' He passed Devereau a piece of paper. 'The flight details are there but there's no information about where he went after he landed. I've already contacted the three clan alphas in Berlin and they're passing word around the entire supe community. Everyone is on the alert for him.'

All three of them exchanged grim looks.

'If they spot him,' Devereau said, 'they can't approach him. We don't want to spook him, especially when he might not be the mastermind.'

Moretti's eyes narrowed. 'You think there's someone else pulling the strings?'

'Yeah.' He grimaced. 'I do.'

'Very well. I will pass your request along. I cannot promise, however, that the Germans will abide by it. Not after what has happened here.'

Devereau nodded. He could understand that. He'd have to hope that cooler heads prevailed. 'Is there any way you can help us get to Berlin without using our own passports?'

'Not Berlin,' he answered, 'but I have a private plane that can get you to an airfield fifty miles out of the city.'

That would have to do. 'Thank you.'

Moretti waved him off. 'This has not been a good night for Rome,' he said stiffly. 'Or for Europe. Vissier was right, you know. My contacts tell me that three hours before the bombs went off, an anonymous message was left. It was a demand for one thousand bitcoin to be paid into an online wallet or Rome would suffer the consequences. I am told that such methods of money transfer are virtually untraceable and that the dollar equivalent is close to sixty million. In any case, the demand was ignored.' He sniffed. 'As one would have expected. We all know what happened after that.'

Devereau's stomach tightened. 'The die has already been cast and the operation is under way.'

'Indeed it is.' Moretti clenched his fists. 'We have passed custody of Vissier to the Italian police. Given what he has been involved in, we had to do so. It won't be long before the authorities across Europe know everything that we do. Vissier was already screaming Avanopoulos's name when we handed him over.'

That was good. The more people on the lookout for the Greek fucker, the less chance there was that more bombs would go off. Organisations like MI5 had the means to track the explosives used and look at how security at the Pantheon had been breached. Such information could lead directly to the money hungry terrorists. It would also be far harder for Stefan Avanopoulos to escape detection if everyone was searching for him. And at least Greensmith wouldn't be able to accuse him of withholding vital details. They were still on the same team at the end of the day.

'Do not let them win, Englishman,' Moretti said. 'Not under any circumstances. These bastards will not waste time and they will make their next move swiftly. They are counting on a domino effect for their plans to work and they will not allow any country or any security services the chance to find them and stop them. Speed is their ally and your enemy.'

'In which case,' Scarlett said, 'We ought to go now.' She stepped forward and kissed Moretti on the cheek. Devereau fought a flare of irrational jealousy. 'Take care.'

The Italian nodded. 'Arsenio will take you to the air strip immediately. He has your suitcases all ready to go.' Moretti paused. 'Happy hunting.'

Devereau grimaced. It wouldn't be happy at all, but it would certainly be a hunt. And an increasingly desperate one. He couldn't fail again; he wouldn't have more innocent blood on his hands. Not for the world.

CHAPTER TWENTY-FIVE

BERLIN FELT COLDER THAN ROME. IN FACT IT HAD AN ENTIRELY different atmosphere to the Italian capital, although it was no less striking. If Rome was an educated statesman in a sharp suit and with impeccable manners, Berlin was a brash, kooky teenager with edge and undeniable levels of cool. On any other occasion, he would have relished wandering around the city but Devereau wasn't interested in seeing the sights this time around. The situation had escalated dramatically in the last twelve hours and, when he stared out of the window of the taxi at what Berlin had to offer, it was with unseeing eyes. He was in yet another unfamiliar city tracking down an unfamiliar man. And time was against them.

'You are English?' the taxi driver asked, in a bid to make small talk and pass the journey time quicker.

It was Scarlett who answered. 'Yes.'

'Vampire, yes?'

'Yes.'

His eyes slid to Devereau who wasn't in the mood for any chat. 'You are here for business or pleasure? Because today is not a good day to be a tourist in Berlin.'

Now, Devereau was interested. 'What do you mean?'

'The government they close all the tourist buildings. All the public places.' He gestured towards the radio. 'It was on news. Charlottenburg Palace closed. Berlin Cathedral closed. Holocaust Memorial. Closed. Even Brandenburg Gate. You cannot get close to it today. It all closed.' He took a hand off the steering wheel and waved it around to indicate his bafflement. 'I do not understand why. They say maybe because of what happened in Rome last night. That maybe next attack will be here.' He shook his head in dismay, causing his shaggy silver hair to bounce. 'I am sorry you come here today. My friend told me police and army are everywhere. They are checking IDs and passports and bags. They close Christmas markets.' He sucked air in through the gap in his teeth. 'These terrorists. They ruin everything.'

'You got that right,' Scarlett murmured. She glanced at Devereau. 'So all potential targets are closed. And being searched. It will be very difficult for anyone to plant a bomb somewhere. If not impossible. At least we know that MI5 are taking the information we found seriously and they're working with other authorities instead of sneaking around on their own.'

Devereau scratched his chin. 'On the surface, that would be a good thing. But now it's obvious to anyone with half a brain that Berlin has been identified as the next target. Avanopoulos or Alina Bonnet or whoever else is now running Solentino's show must know that we're onto RBPL. That could be disastrous. If they alter their plans to avoid detection, we won't know about it until it's too late.'

'Unless your theory about Bonnet leaving Vissier alive so he could point the finger at Avanopoulos is correct,' Scarlett said. 'Because if that's the case, then she would already know he would also confirm what RBPL meant. Maybe it's not a coincidence that we found that scrap of paper at Solentino's place. Maybe we're supposed to know where they're targeting. Terrorists spread terror by definition and there's nothing more terrifying than waiting for an inevitable attack to happen *and* knowing where it's going to happen but still being unable to stop it. Advance knowledge also gives governments enough time to get the money together that they need to meet the demands and prevent the attacks from happening.'

Hmm. 'Advertising the targets in advance would be an incredibly risky move on her part,' he said thoughtfully, 'but the entire operation is risky beyond belief. Either Alina Bonnet is incredibly smart and has planned for every eventuality or we're barking up the wrong tree completely and she's already dead in a ditch somewhere.'

The taxi driver gave them a nervous look in the mirror. Devereau and Scarlett exchanged glances then, by silent mutual agreement, stayed quiet until he dropped them off near the train station at Potsdamer Platz.

He had certainly been right about the increased security. Everywhere Devereau looked, he could see armed police and soldiers. Their presence didn't reassure him; if anything they only increased his sense of dread.

'Fraulein Cook? Herr Webb?'

They both turned. Standing a few metres away was quite the welcome party. Three vampires, three werewolves, a pixie and a gremlin. And a human woman. Devereau stared hard at the woman. She smiled faintly back. Then one of the vampires stepped forward.

'Meister Meyer,' Scarlett said, with considerable respect in her voice. 'Thank you for coming to meet us.'

'I have told you before to call me Jurgen,' the German replied. He glanced at Devereau. He didn't smile but his expression wasn't unfriendly. 'I have heard a great deal about you, Herr Webb. It is good to finally make your acquaintance.'

Devereau nodded soberly back and then addressed the werewolves specifically. 'I understand,' he said, 'that there will be considerable protocol that should be addressed concerning my presence here in Rome. I hope that under the circumstances, we can set aside such traditions for now.' The last thing he needed right now was a similar situation to the one he'd ended up in at the Colosseum.

All three werewolves stared at him. Then they burst out laughing. 'You've just come from Rome,' the tall female wolf said. 'Don't worry. We're more relaxed here about such things. We don't tend to adhere to the old ways like Nicolo Moretti does. Outsiders always think that us Germans are sticklers for the rules when the truth could not be more different.' She shrugged ambivalently. 'I am Mila, alpha of the Konig clan. This is Franz, the Fuchs alpha,' she said, 'and Tomas, the alpha of the Jager clan.'

No prizes for guessing which German clan was the strongest. Devereau greeted them all, making sure to be particularly deferential towards Mila Konig, before the pixie introduced himself as Rosafarben. The gremlin merely grunted and the remaining two vampires only bowed their heads in greeting.

'Hello Mr Webb,' Sarah Greensmith said, with far too much uncharacteristic cheer. She stuck her hand out towards Scarlett. 'Miss Cook. It's nice to meet you. I'm Sarah.'

Scarlett threw Devereau an alarmed look before shaking Greensmith's hand. 'Hi.'

The MI5 agent was unable to stop herself from smirking. 'You both look surprised to see me. You didn't really think that we wouldn't know you'd left Rome and were heading here? That because you managed to run away from one minor embassy staff member, we wouldn't be able to find you?'

Jurgen Meyer looked vaguely apologetic. 'She insisted she came along here and did not give us much choice in the matter.'

'Choice?' Greensmith scoffed. 'We're all in this together.' Her amusement was replaced by a steely edge. 'We are all under threat.'

Konig muttered something in German under her breath.

'Some of us,' she said in English, 'have to deal with more of an immediate threat than others.'

Sarah Greensmith waved an airy hand. 'And that's why it's good that we're all working together even if I remain disappointed that my German counterpart is not also here.'

'The humans are somewhat preoccupied right now,' Konig returned icily. 'And our government trusts its supes more than yours does.'

Greensmith didn't so much as blink. 'I doubt that very much.' She sniffed with the sort of imperious air only an English woman could manage before turning her attention to Devereau and Scarlett. 'Don't get your hackles up, Mr Webb. I'm only here to deliver a message. This would be easier if your phone wasn't turned off or if you actually checked the damned emails.'

'I've been somewhat busy,' he said shortly, wariness bristling through him along with a healthy dose of guilt, 'and my phone is broken. So tell me now. What's the message?'

Greensmith sighed with vague exasperation. 'As you seem so determined to go it alone, we have decided to play along. For now anyway. It took some persuading to get my own superiors to see the light but it helps that you have had some modicum of success with your mission, despite what happened to the Pantheon.' She gestured towards the German supes. 'And you have connections and access to abilities that we are unable to match. You can continue down your current path to locate the terrorists behind all this. The rest of MI5 is working with Interpol and other European security services to do the same. Locate these bastards, stop the attacks, and we will treat you both like heroes. You will have carte blanche going forward.' She paused. 'We'll probably find them before you do but,' she shrugged, 'have at it. What's the worst that could happen?'

The worst? That would be hundreds of dead European citizens and the destruction of several historical monuments. They were all aware of that.

'And if none of us find them? If none of us can stop them?' Scarlett asked.

Greensmith gave her a steady look. 'I'm glad you asked that question,' she said softly. 'In these sorts of circumstances, we usually require a scapegoat. Someone has to take the fall for our mistakes. Unfortunately, on this occasion, we will blame you for the failure.'

Great. Although if they failed and more people died, Devereau would have no problem with blaming himself. He raised his eyes heavenward while every single German supe looked on stony-faced. 'I thought you said we were all in this together?'

'You're the one who decided to ignore your orders and piss off around Europe,' she said with a shrug. Her eyes shifted away from him and Devereau had the sudden sense that she felt far more discomfort than she was letting on. 'That is on you. Don't take it personally though, Mr Webb. After all, I'm not taking your decision to abscond personally, either.' She gave him a mock curtsey. 'Miss Cook, as you are not officially part of MI5, if you choose to come back to London now, we will forget you were ever involved. We will not make this offer again, however. It's a one time deal. Stay with Mr Webb and his successes become your successes. Unfortunately, the same will go for his failures.' She raised her eyebrows at Devereau. 'This wouldn't have happened if you'd only done what you were told. And don't think of it as a punishment. It's only politics.'

Yeah, yeah. Devereau didn't know why he would have ever expected anything less.

Scarlett moved closer to him and put an arm around his waist. Startled, he glanced at her, the warmth of her touch already lifting his spirits. 'I'm no Bond girl,' she sneered, matching Greensmith's attitude with her own. 'But I'm with him.'

From deep underneath his skin, Devereau's wolf yipped in delight.

Greensmith didn't look surprised. 'Very well.' She reached

into her pocket and everyone stiffened. It was only a business card that she pulled out, however. 'I gather you still possess a phone?' she said to Scarlett, who nodded. 'Take my personal phone number then. You might need it in an emergency. You will also need to keep me updated with any new information you uncover.' For the briefest moment, her face softened and Devereau had the sudden thought that she was on his side and wishing him the best, regardless of what machinations might be going on behind the scenes in London. 'Good luck to you both.' She hesitated. 'Good luck to us all.' She turned on her heel and clicked away.

They all watched her go. Scarlett frowned. 'I feel like I should despise her for that little chat. But instead I think I admire her honesty. At least we don't have to run away any more from any British embassy idiots.'

'Thank heavens for small mercies,' Devereau muttered.

'Sometimes,' Jurgen Meyer said, 'you English can be very strange.'

The other supes, including Mila Konig, bobbed their heads in agreement. 'Shall we get started?' she inquired. 'These fuckers could be anywhere in Berlin. We've had supes searching everywhere for this Avanopoulos and the Bonnet woman.' She gestured towards Rosafarben. 'You had a lead, didn't you?'

The pixie raised his chin. 'Yes. I have passed the information onto the German police. Regardless of that horrible English woman just now, we are all trying to achieve the same thing. The only competition should be between us and the terrorists.'

Devereau wasn't going to argue with that. Not at all. 'What is it? What have you discovered?'

Rosenfarben cleared his throat. 'A group of young pixies are certain that very early this morning they saw a man matching the description of Stefan Avanopoulos at Venusbassin in Tiergarten. He approached them and asked for the time. They remember him because he was quite obviously wearing a watch.'

Devereau frowned. That seemed odd - unless Avanopoulos had wanted his presence to be noted. Devereau had the uneasy feeling that they were being played. But right now there was nowhere else to go.

'The Tiergarten is within walking distance,' Mila Konig said. 'It's the public park we use during the full moon. The police haven't closed it off. It's a big green space. There's a zoo but I doubt it would be the terrorists' target. There's very little there to blow up.'

Devereau straightened his shoulders. It was hard not to notice that Scarlett's arm was still round his waist. He flicked a look at her and she jerked in sudden self-awareness. She stepped away and he felt a moment of loss. 'The park might not be the actual target but it's the only intelligence we've got right now.' He gestured to the small group of supes. 'Lead the way.'

* * *

IT WAS an icy wind that rustled through the Tiergarten and Devereau was forced to put up his collar as a guard against the wind. He didn't like the idea of having to transform to a wolf in a hurry – and then shift into his vulnerable human state without any clothes to protect him from the effects of winter. It had been bad enough doing that in Rome.

'How do you manage transformations at this time of year?' he asked Konig, as they walked briskly towards the area where Avanopoulos had been spotted. 'When you have to change in a hurry but your clothes have been ripped to shreds by your initial shift, what do you do?'

Konig seemed amused. 'It is rare that we do not plan in advance for such things. On the odd occasion when we are caught unprepared and are forced to transform in a hurry, we have caches of unisex clothes ready at various spots around the city. There is actually one up at the Venusbassin. Supes congregate here frequently and sometimes ... accidents, shall we say ... happen. The pixies who saw Avanopoulos are here most days. They peddle supe moonshine to passersby. It's little more than vodka with a few herbs thrown in but humans lap that sort of ridiculous stuff up. The younger pixies weave tall tales of magic antidotes for all manner of ailments. We used to try and stop them from such scams but they're incorrigible at that sort of age.' She glanced at Rosenfarben, who was skipping along next to Scarlett at the front of their small group, and lowered her voice. 'Truthfully, pixies are incorrigible at any age.'

Devereau suppressed a smile. 'The human woman who was here before,' he said. 'I got mixed up with her in the first place because of my pixie neighbour. Sort of.'

Konig clicked her tongue. 'I am not surprised. Pixies get away with a great deal because they are small and possess limited powers. But they meddle a great deal in sorts of affairs. We have a saying here. It doesn't translate directly but it's along the lines of *the pixie goes crazy in the pan*. Or rather that they're unbelievable and not to be trusted.' She raised her shoulders in a shrug. 'It's a stereotype but it often fits. They have their own less than complimentary sayings about us.'

Devereau could well imagine.

Rosenfarben cleared his throat. 'I can hear what you're telling that poor wolf, you know. Don't put ideas into his head, Alpha Konig.'

Konig's answering grin looked genuine. There was far more warmth and camaraderie amongst all the supes here, despite the teasing. Devereau's gaze drifted momentarily towards Scarlett and wondered if things would be easier between them if London supes were more like this. Probably not. She was her own person regardless of what other people did or said. He sighed to himself and pulled his coat tighter around him.

'It's there,' Rosenfarben announced. 'See?'

Devereau squinted, spotting the serene rectangular pool with a small monument at the far end. It was pretty, and there were still plenty of people wandering around it despite the threats to Berlin's security. There was, however, no sign of anyone who might fit Stefan Avanopoulos's description. That was hardly surprising, of course. It had been hours since he was seen here and the German police had no doubt conducted their own thorough sweeps. In any event, it still seemed an odd place for the Greek to come. And why would he have approached a group of pixies and asked for the time? Surely, he would have wanted to keep a low profile. There was more to this than met the eye. Devereau was sure of it.

Konig's phone began to ring. A half second later so did Jurgen Meyer's. It was swiftly followed by beeping alerts from the phones of every single German supe. Devereau and Scarlett exchanged dark, alarmed glances.

'What?' she asked. 'What is it?'

'The police have found an explosive device outside the Reichstag,' Konig said, her voice vibrating with urgency. 'The fucking German Parliament. That's virtually around the corner from here.'

CHAPTER TWENTY-SIX

Devereau had never seen so many police in one place. They'd better hope that damned bomb didn't go off or it would decimate the infrastructure of Germany's security and protection services for decades to come. He paused. Huh.

Meyer marched back from the official he'd been arguing with. 'They won't let us get any closer,' he hissed, his jaw tight with frustration. 'So far they think they've identified two separate devices but they think there might be more. Neither device is inside the actual building itself, which is something to be thankful for.'

Devereau swept his gaze round. It was a glorious building. Although it was far larger than the Pantheon, its glass dome and towering pillars at the front somehow put him in mind of the Italian structure as it had been until yesterday evening. He stared at it. And then he shook his head. No. This wasn't right.

'Have there been any demands yet?' he asked. 'Have the German authorities been asked for money?'

'Apparently not.' Meyer sniffed. 'The bombs were found before the terrorists could do so.' As soon as the words left his mouth, he frowned. 'But that doesn't make sense,' he said slowly.

'This is the most heavily guarded building in Berlin. With the police on high alert, those devices were always going to be found quickly.'

Concern flitted across Scarlett's face. 'And as soon as they were discovered,' she said, 'security forces from across the city would leave their other posts and descend here.'

Devereau nodded grimly. 'This isn't the target. Those bombs aren't inside the building because security is too tight. The terrorists would never get explosives inside the Reichstag no matter how well they planned their operation.' He looked round again. Despite the numbers of people milling around, there was an air of unhurried calm. The only palpable excitement was coming from the gaggle of journalists, who were being kept even further away from the scene than they were. Nobody was particularly concerned – and they absolutely should be. 'You need to go and talk to them again. The troops and the police need to be pulled way from here and sent to the other important buildings and landmarks in Berlin. This is a bluff. There's a reason Avanopoulos went to such a public location and made himself known. He wanted the bombs to be found. He wanted everyone to be drawn to this location. In fact ...' His voice trailed off as his eye caught a flurry of movement over by the media crowd. 'Something's happening,' he said. He squared his shoulders. 'We have to find out what.' He began to stride in the journalists' direction, but Scarlett caught his arm.

'What?'

She held up her phone. 'This,' she said. 'This is what's happening.'

Devereau squinted at the screen, his stomach dropping when he saw what was displayed there. All around them, the atmosphere was changing. More people were looking down at their phones, growing horror reflected on all their faces. Konig pushed her way through the crowd towards them.

'I have it too,' she spat. 'It's all over social media in both English and German.'

Scarlett swallowed. 'This is it, Dev. Avanopoulos or Alina or whoever is else is involved? This is definitely them.'

'*The German government has one hour to hand over two thousand bitcoin,*' Devereau read, his stomach dropping with every word. '*Or three specific locations in Berlin will be blown up like the Pantheon was in Rome. Eeny meeny miny mo.*' Shit. 'They're escalating. More targets. More money. And less time.'

'And they're making fun of us with that eeny meeny shit. What's the bet,' Scarlett said in a chilled voice, 'that the targets are more than an hour's travel away from here so we can't find them in time?'

Meyer's jaw tightened. 'We know the shortlisted buildings from what the Dutchman in Rome revealed. They've been swept already. There will still be security forces in those places regardless of what's happening here.'

'The terrorists will know that Vissier was picked up. They must know their original shortlist will have been revealed and have surely adapted their plans accordingly. They're ten steps ahead of us.' Devereau spoke urgently. 'What landmarks might be targeted that aren't on that shortlist but are more than an hour away?'

Meyer threw his hands up. 'There are lots of places! The fucking bombs could be anywhere!'

'Think,' Devereau hissed. 'Museums. Churches. What could be destroyed that would hurt Berliners the most?'

'I don't know!'

Konig lifted up her chin. 'How about the Oberbaum Bridge?'

Meyer stiffened. 'It's not a building.'

'No,' Konig agreed. 'But it has symbolic and economic importance. It formed part of the border between East and West Berlin. It's now seen as a symbol of unity for the entire city. Besides, why are we looking for a museum or a church? They're all closed now because of what happened at the Pantheon. Oberbaumbrucke makes more sense.'

'Except at most,' Meyer said, 'it's only twenty minutes from here.'

Scarlett looked at them both. 'Do you have any other ideas? Anywhere else that might be a target?'

'It's a needle in a haystack.' Meyer's shoulders slumped. 'One of the targets could be the Oberbaum. Who's to say? If we make a mistake, if we go to the wrong place …'

The gremlin, whose name Devereau still didn't know and who up until now, hadn't uttered a single word, interrupted. 'Look at the message,' he said. 'Read it again.'

It was Rosenfarben who spotted it first. 'Scheisse,' he spat. 'One of the targets is definitely Oberbaumbrucke,' he said. 'It has to be.'

'I don't …' Meyer paled. '*Schnick schnack schnuck.*'

Devereau blinked. 'Huh?'

'Instead of eeny meeny miny mo, the German demand is written as *schnick schnack schnuck.*'

'It's not a taunt,' Konig breathed. 'It's a clue. They *want* us to find one of the bombs. They want us to confirm they are not lying.'

Of course. He raised his eyes heavenward as he realised Konig had to be right. It was the only way they'd get their damned money. 'What's the clue?' Devereau demanded. 'What does it mean?'

'When we play rock paper scissors, sometimes in German we say schnick schnack schnuck.'

'So?' Scarlett asked.

'There's an art installation on Oberbaum bridge. A neon sign displaying –'

'Let me guess,' Devereau said, 'rock, paper, scissors.' His body tensed. 'Let's go. Now.'

* * *

THE OBERBAUM BRIDGE was only one location and the demands had stated there were three. In the absence of any other solid leads, however, there was no choice. Meyer, Scarlett and the other German vampires headed for the cars although, alas, they were not parked nearby. Rosenfarben and the taciturn gremlin spun towards the police who were coordinating the scene to demand their attention and tell them what they'd worked out. Konig, Devereau and the other two Berlin alphas didn't need to say a word to each other. They all knew what they had to do. In less than ten seconds, where once there had been five human shaped bodies, there were five werewolves. Some of the nearby humans let out cries of alarm; none of them paid them any attention, however. Let the humans wring their hands and panic. The werewolves were going to take control.

Mila Konig led the way. Devereau was almost twice her size and could have overtaken her with ease but this was her city - and besides, he didn't know the way. The only good thing was that once the Reichstag was behind them, the streets were clear of both people and traffic. The German police had already evacuated the nearby area and any and all traffic had been directed elsewhere. The small troupe of werewolves thundered down the Berlin roads, claws skittering on the cold ground. They ran like hell itself was after them and with such speed and urgency that it wasn't until the bridge itself came into sight that Devereau heard the squeal of sirens as the Berlin emergency services also hurled themselves towards the same spot.

It wasn't quite what Devereau had been expecting. For one thing, the bridge was built as some kind of double decker structure, with trains travelling across the top level and cars and pedestrians beneath. It was made out of some kind of striking red stone, which contrasted sharply with the nearby buildings and added to the dramatic effect. Not only that but the top half of the bridge looked more like a castle than a functional way of crossing the river which split Berlin in two. There were four small turrets stretching up from the centre. It was almost as if he'd suddenly found himself inside a fairy tale. At this point, however, a happy ending was looking increasingly unlikely.

While the other werewolves darted for the lower level, examining the arches and sniffing for bombs, Devereau scrabbled up to the railway line over their heads. A bomb up there would collapse the upper level of the bridge onto the road and pedestrians below and would be far more devastating. A ridge of fur bristled all the way down his spine, from the nape of his neck to his tail, and he could hear the blood rushing in his ears. Coming here to the bridge was a massive gamble regardless of what happened next.

There were shouts from below as police car after fire engine after ambulance appeared, their flashing lights creating an eerie strobe light effect. Satisfied that they would clear the bridge and keep the public away, Devereau focused on the job in hand. Keeping his paws well away from the electrified train tracks, he ran lightly down the length of the bridge, his eyes and nose focused on finding any indication of any sort of bomb. There was old graffiti, smears of oil and an abandoned wasp's nest. But no matter how hard he searched, he couldn't see anything that looked likely to explode. By the time he reached the other end of the bridge, others had joined him. The scene was swarming with werewolves, called no doubt by their three alphas, vampires and humans. He spotted several more pixies, scaling up the side of the bridge to examine every nook and cranny. He heaved in a breath. There was nothing here. There was no bomb. Angling his head downwards, he caught a glimpse of Scarlett's head. She felt his eyes on her and turned, looking upwards with a question in her eyes. He shook his head and she grimaced.

'There's nothing down here either,' she called, raising her

voice to make it heard about the clamour. 'Maybe this bridge isn't one of the targets after all.'

Maybe it wasn't. Or maybe the bastard terrorists had simply placed the bomb somewhere completely out of sight. Devereau leaned out further and gazed down at the river beneath. Slabs of ice were floating down it, passing from one side of the bridge to the other. The water looked treacherous – and bloody freezing. Devereau hissed under his breath. He was an idiot for thinking it. And he would definitely be an idiot for doing it. He glanced at Scarlett again. Her eyes widened as she realised what he was planning to do. She opened her mouth to shout something, but it was too late. Whatever she yelled was swallowed up in the wind and sirens and melee of other voices as Devereau soared out from over her head and plunged straight down into the icy water below.

The temperature was more of a shock than he'd anticipated, and the current was far stronger. He gasped as his head broke above the surface. Fuck, that was cold. And, yes, he was definitely an idiot. The only good thing was that apparently wolves were more than capable of swimming. He allowed the current to carry him under the bridge itself and then used the strength of his own body and limbs to remain there while he searched the arched underside. Someone with a small boat could have sailed under here and surreptitiously planted a bomb without anyone noticing. It wasn't beyond the realms of possibility.

Cold began to seep through his sodden fur and into his skin, leeching to his bones. He forced himself not to think about it. He had to find the fucking explosive. It had to be here.

Something caught his peripheral vision, something dark and misshapen that was caught against the side of one the massive pillars holding the bridge in place. Devereau quickly turned and swam towards it. Was it …?

No. It was simply a piece of driftwood wedged against the side of the bridge. His entire body was shivering now, fighting against the freezing water. He clenched his jaw. Further down perhaps. He had to look everywhere.

He swam hard, pushing against the current that was trying its hardest to pull him away from the Oberbaum and down river. The sheer energy it took to not be carried away exhausted him. He could do this, he told himself. He *had* to do this.

That was the exact moment when he saw it. It was on the underside of the bridge itself, perpendicular to the road above, and stuck to the very centre of the arch he was underneath. Beyond the odd Hollywood film, he'd never seen a bomb in person before. He knew that's what it was the moment he saw it, however, despite its lack of obvious ticking timer or red and blue wires. This was no piece of driftwood. He also knew, with a certainty that chilled him far more than the freezing water, that he couldn't reach it – not as a werewolf and not as a human. It had to be at least nine metres above his head. There was no way to climb up and cling on to the bricks. There was no way to reach the bomb. He possessed excellent climbing skills but he was no Spiderman and he couldn't defeat the laws of gravity. The only thing he could do was alert the others on the bridge above him.

'Devereau!'

It was Scarlett. He breathed out and swam towards the sound of her voice. His limbs felt heavy and sluggish but he had to do it. He had to reach her.

'Devereau!'

He emerged out from underneath the bridge and looked up to see her leaning out from the lower level of the bridge. When she saw him, her face went slack with relief and that alone gave him the surge to swim towards her. As soon as he was directly underneath, he forced himself to shift so he could speak. His body shook and shivered as he managed the transformation while almost entirely submerged in the river. The few seconds it took to change meant that he was dragged away by the current yet again. Cursing, he turned and swam for all his might until he could see Scarlett's pale face yet again.

'It's here!' he yelled through chattering teeth. 'It's underneath the third arch! I can't reach it, Scarlett. Without a boat, nobody can!'

'Get the fuck out of the water, you bloody stupid wolf!' she shouted back.

He managed a grin – but that was about it. Now that he no longer had the protection of his thick lupine fur, he knew he was in trouble. He didn't have the same strength to fight against the current and he certainly couldn't cope with the cold although, oddly, he no longer actually felt cold. Quite the opposite in fact. He suddenly felt very warm indeed. The tiny logical part of his brain that was still in working order told him that was a very bad thing. It meant hypothermia was setting in. He tried to summon up the energy to do something about it. It all seemed so hard though. And he was so very tired. Devereau closed his eyes and allowed himself to relax, just as something splashed down in the water beside him.

'This outfit,' Scarlett's voice said in his ear, 'is dry clean only. You owe me big time, buster.' Her arms went round his body and she began swimming away from the bridge and towards the shore, towing him with her as she went.

And then for some time after that, Devereau heard nothing at all.

CHAPTER TWENTY-SEVEN

THE HOT SWEET COCOA WHICH HAD BEEN THRUST INTO HIS HANDS
was like manna from heaven.

'You do realise, Mr Webb,' Sarah Greensmith said, with a
deeply disapproving look, 'that one of the reasons we recruited
you was your apparently high level of intelligence. In the last day
or so, you have not lived up to that in any way, shape or form.
Leaping into a freezing cold river at the height of a Berlin winter
was not a smart move.' She sniffed. 'We are not in the habit of
hiring martyrs.'

Scarlett pushed herself off the wall she was leaning against
and marched towards Greensmith, positioning herself between
her and Devereau. 'What's your fucking problem? You recruited
him. You pulled him into this with no training, no support and,
from what I can see, nothing but threats against him. You can't
lay all this shit on his shoulders! What are you doing to stop these
bastards? I've not seen one ounce of effort from you or anyone
else in MI5! I get that you're looking for somebody to blame but
we all know none of this is Devereau's fault. He's done a damned
sight more than anyone else has!'

Devereau blinked. The sudden warmth which was spreading

through him wasn't simply because of the syrupy hot chocolate. 'Why, Scarlett,' he croaked, 'I didn't know you cared.'

'Shut up, Devereau!'

Uh, okay then. He leaned back. Sarah Greensmith didn't glance at him; her steady gaze was focused entirely on Scarlett.

'Believe me, Miss Cook,' she said evenly, 'I have conveyed as much to my superiors. You should know that despite his foolishness, the German Chancellor has also privately expressed her gratitude to Mr Webb.'

'Well, that's wonderful,' Scarlett said, every word dripping with heavy sarcasm. 'That makes up for everything.'

'At least nobody died this time.'

Devereau sat up again. 'What happened?' he asked. 'Did the bridge …?' For some reason he couldn't quite form the words to complete the sentence.

'No, Mr Webb. After you confirmed the presence of the bomb, the German government did the unthinkable.'

'They paid the money?'

Greensmith's mouth downturned. 'They did indeed. Nothing exploded. It appears the devices were linked to mobile phones. One call was all it would have taken to trigger the explosives. The other two targets have been discovered. They're both high value buildings on the outskirts of the city. They are being made safe as we speak. There has been no loss of life and no damage to any property. But Berlin have played right into the terrorists' hands.'

'The alternative would have been much worse!' Scarlett shot back.

'This is what they wanted. They left that clue to the Oberbaum bridge because they wanted the bomb found before it blew up. Their end goal is to make money and that's exactly what they've done. You might think that paying them off is for the greater good but if you yield to one terrorist once, then they all think you'll do it again. It opens Germany up to terrible future atrocities. The only alternative left now is to hunt down everyone involved and make sure they never see the light of day. Unfortunately,' Greensmith added grimly, 'that may prove harder than it sounds. Avanopoulos has a lot of contacts. He could go to ground, change his face, hide himself away and we'll never see him again. It's highly unlikely he's no longer in Germany.'

'The Greek might not be the one pulling the strings,' Devereau told her. 'I know it looks that way and I know he very deliberately placed himself near the Reichstag. But I'm not convinced he's the ultimate boss.'

'Most analysts at MI5 think he's the most likely suspect. Solentino already had everything in place and ready to go. All Avanopoulos had to do was persuade everyone left that he could fill Solentino's shoes. If not Avanopoulos then who?'

'Alina Bonnet.'

Greensmith jerked. 'You have reason to believe she's still alive?'

'Nothing concrete. And I have nothing more than speculation as to her actual involvement in all this crap. But it's educated speculation and I can't shake the feeling that she's tied up with this far more than we realise.'

She pursed her lips. 'We did consider her. We've not blindly run towards Stefan Avanopoulos as terrorist boss numero uno. But almost nobody believes Alina Bonnet has the ability, the power or the damned cold-hearted viciousness to pull off such a thing. She doesn't have any form for this type of thing and she's likely already dead.'

Devereau shook his head. 'She's involved. I'm convinced of it. I don't have any proof but there was something about her …' He ground his teeth in frustration that he couldn't put his feelings about Solentino's supposed girlfriend into words. 'She shouldn't be underestimated.'

'That's as may be.' Greensmith raised her shoulders. 'There's no actual evidence to prove she's anything more than an unwilling participant, however. Or that she's even alive. Still, I will pass along your theory, however, and I'm not saying it doesn't have some merit. You realise that if Ms Bonnet is somehow part of it, we don't know where she is any more than we know where Avanopoulos is. We have been looking. Hard.'

'I suppose that's what happens when you're the handyman of the terrorist world. You've got contacts and unsavoury friends all over the place who can help you hide.' Devereau grimaced and stood shakily up to his feet. 'We don't know where they are but we know where they're going. Paris is next on the list. We need to get there now.'

'And do what?' Greensmith inquired. 'Find them how?'

'We came close this time,' Devereau growled. 'All we need is for the bastards to make one mistake and –'

He was interrupted by a ping from Greensmith's pocket. She slid out her phone and glanced down at the screen, her face suddenly turning several shades paler. 'I have to make a call,' she muttered. 'Don't go anywhere.' She turned on her heel and marched out of the door. That didn't bode well.

Devereau massaged the back of his neck. 'Where are we right now?' he asked Scarlett.

'Some kind of MI5 safe house near the centre of Berlin. I wanted a hospital but that Greensmith woman seemed to think it would be wiser to bring you somewhere anonymous to recover. Avanopoulos or Bonnet or whoever will be more than aware Vissier was picked up. They know their early plans are compromised.' She pointed at him. 'But it's likely that they still don't know you've been working against them all this time. She thought it was prudent to keep it that way. Just in case.' Scarlett gave him a meaningful look. 'We don't know what will happen next but you've been a damned sight more successful in getting close to those wankers than the rest of MI5 have been.' She tossed her head. 'Greensmith was right about something else too. Jumping into that river was a dick move, Devereau.'

Devereau caught her gaze and held it. 'You risked your own life by jumping in after me,' he said quietly.

Scarlett snorted. 'Hardly. I'm a vampire, remember? I'm pretty hardy. My kind doesn't tend to get hypothermia.'

'It was still dangerous.'

'You have my ring. If you sank to the bottom of the River Spree, then I'd likely never get it back.'

'Uh huh.' Devereau licked his lips, enjoying himself. 'Keep protesting, Scarlett. Keep pretending you don't care.'

Her dark eyes flashed. 'We've been through this already. I never said I didn't care.'

Devereau smiled.

The door re-opened and Sarah Greensmith walked back in. Her expression was tight and Devereau had the sense that her attention was elsewhere. 'I'll make arrangements to get you to London. Both of you this time.'

He opened his mouth to argue but she was already scowling at him.

'Don't piss me off, Mr Webb. This isn't up for negotiation. Not this time. Going to Paris isn't going to help. It turns out the bad guys are far, far smarter than any of us gave them credit for.'

Both Devereau and Scarlett stilled. 'What? What's happened?' he asked.

All of a sudden, Sarah Greensmith looked incredibly tired. 'They've made their next move and made it very public. They're asking for 3000 bitcoin from the British government in return for not bombing Paris. And they're demanding 3000 bitcoin from the French for not doing the exact same thing to London.'

* * *

IT WAS ALREADY DARK when Scarlett, Devereau and Sarah Greensmith boarded the military plane bound for London. Greensmith took herself away to the far corner, flipped open her laptop and began muttering to herself. Scarlett and Devereau sat further away, both of them with their shoulders slumped.

'It's clever,' Scarlett conceded.

Devereau grunted.

'If Paris pay up and London don't then Britain will forever be castigated as the villain. And vice-versa. They're using politics against the politicians and peer pressure to force both countries' hands. Hell, at this point they don't even need to plant any explosives. By making good on their threats up till now, they've done enough to get the money that they want by doing nothing more than asking for it.' She blew air out through her cheeks. 'What a shitshow.'

'They've not won yet.'

'I'm all for optimism, Devereau, but this is beginning to feel like a lost cause. We've been out-manoeuvred at every turn.'

'The Italians still have Vissier. Maybe he'll yet reveal something vital that we've missed. We have the shortlist of specific targets from him...'

Scarlett interrupted. 'We already know from what happened in Berlin that they're circumnavigating that shortlist. The information we have is useless. You know how many important buildings there are in both London and Paris. You know how much history and meaning is tied up in each one. To cover every single building and every single bridge is next to impossible. You could draft in the entire army from every corner of the world and it still might not be enough. It didn't work in Berlin. There's no reason to think it would work now.'

Devereau drummed his fingers. 'Maybe there's something else we're not thinking of.'

From the corner, Greensmith cleared her throat. '*Maybe* doesn't cut it. In the end, Mr Webb,' she said, 'you're really not James Bond. MI5 are not invincible and most certainly not infallible. And sometimes, sadly, the bad guys do win. We don't know where they are. We don't have any leads. If you can think of anything, by all means, let me know. But they could be in Paris. They could be in London. They could be fucking anywhere,' she said, swearing in front of him for the first time, 'and *we don't know where*. The clock is already ticking. London and Paris have until two o'clock in the morning to pay up.' She held up her watch. 'That's less than six hours from now. And this time the terrorists, whoever they truly are, have not provided any helpful clues to allow us to locate the bombs. Anything we do to stop them now is nothing more than a stab in the dark. It's only pure luck that will help us now and that's in short supply. They've already won.'

Sharp pain stabbed between his shoulder blades. No. She was wrong. There had to be something they could do. This was MI5 for goodness sake.

Something softened in Greensmith's expression. 'Don't get me wrong, we'll catch up to them eventually. It's simply not possible in this day and age to stay hidden forever. But it won't happen today. Today,' she said, gazing off into the distance, 'they win.'

He stared at her, watching the angular shadows of the plane flit across her face. 'No,' he said, 'I'm not going to accept that.'

'Then it'll end up destroying you,' she said simply.

'Not before you destroy me first.' There was more than a trace of bitterness to his tone.

Something flickered in her eyes. 'Despite what I said before, we won't actually blame you for any failures with this operation. Everything you have done this far has proven what an asset you can be and everyone at MI5 now appreciates that.'

Devereau genuinely doubted anyone at MI5 believed he was an asset. It didn't take a super spy to know that she was lying through her teeth.

Greensmith seemed to realise that herself and added lamely, 'You've done everything you could. Finding that device at the Oberbaum bridge will stand you in good stead. Consider yourself off the hook. You won't receive any blowback. On that part, I promise you. The Germans wouldn't stand for it.'

'Just as well,' Scarlett half snarled, 'because none of this is Devereau's fault.'

Greensmith merely gave her a wan smile.

'Somebody will need to be made the scapegoat,' Devereau said. 'Which poor bugger have you decided to pick on now?'

'As it turns out, Mr Webb, there are no shortage of candidates. Other governments have been involved and numerous other nationalities. Not to mention other people at MI5. It's a case of stick a pin into a map and come up with someone to blame. It shouldn't be too hard. They'll find someone.'

He shook his head. Unbelievable. 'They're going to pay the demands, aren't they? The British government will pay up.'

She sighed. 'I believe so. It's a mistake but it's far out of my own hands. We underestimated what these terrorists were capable of. And we will pay the price for that. Literally.' She turned her head and looked away from him. There was something she wasn't saying. He was sure of it. All of a sudden, Devereau realised what it might be.

'I was sent to investigate Solentino on my own,' he said. 'With only you as my guide. There was a limited budget. I've got no experience. And I'm a supe to boot. This was really nothing more than another test, wasn't it?'

Greensmith jerked. '*Another* test?'

Devereau smiled humourlessly. 'Yeah. Nobody at MI5 actually believed Christopher Solentino was a threat. He was on your radar. You knew something was up. But you never thought for a second that it would be something like this or that he could possibly be remotely successful. Sending me to Rome was merely a shot in the dark. You were sticking a pin in a map,' he said, turning her own words against her, 'and seeing what happened. If I fucked up, it didn't really matter. I'm just a werewolf. If I messed up, it would only prove the prejudices.'

Greensmith's eyes slid away.

'Bloody hell,' Scarlett breathed.

'I've always been on your side, Devereau,' Greensmith said.

Perhaps she had. Perhaps she hadn't. He chose not to challenge her on that for now. 'And the rest of MI5?' he asked. 'What about them?'

This time she didn't answer.

CHAPTER TWENTY-EIGHT

NONE OF THEM BREATHED A WORD FOR THE REST OF THE JOURNEY and, when they landed at RAF Northolt, which was far less appealing than Heathrow, there was a small contingent of grim looking men waiting for them at the end of the runway. Sarah Greensmith sighed audibly but Devereau forced himself to plaster on a smarmy grin.

'Hey! Which way to duty free?' he asked. 'I want to pick up some booze and fags before I head home.'

None of the men cracked a smile. That was understandable given the circumstances. The oldest man, a blank faced bloke with thinning hair and the hint of a paunch, lifted up his chin to speak. 'We will transport you back to your home, Mr Webb. You can expect a thorough debrief in the days to come.'

'I only like it when Scarlett here debriefs me.' He winked but his heart wasn't really in it.

The men still didn't smile. Neither did Scarlett come to that.

'Miss Cook will also be debriefed,' the older man said. 'In the meantime, we thank you both for your service to your country and we release you from any further obligations.'

Devereau's pathetic attempts at light-hearted banter vanished. 'That's it? You're giving me the boot?'

'We will take up the hunt for Stefan Avanopoulos from here. We are in a better position to find him.'

'I don't think Avanopoulos is the mastermind.'

The anonymous man barely reacted. 'I've heard your theory. You're talking about Alina Bonnet. It's very doubtful that she is still alive. She wouldn't have the means or the power to pull off an operation like this. Leave the strategy and analysis to us. We're better at it.'

Devereau bit back his anger at such blithe dismissal. 'I think you're under-estimating what she could be capable of.'

'Women rarely do this kind of thing.'

'Actually,' Greensmith broke in, 'that's not true. There are several studies which show –' She faltered in mid-sentence when the man gave her a cold look.

'Regardless, we have this now. You don't have to worry, Mr Webb. We are in charge now. You are done.' He jerked his head to the right. 'Your car is waiting over there.' He stepped aside, folding his hands together and waiting for Devereau and Scarlett to depart.

Devereau remained exactly where he was. His eyes swung from man to man before sliding to Greensmith. 'It's you,' he said quietly. 'You're going to be the scapegoat.'

'You should go, Mr Webb,' Greensmith said.

'You recruited me. You identified Solentino as a target. You ran the operation to infiltrate his little gang. *You* saw the threat. And now you'll be blamed.'

She gazed at him and, for the first time, Devereau thought he saw her mask slip. Beyond her brisk, no-nonsense façade, there was vulnerability. And rage. He knew that the latter wasn't directed at him, however, but at the blank faced men who were standing next to her. There was far more to Sarah Greensmith than he'd given her credit for.

'Go,' she repeated.

'And what if I don't?'

'You're not helping,' she said.

Scarlett moved up beside him and took his elbow. 'Devereau,' she murmured. 'Let's get out of here.'

'It's for the best,' Greensmith said. She bowed her head. 'You did good, Devereau Webb. Don't ever tell yourself otherwise. This is not on you.'

'Let's go, Ms Greensmith.' Two of the men moved up, each one taking one of her arms, as if they thought she was going to make a run for it and sprint across the airfield to get away from them.

Devereau gazed at them all in disgust. 'You people. You fucking people.'

* * *

THE MI5 DRIVER, who was as taciturn as his colleagues, dropped them off in the centre of Soho.

'The entire city is on alert looking for Stefan Avanopoulos,' Scarlett said to Devereau. 'And I'm fresh out of ideas. Unless you've had any brainwaves in the last hour that you've not told me, I don't think there's anything more we can do.'

He desperately wanted to disagree. He knew, however, that he couldn't. Sarah Greensmith had been right. The bad guys were about to win. He gave Scarlett a tight nod and looked away.

'Heart will be too busy right now,' Scarlett said. 'I'm not in the mood for people but I don't want to go home to sit alone and I have no idea what I'll say to Lord Horvath right now. I know a little place near here. Do you feel like a drink before you head home?'

The last thing Devereau was going to do was say no. He nodded once more before allowing her to lead him away from the busier streets and down a small alleyway. The only sign there was a bar there at all was a small mark etched into the stone on the outside wall. Scarlett pushed open the door and he followed her in, glad that she'd been right. It was smoky and dark and seemed to sell only a very limited selection of drinks. The place was perfect.

They sat together in the corner by the door, neither saying very much. The bartender, a grizzled looking vampire who had more scars than teeth, had taken one look at their faces and given them an entire bottle along with two empty glasses. Then he'd retreated to his spot behind the narrow bar and paid them no more attention.

Devereau downed three glasses of whiskey in short succession. He was tired enough that the alcohol went straight to his head, loosening his tongue and releasing a great deal of his pent-up tension.

'I can't get those two choir boys out of my head,' he said as much to himself as to Scarlett.

'Yeah.' She took a sip of her own drink. 'I'm much the same. I've been over and over it though. I don't know what we could have done differently.' She put her hand on his and squeezed. 'It's not your fault, Devereau. None of it is.'

He gave her a baleful look. Several seconds passed as they gazed at each other, the silence of their shared experiences over the last few days hanging heavily between them.

Eventually, Devereau sucked in a deep breath. 'I miss you, Scarlett.'

She stiffened and pulled her hand away. 'Don't go there, Devereau.'

'Why not? We're good together. We *fit* together. No, I don't know your deepest ambitions or desires. I'm willing to take the time to find out though. Together we could be anything. *Do* anything.'

'Apart from stop a terrorist group in their tracks, you mean.'

Damn it. He couldn't stop himself from wincing.

'Sorry,' she muttered. 'That was facetious and uncalled for.' She pressed her lips together. 'You're asking for more than I'm able to give, Devereau. We had fun while it lasted. Can't you leave it at that?'

'No,' he said honestly. 'I can't.' He met her eyes. 'But what I can do and will do is wait until you're ready. For whatever reasons, you're terrified of commitment. I don't know what happened to you to make you feel that way but you can trust me to the grave. If it takes the rest of my life to get you to see that, then that's what I will do. I was yours the day you sat down beside me in Heart. I'm not going anywhere, Scarlett. Not now. Not ever.'

'You know you sound like a crazed stalker, right?' she said. Her tone was light but her eyes were guarded. She wasn't with him yet. Not by a long shot.

'I meant what I said that first night in Rome. I won't touch you unless you ask me to. I won't make a move on you unless you do first.'

'Then what the hell do you call this?' she asked, gesturing towards him with a touch of flame.

'My feeble attempt to get you to see that I'm in love with you, I guess.'

Scarlett stared at him. 'I'm not the type of woman that men fall in love with,' she said finally. There was a tiny tremble in her voice. 'I'm the type they lust after. The type they think they've fallen for until they realise who I really am behind the gloss.' She curled her fingers into tight fists. 'I'm the type who won't let a man take my independence or my freedom.'

'I'm not asking for either of those things. I wouldn't want them.'

'You don't want me either, Devereau. You might think you do because right now I'm the shiny thing that you think is playing hard to get. I'm not a conquest though. I like you. I'm pretty sure I've made it clear on more than one occasion that I fancy the pants off of you. But that's not love. I don't love you. And you definitely don't love me.'

All he could tell her was the stark, absolute truth. 'Yes,' he said simply. 'I do.'

'Then you're a bigger fool than I thought you were.'

This wasn't going particularly well. He grimaced and felt his stomach tighten unpleasantly. 'I'm going to go to the restroom and re-group,' he told her. 'Don't go anywhere, Scarlett. Please.'

In response, she picked up her glass and took another delicate sip although she didn't look him in the eye. And when he returned to their table several minutes later with the newly sanitised Ring of All Seasons in his hand, she'd already gone.

Devereau headed straight for the door, sticking his head out to the narrow street to search for her.

'Scarlett!'

His voice echoed back at him. Damn it. There was no sign of her in either direction and he knew that if she didn't want him to find her, he wouldn't be able to. He supposed that was one thing – the only thing – she had in common with those fucking terrorists. Devereau paused and turned his head, glancing round at the bar.

'What time is it?' he asked.

The bartender looked up. Then he grunted and pointed up at the clock on the wall. Devereau stared at it. It was after two in the morning. There had been no distant explosions of any kind. 'Can you turn on the TV?' he asked.

The bartender sighed but did as he requested, lifting up a dusty remote and pressing a button. The television set, hanging precariously off the far wall, flickered into life.

'If you're just tuning in,' the news anchor intoned, 'we are getting several reports that both the French and British governments have agreed to meet the terrorists' demands. A spokesperson stated that it was a highly unusual step but that it was warranted under the circumstances and that they were confident they could recover the money and locate the terrorists within days if not hours.'

Bullshit. Devereau knew a blatant lie when he heard one. He reached down for his whiskey glass and threw it with all his might at the far wall. It shattered instantly, shards of glass flying across the small room.

The bartender didn't blink. 'Feel better now?' he inquired.

Devereau's shoulders slumped. No. Not in the slightest.

* * *

HE AWOKE in his own bed the next morning with a headache throbbing behind his eyes and a nasty taste in his mouth. Devereau groaned and flipped over onto his back, just as a sharp knock came at his bedroom door.

'I make breakfast,' Dr Yara called. 'Eggs and bacon. Will do you good.'

His stomach rolled. He doubted it. 'Thank you,' he called back anyway. Where Dr Yara was concerned, it was far better to give in to the inevitable rather than attempting to argue.

Shrugging on a dressing gown, he padded downstairs. 'You don't have to cook for me,' he told her. It was an old argument.

'I know.' She waved at him, her eyes indicating that she wouldn't brook any kind of disagreement. 'Now eat.'

'I thinking while you are away,' she told him. 'I like to set up clinic. I know I am not allowed to be doctor here but maybe if I work only for supes it is okay. Supes will be happy to have doctor and government will not care because I do not treat humans.'

He reached for a slice of toast. 'That's a really good idea.'

She beamed at him. 'You think?'

'I do.' The vampires and the clans had their own medical teams but the smaller supe groups find it much harder to get treatment. Not to mention that such a thing would be much better for Dr Yara than cooking him breakfast. 'Let's sit down together later and discuss how it could work. I'll do whatever I can to help you set it up.'

She widened her eyes. 'Oh no. You too busy. I can do it myself.'

'I'm not busy,' he told her. He sighed. 'Not any more.'

'Is full moon again soon,' she reminded him.

How could he forget? 'Yeah.' Life went on. He should be pleased.

From the other room, the landline began to ring. Devereau began to get to his feet but Dr Yara glared at him. 'You stay. You eat. I answer phone.'

He gave her a mock salute and picked up his knife and fork. Then it occurred to him that maybe it was Scarlett calling and he quickly placed them down on the table again and sprang up.

'Is for you!' Dr Yara called through.

He all but sprinted to the living room. 'Hello?' he said into the receiver.

'Good morning, Mr Webb.'

Devereau's heart sank. 'Greensmith. I didn't think I'd hear from you again.'

'You probably won't after today,' she told him. 'I'm not supposed to be calling you now but everyone else is busy and not paying attention to what I'm doing. And I still have some friends who are on my side.'

He tensed. 'What?' he asked. 'What is it?'

'I have some new information that I thought you'd want to hear before ends up on the national news.'

He tensed. 'Go on.'

'After an anonymous phone call, the remains of Stefan Avanopoulos, along with several others, were discovered early this morning in a farmhouse not far from London. It appears they died as a result of some kind of unfortunate accident.'

Devereau remained perfectly still. 'What do you mean?'

'Somehow, Avanopoulos blew himself up with one of his own bombs. By all accounts it's very messy and there are no survivors.'

He sucked in a sharp breath. 'Alina Bonnet?'

'It does not look like there are any female casualties.' Greensmith paused. 'And from what I've heard, there's nothing to be found which might allow either France or Britain to recover the bitcoin they sent mere hours ago.'

'How very convenient,' he murmured.

'Indeed,' she said drily. 'The manhunt to find those responsible for all that has occurred would have been unprecedented. Four separate countries were involved. The entire international community would have been searching for those terrorists. Despite their success thus far, they would have been located eventually. Now they're dead, no-one will be searching. Avanopoulos's unexpected death has saved everyone a great deal of time, hassle and money.'

'It was very thoughtful of him to die at this particular moment then. And for someone to phone it in too.'

'Oh yes,' she said, 'it's all very caring. We didn't recover our money but the bad guys didn't get away and we can all relax now.' She sniffed. 'Go us. It will be publicised as our great success rather than a horrific failure and, because of the optics, nobody will stop to question the dramatic coincidence that Avanopoulos blew himself up mere hours after achieving his goals.'

Devereau chewed on his bottom lip. 'You know, you are thoughtful and caring too.'

'I am?'

'Yep. You kept me out of German hospital last night. You kept my involvement secret from the world at large. And you're calling me now.'

'Don't thank me for that,' Greensmith said. 'I understand the same as you,' she told him bitterly, 'how it feels to be left out in the cold from your own operation. This is an entirely selfish phone call.'

Devereau smiled to himself. His headache had all but gone. 'Yes. I suppose it is.'

'I take back what I said before, Mr Webb. You're more intelligent than I'd realised. Than any of us realised. Trust that furry gut of yours. I strongly suspect your theories about the truth of this entire operation are right.'

He envisioned Alina Bonnet for a moment. 'We underestimate others only at our own peril.'

'Then we understand each other, Mr Webb. Good luck.' And with that she hung up.

CHAPTER TWENTY-NINE

IIT WAS ALL ABOUT USING THE RIGHT LURE IN THE RIGHT WAY.
There was only one thing which Devereau had that might work.
It was a gamble and it might all come to naught. But he had
nothing to lose. He swallowed down the last of his breakfast and
made several phone calls. By the time he was finished and heard
the burble from the television set in the next room, the news was
already filtering through to the world at large.

Devereau wandered through. Dr Yara was watching the
screen with wide eyes.

The newscaster's expression was bright. 'A spokesperson for
British security services told us that the events which occurred in
the early hours of this morning will serve as an important
deterrent to anyone who thinks they can threaten the security of
either our country or our European neighbours.'

He snorted to himself. Yeah. The PR machine was already in
full swing. If he was right about Alina Bonnet, however, the real
culprit behind all the bombs and threats was still at large.

'Plans are already underway for an inquiry into the security
failings which led to this point,' the newscaster continued. 'The
Prime Minister has said that he will give it his full backing.'

There it was. If he wasn't going to be pinpointed as the reason why the terrorists weren't stopped earlier, then there was no doubt that any inquiry would land blame squarely at Sarah Greensmith's feet instead. Somebody had to be the fall guy. Stefan Avanopoulos fitted that bill for the terrorists. Greensmith would play the same role for MI5. Devereau shook his head. The powers that be would allow themselves to believe that everything was over and done with and wrapped up in a neat little bow. He knew differently – and if he played his cards right, he'd prove that knowledge to the rest of the world.

'You is angry,' Dr Yara observed. She gestured to his hands. He glanced down, noting the fur which had sprouted across his skin.

'Yes,' Devereau said. 'I'm angry.' A ghost of a smile crossed his face. 'But I'm not done yet either.'

* * *

THE FIRST PHONE call came at midday.

'I've got a buyer for you.'

Devereau's hand tightened round the phone. 'Go on.'

'A Russian guy. He's bought similar items in the past. He'll give you two million in cash no questions asked.'

'Not interested.'

'It's a good offer.'

'Nope.'

'You have something against Russians?'

He shrugged. 'Let's just say I'm picky.'

The speaker on the other end of the line sighed. 'Suit yourself.'

By the end of the day, Devereau had fielded three more similar calls. There was an English businessman was well known for purchasing expensive works of art with dubious histories who offered one point five. An Irish company were prepared to hand over one million and the deeds to a large house on the outskirts of Dublin. An upstart hereditary Lord with investments in various diamond mines put another two million on the table. Devereau politely declined them all.

'You're not making my life very easy.'

'Easy is over-rated,' Devereau answered.

'If we could open bids up to supes, you'd make more money.'

'No.' He was adamant. 'No supes. I told you already. I don't want a single supe anywhere to hear so much as a whisper about what I'm selling.'

'Everything I've brought you so far is a genuine offer. The buyers are known to me personally. You could be quids in.'

He remained unruffled. 'Let's wait for now. I'll know the right offer when I hear it.'

The broker grumbled. 'You didn't used to cause me these many headaches.'

'Bear with me. It'll be worth it,' Devereau promised.

'Yeah, yeah.'

'Are you sure you're feeling alright? I don't hear from you for months. Then when I do, you're acting like some kind of lunatic. I know you turn furry these days but I didn't think you'd turn into an idiot as well as a damned werewolf.'

'There's method to my madness.'

'Whatever.'

He hung up. Devereau massaged the back of his neck. If he'd gotten into the business of stealing and selling magical rings before he'd become a werewolf, he'd have been a very rich man indeed. Regret twanged at him. As much as it pained him to decline so many lucrative offers, he had to be patient. It was early days. This might still work.

The last call came a few minutes after midnight. Dr Yara had long since loped off to her bed. Devereau was lying on the shabby sofa in the living room and dozing off himself. He wiped away the line of drool from the side of his mouth and answered.

'Alright.' The broker's voice was heavy. 'I know what you're going to say but hear me out. I've got someone who's willing to pay around one point five. I know we've had higher offers and this one is only for cryptocurrency but when it's converted to sterling –'

He sat bolt upright. 'Bitcoin?'

'Yes. She said she can transfer it to any online account of your choosing. You might prefer to be old-fashioned and receive cold, hard cash. I'm the same. There's a lot to be said for this internet shit though.' From the way the broker spoke, he was unconvinced, despite his attempt to persuade Devereau otherwise.

'Make the trade.'

There was a beat of silence. 'You're sure?'

A slow self-congratulatory smile spread across Devereau's face. 'I'll be at the pub on Bell Street in the East End at midday tomorrow to hand it over.'

'It's almost the Winter Solstice. Don't you want to wait another day and see for yourself if this daft ring even works?'

Devereau grinned. 'Accept the offer, make the trade,' he repeated. 'This is exactly what I want.'

* * *

Devereau pushed open the door to the grubby pub at two minutes past twelve. The bartender glanced up, his eyes widening in alarm as he registered who had just walked in. The white haired woman in the corner was already getting up to her feet.

'Get out of here, you mangy dog,' she hissed.

Devereau ignored her and strode up the bar. 'Pint of beer,' he ordered. There was no sign of Ronnie Hitchens. But then that was probably a good thing.

The bartender's gaze flicked to the woman then back to him. 'I don't think –'

The pub door opened again. Devereau's nostrils twitched but

he didn't turn round. 'Just pour the drink,' he growled. 'And don't try and slip anything in it this time.'

There was the click of high heels. A moment later, Alina Bonnet appeared by his side. 'Well, well, well,' she drawled. 'This is an interesting establishment.' She looked round, taking in the old woman and the bartender and obviously dismissing both of them as threats.

'It might be a little less salubrious than what you're used to,' Devereau answered. 'And it's not the sort of place where someone as rich as you would want to spend their time.' He watched the bartender as he placed the foaming drink in front of him. 'But it has its charms. What would you like to drink?'

'A glass of dry white wine.'

The bartender stared at her.

'You don't serve wine?' She rolled her eyes. 'Prosecco?'

'We're not that kind of place.'

Alina sniffed. 'Apparently. I'll have a glass of water then. No ice.'

The bartender reached for a smudged glass and filled it up with tap water before putting it down in front of her. Both Alina and Devereau looked at it.

'There's something floating in that water,' she said faintly. 'Tell you what. I'll go without.' She sniffed and turned round, her eyes falling on a nearby table and chairs. 'Shall we sit?'

Devereau gestured. 'Ladies first.'

She did as he suggested. Devereau took the chair opposite and leaned back. He had to admit that she looked good. Her eyes were clear, her appearance was immaculate and, when he delicately sniffed the air, he could scent nothing beyond confident pleasure emanating from her. Alina Bonnet was not suffering from any sleepless nights or traces of guilt about what she'd done. Far from it.

'If you know I'm rich, Mr Webb, then you know what I've done.'

Devereau didn't miss a beat. 'I've been following the news. I know what happened to Solentino. Given what he'd already implied about his upcoming plans, it doesn't take a genius to work out what happened next.' He met her gaze. 'Does it bother you that I know?'

She crossed her legs. 'Not particularly. You've not told that vampire of yours, have you?'

'She's not like us. She wouldn't understand.'

Alina permitted herself a small smile. 'I knew you of all people would get it. Christopher did too. It's why he was so willing to bring you on board in the first place.' Her eyes gleamed. 'The pursuit of wealth is a glorious thing.'

For the briefest moment, Devereau had a flashback to the Pantheon, and two young boys dressed covered in blood and dust and pain. 'Indeed,' he murmured. 'Indeed.'

'I tried to keep you out of it, you know. I persuaded Christopher to let you go so you wouldn't be there when everything went down. It was thanks to me that you weren't present.' She licked her lips, enjoying the memory. 'If you'd been in the apartment, you'd have met the same fate as he did. I liked you and I wanted to spare you that sort of ending.'

Possibly. But it was more likely the prospect of a werewolf and a vampire had been too much and she'd done what she could to keep both him and Scarlett out of the way. Alina had needed to control the situation. Two powerful supes would not have aided her cause in any way.

'In that case,' he answered aloud, 'I should thank you.'

'Yes,' she said. 'You certainly should.'

He reached across the table and took her hand before lifting it to his lips. 'Thank you,' he murmured, pressing his mouth to her skin with slow, deliberate languidity.

Alina couldn't stop herself from shuddering in delight, although whether it was his open gratitude or the feeling of his lips on her hand, he wasn't sure.

'What you accomplished in that apartment,' he said, 'was so very impressive. Did you kill them all yourself?'

She laughed slightly. 'Do you think I'm afraid of getting my hands dirty? Of course I did. At the end of the day, the only person I can truly trust is myself. Those idiots didn't see it coming for a second. To them I was nothing more than Solentino's bit of fluff. But I showed them all.'

'You certainly did.' Devereau injected the right amount of admiration into his voice. 'And leaving your own blood at the scene was a particularly deft touch.'

'That wasn't just for you although it helped that your fangy friend had drunk from me earlier. I was painting a picture for the world to see. Christopher already had everything in place and ready to go, you see. It didn't matter if he was alive or dead. Everything was set up and the rest of our people in Rome, Berlin, Paris and London were ready to go. They wanted to be paid and they didn't care who paid them.'

'Solentino didn't die easily.'

'I wanted everyone to think he'd been forced to give up the information that I already knew.'

Devereau watched her. He knew that wasn't the real reason Solentino had been tortured. It was only the excuse. Maybe part of the reason had been to pay him back for the way he'd treated her but Devereau suspected that mostly Alina had just enjoyed it. The cold light in her eyes suggested it.

'You let Vissier go.'

'Gee was weak. Plus, I knew what he knew. There was no doubt that sooner or later, he would be arrested and he would give up every detail of our plans. I wanted every government to know I was coming for them. It was perfect misdirection and the best way to get what I wanted. Gee Vissier was under my control at every moment.' She shrugged casually. 'And I had a bit of a soft spot for him. I didn't need him to die.'

'What about Stefan Avanopoulos?'

Alina actually giggled. 'Oh, he was so very pliable. I knew Bartan wouldn't accept me taking over if Solentino died so I persuaded Avanopoulos to get on board instead. He killed Bartan for me and then stepped up with barely a moment's pause. Stefan was *so* very helpful. And I needed someone to take the blame. I'd never get away with the money otherwise. It was really very easy to rig one more bomb up and get rid of Stefan and the others at the end.'

She really was very pleased with herself. 'You planned for everything,' Devereau said.

'Everything apart from this.' She gazed at him. 'I'm supposed to be the only one left who knows the truth. But now there's also you.' She paused. 'Do you have the Ring of All Seasons with you?'

'Why do you want it now? You've achieved everything you wanted.'

'I told you when we first met,' she said almost dreamily, 'that ring is power.'

Devereau raised his shoulders. 'In that case,' he said, 'here you go.' He reached into his pocket and drew the ring out, placing it in the centre of the table between them.

Greed lit her face. 'You're a good man, Devereau Webb,' Alina said. 'And a very stupid one.' Her hand dropped under the table, delving into the bag she'd left by her feet.

The air to Alina's right shimmered. She barely had time to raise the gun to chest height when something smacked into her arm, forcing her to drop it.

'That's the second time I've been called stupid inside this pub,' Devereau said, 'and it's not any more true on this occasion than it was last time.'

The air shimmered again, coalescing into the familiar shape of Tatton O'Brien. With near lightning speed, he bent down and scooped the gun up before backing away and inspecting it.

'Fully loaded,' he said. 'With silver bullets. What was the plan, lovie? Put one of these babies in poor Devereau's head, take out the barman and the old woman and run for the hills?'

Alina's face twisted into a vicious snarl. Then she lunged towards the leprechaun, flipping the table and sending the Ring of All Seasons, Devereau's barely touched pint and several sticky coasters flying in all directions. O'Brien laughed and danced out of her reach. Devereau spun and grabbed her by the shoulders, hauling her back. 'Give it up, Alina. You're done.'

'Fuck you.' She rammed her elbows into his midriff. Devereau gasped but didn't let go. Then, however, she reached for her belt and, seemingly from nowhere, produced a knife she'd had concealed under top. In one swift movement, she twisted the blade and arced it round, slicing deeply into Devereau's forearm. His blood splattered across the sticky pub floor and he released her.

She twisted her head left then right, assessing the situation. 'You bastard,' she hissed. 'Devereau fucking Webb. Who are you really?'

From the doorway at the back of the pub, the one which led down to the basement, a voice appeared. 'That furry fucker's one of us.'

They all turned. It was Ronnie Hitchens, holding a gun of his own. He was pointing it steadily towards Alina's head.

She screamed in rage and ran at him. He loosed off a single shot. Alina screamed again as the bullet slammed into her upper arm, throwing her off balance. She wasn't giving up yet, however. She staggered forward, still clutching the knife, and reached for the old woman to use her as a shield. 'I'm walking out of here,' she spat. 'Lower your gun or this old biddy gets it.' She wrapped her injured arm round the woman's waist and pressed the blade against her throat.

Nobody moved. Alina glared at Ronnie and, with obvious reluctance, he lowered his gun. Then she swung her head towards O'Brien. He looked at Devereau.

'Put it down,' Devereau said quietly.

'Yeah,' Alina sniped. 'Do what the wolf says.'

O'Brien's eyes flashed but he too lowered the muzzle of the gun. Alina smiled nastily and began dragging the old woman to the door. The bartender twitched. Devereau shook his head at him.

'Don't,' he said.

Alina smirked. Then, with the woman pressed tightly against her, she kicked the door open and disappeared.

'Well, this is a fecking shitshow,' O'Brien muttered.

Devereau grimaced. Then he sprinted out after Alina.

She hadn't gotten very far. She was curled into a ball in the middle of the pavement. The white haired woman was holding the knife and frowning at it while two werewolves, both in animal form and both with their jaws snapping, flanked Alina on either side. The smaller wolf growled, her fur bristling.

'It's alright, Martina,' Devereau murmured. 'You can stand down.'

The young werewolf immediately relaxed.

'Good work,' Devereau said. 'You didn't let her get far at all.' He peered down at Alina's body. 'You've not hurt her much, have you? We need her alive.'

The second werewolf blinked, transforming into his human form. 'Wasn't us, boss,' Morty said. 'It was the old lady that did that.'

The old lady in question glared at Morty and his now naked body. 'For goodness sake,' she said. 'Put that away. This is a respectable neighbourhood and we have appearances to maintain.'

To Devereau's genuine surprise, Morty blushed brick red and used his hand to cover his groin.

'Are you alright, ma'am?' Ronnie Hitchens asked, appearing in the doorway.

'Of course I am,' she snapped. 'It's a cold day in hell when someone like that gets the better of me.' She stared at them. 'Well, come on then! Get her inside before somebody sees! I'm quite sure the cavalry is already on its way.'

'They've been called,' Hitchens said, picking up Alina and backing into the pub. She was quite clearly out for the count.

Devereau scratched his head, still not entirely sure what had happened. 'Uh …'

'I suppose, young man, you thought you were being clever by bringing her here,' the woman said to him. With some distaste, she dropped the knife to the ground. 'Well,' she continued, 'you were. It was a clever move. I heard the entire conversation.' She held her hand out. 'As you may have guessed, I work for the same outfit as you do. You can call me Em.'

'M?'

She gritted her teeth. 'Em. Short of Emma.'

Devereau nodded and tried to suppress his smirk. 'Sure. Nice to meet you, M.' Then he bowed. It seemed the right thing to do.

CHAPTER THIRTY

Six days later

DEVEREAU SHIFTED UNCOMFORTABLY on the park bench. It was a bitterly cold day and he was certain that snow was beckoning. Given all that he'd achieved, he'd been sure that he at least he could graduate to being allowed to meet in a coffee shop instead of a frozen park.

'Happy Christmas.'

Sarah Greensmith eyed him. 'It's not quite Christmas yet. And if this is where you produce a perfectly wrapped present, know that I didn't buy you anything and that I bloody hate Christmas.'

'Yeah,' Devereau said, 'all that peace on earth and goodwill to all men stuff is rather tiring, isn't it?'

She gave him a long look. 'In any case, thank you for putting a word in for me with the higher-ups,' she told him. 'It is appreciated. My present is that I get to keep my job.'

'Maybe we'll both be treated with a bit more respect from now on,' Devereau said.

She smiled slightly. 'Stranger things have happened.'

He grunted.

'You should know,' Greensmith told him, 'that we have recovered almost all of the money which Alina Bonnet accrued from the German, French and British governments. She was persuaded to return it all and she is being … taken care of. I doubt we'll be seeing or hearing from her ever again.'

'I'm glad to hear it.'

'Roughly one and a half million pounds are still missing. It looks like that amount was transferred to an online bitcoin wallet shortly before you met Ms Bonnet in the Bell Street pub. You wouldn't know anything about what happened to that money, would you, Mr Webb?'

He blinked innocently. 'Not a clue.'

'Hmmm.' Greensmith gave him a pointed frown but didn't pursue it further. 'Well, in any case, you're being lauded across MI5 for your actions. I do believe that going forward, you will have your pick of assignments. I could be persuaded to continue working with you now that I'm no longer being thrown under the bus.' She shrugged awkwardly and looked away. 'It's up to you.'

He didn't hesitate. 'I'd be delighted.'

Greensmith only just managed to mask her smile. 'As you wish,' she said blandly. 'But don't think that being a maverick hero will give you carte blanche from here on. You still need to work on being a team player.'

'I'll do my best,' Devereau promised her. 'Scout's honour.'

'I do not believe for one second, Mr Webb, that you were ever a Boy Scout.'

He raised three fingers to his eyebrow. 'Dib dib dib.'

Greensmith gave him a disbelieving sniff. 'If you say so.' She held out her hand. 'Now,' she said briskly. 'Hand it over.'

'Hand what over?'

'The Ring of All Seasons. We know it fell to the floor when Ms Bonnet attempted to escape. We've searched for it but we can't find it. It's potentially a powerful object that could do a great deal of good.'

'It doesn't belong to MI5,' he said gently.

'It doesn't belong to you either, Mr Webb.'

He held up his hands. 'I don't have it.'

'Hmmm.' She gave him a hard look. 'Hmmm. If I'm not mistaken, it was the Winter Solstice last night. If someone were to put on a magical ring that told the future and they saw something that related to their job perhaps or the safety of their country, then I would expect that someone to pass that sort of information on.'

'I am sure,' Devereau agreed, 'that someone would indeed do that.' He paused. 'If that were the case.'

Greensmith gave him a long look. 'Very well, Mr Webb.' She stood up and slid her hands into her pockets. 'I'm sure I'll be seeing you again very soon.'

Devereau grinned. 'I'll look forward to it.'

* * *

THE FANGED BOUNCERS outside Heart did not look very pleased to see him. 'You,' the nearest one growled. 'We have told you before. You need to stop coming here.'

'I only need to speak to Scarlett. Once I've done that, I will indeed stop coming here.'

'She doesn't want to see you. So fuck off.'

There was a brief whine and both bouncers tilted their heads, their expressions darkening. Devereau felt himself relax. Someone was talking to them through their tiny earpieces. He reckoned he knew who. It was about time.

'She'll meet you at the bar,' the bouncer told him with heavy reluctance. 'But don't try any funny business, wolf.'

'We all know that Scarlett could take us all down if she wanted to. I don't think you've got anything to worry about.' He patted the vampire on the shoulder and wandered into the club, pretending that he didn't feel relieved she was agreeing to meet him.

There was already a glass of whiskey waiting for him on the bar top. The bartender gave him a nod and moved away to a discreet distance. A moment later, Scarlett glided into view. She didn't smile. She didn't say hello.

'You took Alina Bonnet down and you didn't contact me, Devereau. I should have been there too. I deserved to be there too.'

'You walked out on me.'

Her expression was stony. 'So you were punishing me by keeping me out of the way?'

'No. If she'd glimpsed you, she'd have run a mile. She threatened London and you'd already made it clear how you feel about this city. I had to make her believe I was on her side for as long as I possibly could. I wasn't trying to shut you out. I was trying to catch a terrorist.' He hesitated. 'But I am sorry you weren't there to see it. Truly.'

Scarlett glared at him. 'Don't fucking do it again.'

'Does that mean you'll work with me again?'

She didn't answer. Instead, she folded her arms. 'Is that why you're here? You wanted to apologise? Because if you're here because you think that another stupid declaration of love is going to make me melt into your arms and then we'll waltz off into the sunset together, you are sadly mistaken.'

The walls she'd built around her heart were very high indeed. 'That's not why I'm here. I came to bring you a present. It is nearly Christmas after all.' He took out the small velvet lined box and held it out to her.

'What?' she asked with the edge of a taunt. 'You're not going to get down on one knee?'

He watched her carefully, hoping his expression didn't give him away. 'Are you disappointed that I'm not?'

Scarlett snorted. 'Don't be ridiculous.' She took the little box from him and flipped it open. Then she stared at the Ring of All Seasons for a moment. 'The Winter Solstice was yesterday, Devereau. The ring is all but useless for another year.'

'That's assuming it even works at all.'

'You mean to tell me you didn't put it on last night to see?'

Devereau grinned and tapped the side of his nose, indicating his lips were sealed. 'Would you like to go out for dinner tonight?'

'No.'

'Tomorrow night?'

'No.'

'Wednesday?'

Scarlett muttered something under her breath. 'That's Christmas Eve.'

'I'm free if you are.'

Something passed across her eyes. 'Fine. But only because I have to eat. Not for any other reason.'

'I wouldn't dream of thinking otherwise.' Devereau doffed an imaginary cap and took a moment to gaze at her. Of course he'd tried the Ring of All Seasons last night. He'd have been a fool not to. There was only one flickering image that he'd seen, emerging in front of him like a leprechaun with a Candy Crush addiction. It had been Scarlett, smiling at him like the happiest vampire in the world. And she'd been dressed in white with a veil.

'What?' she asked suspiciously. 'Why are you looking at me like that?'

'No reason.' He gave her another smile. 'See you soon, Scarlett.' Then he downed the whiskey and walked away. He glanced over his shoulder as he reached the exit and caught her staring at his arse before she hastily turned away.

Devereau's smile broadened until it stretched from ear to ear. The future looked very bright indeed.

ABOUT THE AUTHOR

After teaching English literature in the UK, Japan and Malaysia, Helen Harper left behind the world of education following the worldwide success of her Blood Destiny series of books. She is a professional member of the Alliance of Independent Authors and writes full time, thanking her lucky stars every day that's she lucky enough to do so!

Helen has always been a book lover, devouring science fiction and fantasy tales when she was a child growing up in Scotland.

She currently lives in Devon in the UK with far too many cats – not to mention the dragons, fairies, demons, wizards and vampires that seem to keep appearing from nowhere.

The *WolfBrand* series

Devereau Webb is in uncharted territory. He thought he knew what he was doing when he chose to enter London's supernatural society but he's quickly discovering that his new status isn't welcome to everyone.

He's lived through hard times before and he's no stranger to the murky underworld of city life. But when he comes across a young werewolf girl who's not only been illegally turned but who has also committed two brutal murders, he will discover just how difficult life can be for supernaturals - and also how far his own predatory powers extend.

Book One – The Noose Of A New Moon

Book Two - Licence To Howl

The complete *Blood Destiny* series

"A spectacular and addictive series."

Mackenzie Smith has always known that she was different. Growing up as the only human in a pack of rural shapeshifters will do that to you, but then couple it with some mean fighting skills and a fiery temper and you end up with a woman that few will dare to cross. However, when the only father figure in her life is brutally murdered, and the dangerous Brethren with their predatory Lord Alpha come to investigate, Mack has to not only ensure the physical safety of her adopted family by hiding her apparent humanity, she also has to seek the blood-soaked vengeance that she craves.

Book One - Bloodfire

Book Two - Bloodmagic

Book Three - Bloodrage

Book Four - Blood Politics

Book Five - Bloodlust

Also
Corrigan Fire
Corrigan Magic
Corrigan Rage
Corrigan Politics
Corrigan Lust

The complete *Bo Blackman* series

A half-dead daemon, a massacre at her London based PI firm and evidence that suggests she's the main suspect for both ... Bo Blackman is having a very bad week.

She might be naive and inexperienced but she's determined to get to the bottom of the crimes, even if it means involving herself with one of London's most powerful vampire Families and their enigmatic leader.

It's pretty much going to be impossible for Bo to ever escape unscathed.

Book One - Dire Straits

Book Two - New Order

Book Three - High Stakes

Book Four - Red Angel

Book Five - Vigilante Vampire

Book Six - Dark Tomorrow

The complete *Highland Magic* series

Integrity Taylor walked away from the Sidhe when she was a child. Orphaned and bullied, she simply had no reason to stay, especially not when the sins of her father were going to remain on her shoulders. She found a new family - a group of thieves who proved that blood was less important than loyalty and love.

But the Sidhe aren't going to let Integrity stay away forever. They need her more than anyone realises - besides, there are prophecies to be fulfilled, people to be saved and hearts to be won over. If anyone can do it, Integrity can.

Book One - Gifted Thief

Book Two - Honour Bound

Book Three - Veiled Threat

Book Four - Last Wish

The complete *Dreamweaver* series

"I have special coping mechanisms for the times I need to open the front door. They're even often successful..."

Zoe Lydon knows there's often nothing logical or rational about fear. It doesn't change the fact that she's too terrified to step outside her own house, however.

What Zoe doesn't realise is that she's also a dreamweaver - able to access other people's subconscious minds. When she finds herself in the Dreamlands and up against its sinister Mayor, she'll need to use all of her wits - and overcome all of her fears - if she's ever going to come out alive.

Book One - Night Shade

Book Two - Night Terrors

Book Three - Night Lights

magical helping hand. If it were down to Ivy, she'd spend all day every day on her sofa where she could watch TV, munch junk food and talk to her feline familiar to her heart's content.

However, when a bureaucratic disaster ends up with Ivy as the victim of a case of mistaken identity, she's yanked very unwillingly into Arcane Branch, the investigative department of the Hallowed Order of Magical Enlightenment. Her problems are quadrupled when a valuable object is stolen right from under the Order's noses.

It doesn't exactly help that she's been magically bound to Adeptus Exemptus Raphael Winter. He might have piercing sapphire eyes and a body which a cover model would be proud of but, as far as Ivy's concerned, he's a walking advertisement for the joyless perils of too much witch-work.

And if he makes her go to the gym again, she's definitely going to turn him into a frog.

Book One - Slouch Witch

Book Two - Star Witch

Book Three - Spirit Witch

Sparkle Witch (Christmas short story)

The complete *Fractured Faery* series

One corpse. Several bizarre looking attackers. Some very strange magical powers. And a severe bout of amnesia.

It's one thing to wake up outside in the middle of the night with a decapitated man for company. It's another to have no memory of how you got there - or who you are.

She might not know her own name but she knows that several people are out to get her. It could be because she has strange magical powers seemingly at her fingertips and is some kind of fabulous hero. But then why does she appear to inspire fear in so many? And who on earth is the sexy, green-eyed barman who apparently despises her? So many questions ... and so few answers.

At least one thing is for sure - the streets of Manchester have never met someone quite as mad as Madrona...

Book One - Box of Frogs

SHORTLISTED FOR THE KINDLE STORYTELLER AWARD 2018

Book Two - Quiver of Cobras

Book Three - Skulk of Foxes

The complete *City Of Magic* series

Charley is a cleaner by day and a professional gambler by night. She might be haunted by her tragic past but she's never thought of herself as anything or anyone special. Until, that is, things start to go terribly wrong all across the city of Manchester. Between plagues of rats, firestorms and the gleaming blue eyes of a sexy Scottish werewolf, she might just have landed herself in the middle of a magical apocalypse. She might also be the only person who has the ability to bring order to an utterly chaotic new world.

Book One - Shrill Dusk

Book Two - Brittle Midnight

Book Three - Furtive Dawn